Early F. Scott Fitzgerald

Start Publishing PD LLC

Manufactured in the United States of America

Cover art: Shutterstock/Taisiya Kozorez

Cover design: Jennifer Do

10 9 8 7 6 5 4 3 2 1

ISBN 979-8-8809-0409-9

Early F. Scott Fitzgerald

by F. Scott Fitzgerald

Contents

Sentiment—and the Use of Rouge

I

This story has no moral value. It is about a man who had fought for two years and how he came back to England for two days, and then how he went away again. It is unfortunately one of those stories which must start at the beginning, and the beginning consists merely of a few details. There were two brothers (two sons of Lord Blachford) who sailed to Europe with the first hundred thousand. Lieutenant Richard Harrington Syneforth, the elder, was killed in some forgotten raid; the younger, Lieutenant Clay Harrington Syneforth is the hero of this story. He was now a Captain in the Seventeenth Sussex and the immoral thing in the story happens to him. The important part to remember is that when his father met him at Paddington station and drove him up town in his motor, he hadn't been in England for two years—and this was in the early spring of nineteen-seventeen. Various circumstances had brought this about, wounds, advancement, meeting his family in Paris, and mostly being twenty-two and anxious to show his company an example of indefatigable energy. Besides, most of his friends were dead and he had rather a horror of seeing the gaps they'd leave in his England. And here is the story.

He sat at dinner and thought himself rather stupid and unnecessarily moody as his sister's light chatter amused the table, Lord and Lady Blachford, himself and two unsullied aunts. In the first place he was rather doubtful about his sister's new manner. She seemed, well, perhaps a bit loud and theatrical, and she was certainly pretty enough not to need so much paint. She couldn't be more than eighteen, and paint—it seemed so useless. Of course he was used to it in Lois mother, would have been shocked had she appeared in her unrouged furrowedness, but on Clara it merely accentuated her youth. Altogether he had never seen such obvious paint, and, as they had always been a shockingly frank family, he told her so.

"You've got too much stuff on your face." He tried to speak casually and his sister nothing wroth, jumped up and ran to a mirror.

"No, I haven't," she said, calmly returning.

"I thought," he continued rather annoyed, "that the criterion of how much paint to put on, was whether men were sure you'd used any or not."

His sister and mother exchanged glances and both spoke at once.

"Not now, Clay, you know—" began Clara.

"Really, Clay," interrupted his mother, "you don't know ex- actly what the standards are, so you can't quite criticize. It happens to be a fad to paint a little more."

Clayton was now rather angry.

"Will all the women at Mrs. Severance's dance tonight be striped like this?"

Clara's eyes flashed.

"Yes!"

"Then I don't believe I care to go."

Clara, about to flare up, caught her mother's eye and was silent.

"Clay, I want you to go," said Lady Blachford hastily. "Peo- ple want to see you before they forget what you look like. And for tonight let's not talk about war or paint."

In the end Clay went. A navy subaltran called for his sister at ten and he followed in lonesome state at half-past. After half an hour he had had all he wanted. Frankly, the dance seemed all wrong. He remembered Mrs. Severance's ante-bellum affairs—staid, correct occasions they were, with only a mere scattering from the faster set, just those people who couldn't possibly be left out. Now it all was blent, some how, in one set. His sister had not exaggerated, practically every girl there was painted, overprinted; girls whom he remembered as curate-hunters, holders of long conversations with earnest young men on incence and the validity of orders, girls who had been terrifyingly masculine and had talked about dances as if they were the amusement of the feeble minded—all were there, trotting through the most extreme steps from over the water. He danced stiffly with many who had de- lighted his youth, and he found that he wasn't enjoying himself at all. He found that he had come to picture England as a land of sorrow and acetisism and while there was little extravagance displayed tonight, he thought that the atmosphere had fallen to that of artificial gayety rather than risen to a stern calmness. Even under the carved, gilt ceiling of the Severances' there was strangely an impression of dance-hall rather than dance, people arrived and departed most informally and, oddly enough, there was a dearth of older people rather than of younger. But there was something in the very faces of the girls, something which was half enthusiasm and half recklessness, that depressed him more than any concrete thing.

When he had decided this and had about made up his mind to go, Eleanor Marbrooke came in. He looked at her keenly. She had not lost, not a bit. He fancied that she had not quiet so much paint on as the others, and when he and she talked he felt a social refuge in her cool beauty. Even then he felt that the difference between she and the others was in degree rather than in kind. He stayed, of course, and one o'clock found them sitting apart, watching. There had been a drifting away and now there seemed to be nothing but officers and girls; the Severances them- selves seemed out of place as they chattered volubly in a corner to a young couple who looked as if they would rather be left alone.

"Eleanor," he demanded, "why is it that everyone looks so– well, so loose–so socially slovenly?"

"It's terribly obvious, isn't it?" she agreed, following his eyes around the room.

"And no one seems to care" he continued.

"No one does," she responded, "but my dear man, we can't sit here and criticize our hosts. What about me? How do I look?"

He regarded her critically.

"I'd say on the whole, that you've kept your looks."

"Well, I like that," she raised her brows at him in reproof. "You talk as if I were some shelved, old play-about, just over some domestic catastrophy."

There was a pause; then he asked her directly.

"How about Dick?"

She grew serious at once.

"Poor Dick–I suppose we were engaged."

"Suppose," he said astonished, "why it was understood by everyone, both our families knew. I know I used to lie awake and envy my lucky brother."

She laughed.

"Well, we certainly thought ourselves engaged. If war hadn't come we'd be comfortably married now, but if he were still alive under these circumstances, I doubt if we'd be even engaged."

"You weren't in love with him?"

"Well, you see, perhaps that wouldn't be the question, perhaps he wouldn't marry me and perhaps I wouldn't marry him."

He jumped to his feet astounded and her warning hush just prevented him from exclaiming aloud. Before he could control his voice enough to speak she had whisked off with a staff officer. What could she mean?–except that in some moment of emotional excitement she had–but he couldn't bear to think of Eleanor in that light. He must have misunderstood–he must talk more with her. No, surely–if it had been true she wouldn't have said it so casually. He watched her–how close she danced. Her bright brown hair lay against the staff officer's shoulder and her vivacious face was only two or three inches from his when she talked. All things considered Clay was becoming more angry every minute with things in general.

Next time he danced with her she seized his arm, and before he knew her intention, they had said goodbyes to the Severances' and were speeding away in Eleanor's limousine.

"It's a nineteen-thirteen car—imagine having a four year old limousine before the war."

"Terrific privation," he said ironically. "Eleanor, I want to speak to you—"

"And I to you. That's why I took you away. Where are you living?"

"At home."

"Well then we'll go to your old rooms in Grove Street. You've still got them, haven't you?"

Before he could answer she had spoken to the chauffer and was leaning back in the corner smiling at him.

"Why Eleanor, we can't do that—talk there—."

"Are the rooms cleaned?" she interrupted.

"About once a month I think, but—."

"That's all that's necessary. In fact it'll be wonderfully proper, won't be clothes lying around the room as there usually are at bachelor teas. At Colonel Hotesane's farewell party, Gertrude Evarts and I saw—in the middle of the floor, well, my dear, a series of garments and—as we were the first to arrive we—."

"Eleanor," said Clay firmly, "I don't like this."

"I know you don't, and that's why we're going to your rooms to talk it over. Good heavens, do you think people worry these days about where conversations take place, unless they're in wire- less towers, or shoreways in coast towns?"

The machine had stopped and before he could bring further argument to bear she had stepped out and scurried up the steps, where she announced that she would wait until he came and opened the door. He had no alternative. He followed, and as they mounted the stairs inside he could hear her laughing softly at him in the darkness.

He threw open the door and groped for the electric light, and in the glow that followed both stood without moving. There on the table sat a picture of Dick, Dick almost as they had last seen him, worldly wise and sophisticated, in his civilian clothes. Eleanor was the first to move. She crossed swiftly over, the dust rising with the swish of her silk, and elbows on the table said softly

"Poor old handsome, with your beautiful self all smashed." She turned to Clay

"Dick didn't have much of a soul, such a small soul. He never bothered about eternity and I doubt if he knows any—but he had a way with him, and oh, that magnificent body of his, red gold hair, brown eyes—" her voice trailed off and she sank lazily onto the sofa in front of the hearth.

"Build a fire and then come and put your arm around me and we'll talk." Obediently he searched for wood while she sat and chatted. "I won't pretend to busybody around and try to help—I'm far too tired. I'm sure I can give the impression of home much better by just sitting here and talking, can't I?"

He looked up from where he knelt at her feet manipulating the kerosene can, and realized that his voice was husky as he spoke.

"Just talk about England—about the country a little and about Scotland and tell me things that have happened, amusing pro- vincial things and things with women in them—put yourself in" he finished rather abruptly.

Eleanor smiled and kneeling down beside him lit the match and ran it along the edge of the paper that undermined the logs. She twisted her head to read it as it curled up in black at the corners, "August 14h, 1915. Zeppelin raid in—there it goes" as it disappeared in little, licking flames. "My little sister—you remember Katherine; Kitty, the one with the yellow hair and the little lisp—she was killed by one of those things—she and a governess, that summer."

"Little Kitty," he said sadly, "a lot of children were killed I know, a lot, I didn't know she was gone," he was far away now and a set look had come into his eyes. She hastened to change the subject.

"Lots—but we're not on death tonight. We're going to pretend we're happy. Do you see?" She patted his knee reprovingly, "we are happy. We are! Why you were almost whimsical awhile ago. I believe you're a sentimentalist. Are you?

He was still gazing absently at the fire but he looked up at this.

"Tonight, I am—almost—for the first time in my life. Are you, Eleanor?"

"No, I'm romantic. There's a huge difference; a sentimental person thinks things will last, a romantic person hopes they wont."

He was in a reverie again and she knew that he had hardly heard her.

"Excuse please," she pleaded, slipping close to him. "Do be a nice boy and put your arm around me." He put his arm gingerly about until she began to laugh quietly. When he hastily withdrew it, and bending forward, talked quickly at the fire.

"Will you tell me why in the name of this mad world we're here tonight? Do you realize that this is—was a bachelor apart- ment before the bachelors all married the red widow over the channel—and you'll be compromised?"

She seized the straps of his shoulder belt and tugged at him until his grey eyes looked into hers.

"Clay, Clay, don't—you musn't use small petty words like that at this time. Compromise! What's that to words like Life and Love and Death and England. Compromise! Clay I don't believe anyone uses that word except servants." She laughed. "Clay, you and our butler are the only men in England who use the word compromise. My maid and I have been warned within a week—How odd—Clay, look at me."

He looked at her and saw what she intended, beauty heightened by enthusiasm. Her lips were half parted in a smile, her hair just so slightly disarranged.

"Damned witch," he muttered. "You used to read Tolstoy, and believe him."

"Did I?" her gaze wandered to the fire. "So I did, so I did." Then her eyes came back to him and the present. "Really, Clay, we must stop gazing at the fire. It puts our minds on the past and tonight there's got to be no past or future, no time, just tonight, you and I sitting here and I most tired for a military shoulder to rest my head upon." But he was off on an old tack thinking of Dick and he spoke his thoughts aloud.

"You used to talk Tolstoy to Dick and I thought it was scan- dalous for such a good-looking girl to be intellectual."

"I wasn't, really," she admitted. "It was to impress Dick."

"I was shocked, too, when I read something of Tolstoy's, I struck the something Sonata."

"Kreutzer Sonata," she suggested.

"That's it. I thought it was immoral for young girls to read Tolstoy and told Dick so. He used to nag me about that. I was nineteen."

"Yes, we thought you quite the young prig. We considered ourselves advanced."

"You're only twenty, aren't you?" asked Clay suddenly. She nodded.

"Don't you believe in Tolstoy any more?" he asked, almost fiercely.

She shook her head and then looked up at him almost wistfully.

"Won't you let me lean against your shoulder just the smallest bit?" He put his arm around her, never once taking his eyes from her face, and suddenly the whole strength of her appeal burst upon him. Clay was no saint, but he had always been rather decent about women. Perhaps that's why he felt so helpless now. His emotions were not complex. He knew what was wrong, but he knew also that he wanted this woman, this wallet creature of silk and life who crept so close to him. There were reasons why he oughtn't to have her, but he had suddenly seen how love was a big word like Life and Death, and she knew that he realized and was glad. Still they sat without moving for a long while and watched the fire.

II

At two-twenty next day Clay shook hands gravely with his father and stepped into the train for Dover. Eleanor, comfortable with a novel, was nestled into a corner of his compartment, and as he entered she smiled a welcome and closed the book.

"Well," she began. I felt like a minion of the almighty secret service as I slid by your inspiring and impecable father, swathed in yards and yards of veiling."

"He wouldn't have noticed you without your veil," answered Clayton, sitting down. "He was really most emotional under all that brusqueness. Really, you know he's quite a nice chap. Wish I knew him better."

The train was in motion; the last uniforms had drifted in like brown, blown leaves, and now it seemed as if one tremendous wind was carrying them shoreward.

"How far are you going with me?" asked Clayton.

"Just to Rochester, an hour and a half. I absolutely had to see you before you left, which isn't very Spartan of me. But really, you see, I feel that you don't quite understand about last night, and look at me, as" she paused "well—as rather exceptional."

"Wouldn't I be rather an awful cad if I thought about it in those terms at all?"

"No," she said cheerily, "I, for instance, am both a romantiscist and a psychologist. It does take the romance out of anything to analyze it, but I'm going to do it if only to clear myself in your eyes."

"You don't have to—" he began.

"I know I don't," she interrupted, "but I'm going to, and when I've finished you'll see where weakness and inevitability shade off. No, I don't believe in Zola."

"I don't know him."

"Well, my dear, Zola said that environment is environment, but he referred to families and races, and this is the story of a class."

"What class?"

"Our class."

"Please," he said, "I've been wanting to hear.

She settled herself against his shoulder, and gazing out at the vanishing country, began to talk very deliberately.

"It was said, before the war, that England was the only country in the world where women weren't safe from men of their own class."

"One particular fast set," he broke in.

"A set, my dear man, who were fast but who kept every bit of their standing and position. You see even that was reaction. The idea of physical fitness came in with the end of the Victorians. Drinking died down in the Universities. Why you yourself once told me that the really bad men never drank, rather kept themselves fit for moral or intellectual crimes."

"It was rather Victorian to drink much," he agreed. "Chaps who drank were usually young fellows about to become curates, sowing the conventional wild oats by the most orthodox tippling."

"Well," she continued, "there had to be an outlet—and there was, and you know the form it took in what you called the fast set. Next enter Mr. Mars. You see as long as there was moral pres- sure exerted, the rotten side of society was localized. I won't say it wasn't spreading, but it was spreading slowly, some people even thought, rather normally, but when men began to go away and not come back, when marriage became a hurried thing and widows filled London, and all traditions seemed broken, why then things were different."

"How did it start?"

"It started in cases where men were called away hurriedly and girls lost their nerve. Then the men didn't come back—and there were the girls.—."

He gasped.

"That was going on at the beginning?—I didn't know at all."

"Oh it was very quiet at first. Very little leaked out into daylight, but the thing spread in the dark. The next thing, you see, was to weave a sentimental mantle to throw over it. It was there and it had to be excused. Most girls either put on trousers and drove cars all day or painted their faces and danced with officers all night."

"And what mighty principle had the honor of being a cloak for all that?" he asked sarcastically.

"Now here, you see, is the paradox. I can talk like this and pretend to analyze, and even sneer at the principle. Yet I'm as much under the spell as the most wishy-washy typist who spends a week end at Brighton with her young man before he sails with the conscripts."

"I'm waiting to hear what the spell is."

"It's this—self sacrifice with a capitol S. Young men going to get killed for us.—We would have been their wives—we can't be—therefore we'll be as much as we can. And that's the story."

"Good God!"

"Young officer comes back," she went on; "must amuse him, must amuse him; must give him the impression that people here are with him, that it's a big home he's coming to, that he's ap- preciated. Now you know, of course, in the lower classes that sort of thing means children. Whether that will ever spread to us will depend on the duration of the war."

"How about old ideas, and standards of woman and that sort of thing?" he asked, rather sheepishly.

"Sky-high, my dear—dead and gone. It might be said for utility that it's better and safer for the race that officers stay with women of their own class. Think of the next generation in France."

To Clay the whole compartment had suddenly become smothering. Bubbles of conventional ethics seemed to have burst and the long stagnant gas was reaching him. He was forced to seize his mind and make it cling to whatever shreds of the old still floated on the moral air. Eleanor's voice came to him like the grey creed of a new materialistic world, the contrast was the more vivid because of the remains of erratic honor and sentimental religiosity that she flung out with the rest.

"So you see, my dear, utility, heroism and sentiment all com- bine and levoice. And we're pulling into Rochester," she turned to him pathetically. "I see that in trying to clear myself I've only indicted my whole sex," and with tears in their eyes they kissed.

On the platform they talked for half a minute more. There was no emotion. She was trying to analyze again and her smooth brow was wrinkled in the effort. He was endeavoring to digest what she had said, but his brain was in a whirl.

"Do you remember," he asked, "what you said last night about love being a big word like Life and Death?"

"A regular phrase; part of the technique of—of the game; a catch word." The train moved off and as Clay swung himself on the last car she raised her voice so that he could hear her to the last—"Love is a big word, but I was flattering us. Real Love's as big as Life and Death, but not that love—not that—" Her voice failed and mingled with the sound of the rails, and to Clay she seemed to fade out like a grey ghost on the platform.

III

When the charge broke and the remnants lapped back like spent waves, Sergeant O'Flaherty, a bullet through the left side, dropped beside him, and as weary castaways fight half listlessly for shore, they crawled and pushed and edged themselves into a shell crater. Clay's shoulder and back were bleeding profusely and he searched heavily and clumsily for his first aid package.

"That'll be that the Seventeenth Sussex gets reorganized," remarked O'Flaherty, sagely. "Two weeks in the rear and two weeks home."

"Damn good regiment, it was, O'Flaherty," said Clay. They would have seemed like two philosophic majors commenting from safe behind the lines had it not been that Clay was flat on his back, his face in a drawn ecstasy of pain, and that the Irishman was most evidently bleeding to death. The latter was twining an improvised tourniquet on his thigh, watching it with the careless casual interest a bashful suitor bestows upon his hat.

"I can't get up no emotion over a regiment these nights," he commented disgustedly. "This'll be the fifth I was in that I seen smashed to hell. I joined these Sussex byes so I needn't see more o' me own go."

"I think you know every one in Ireland, Sergeant.

"All Ireland's me friend, Captain, though I niver knew it 'till I left. So I left the Irish, what was left of them. You see when an English bye dies he does some play actin' before. Blood on an Englishman always calls rouge to me mind. It's a game with him. The Irish take death damn serious."

Clayton rolled painfully over and watched the night come softly down and blend with the drifting smoke. They were certainly between the devil and the deep sea and the slang of the next generation will use "no man's land" for that. O'Flaherty was still talking.

"You see you has to do somethin'. You haven't any God worth remarkin' on. So you pass from life in the names of your holy principles, and hope to meet in Westminster."

"We're not mystics, O'Flaherty," muttered Clay, "but we've got a firm grip on God and reality."

"Mystics, my eye, beggin' your pardon, lieutenant," cried the Irishman, "a mystic ain't no race, it's a saint. You got the most airy way o' thinkin' in the wurruld an yit you talk about plain faith as if it was cloud gazin'. There was a lecture last week behind Vimy Y. M. C. A., an' I stuck my head in the door; 'Tan-gi-ble,' the fellow was sayin' 'we must be Tan-gi-ble in our religion, we must be practicle' an' he starts off on Christian brotherhood an' honorable death—so I stuck me head out again. An' you got lots a good men dyin' for that every day-tryin' to be tan-gi-ble, dyin' because their father's a Duke or because he ain't. But that ain't what I got to think of. An' right here let's light a pipe before it gets dark enough for the damn burgomasters to see the match and practice on it."

Pipes, as indispensible as the hard ration, were going in no time, and the sergeant continued as he blew a huge lung full of smoke towards the earth with incongruous supercaution.

"I fight because I like it, an' God ain't to blame for that, but when it's death you're talkin' about I'll tell you what I get an' you don't. Pere Dupont gets in front of the Frenchies an' he says: 'Allon, mes enfants!' fine! an' Father O'Brien, he says: 'Go on in byes and bate the Luther out o' them'—great stuff! But can you see the reverent Updike—Updike just out o' Oxford—yellin' 'mix it up, chappies,' or 'soak 'em blokes?'—NO, Captain, the best leader you ever get is a six foot rowin' man that thinks God's got a seat in the House o' Commons. All sportin' men have to have a bunch o' cheerin' when they die. Give an Englishman four inches in the sportin' page this side of the whistle an' he'll die happy—but not O'Flaherty."

But Clay's thoughts were far away. Half delirious, his mind wandered to Eleanor. He had thought of nothing else for a week, ever since their parting at Rochester, and so many new sides of what he had learned were opening up. He had suddenly realized about Dick and Eleanor, they must have been married to all intents and purposes. Of course Clay had written to Eleanor from Paris, asking her to marry him on his return, and just yesterday he had gotten a very short, very kind, but definite refusal. And he couldn't understand at all.

Then there was his sister—Eleanor's words still rang in his ear. "They either put on trousers and act as chauffers all day or put on paint and dance with officers all night." He felt perfectly sure that Clara was still well—virtuous. Virtuous—what a ridiculous word it seemed, and how odd to be using it about his sister. Clara had always been so painfully good. At fourteen she had been sent to Boston for a souvenir picture of Louisa M. Alcott to hang over her bed. His favorite amusement had been to replace it by some startling soubrette in tights, culled from the pages of the Pink Un. Well Clara, Eleanor, Dick, he himself, were all in the same boat, no matter what the actuality of their innocence or guilt. If he ever got back–.

The Irishman, evidently sinking fast, was talking rapidly.

"Put your wishy-washy pretty clothes on everythin' but it ain't no disguise. If I get drunk it's the flesh and the devil, if you get drunk it's your wild oats. But you ain't disguisin' death, not to me you ain't. It's a damn serious affair. I may get killed for me flag, but I'm goin' to die for meself. 'I die for England' he says. 'Settle up with God, you're through with England' I says."

He raised himself on his elbow and shook his fist toward the German trenches.

"It's you an' your damn Luther," he shouted. "You been pro- testin' and analyzin' until you're makin' my body ache and burn like hell; you been evolvin' like mister Darwin, an' you stretched yourself so far that you've split. Everythin's in-tan-gi-ble except your God. Honor an' Fatherland an' Westminster Abbey, they're all in-tan-gi-ble except God an' sure you got him tan-gi- ble. You got him on the flag an' in the constitution. Next you'll be writin' your bibles with Christ sowin' wild oats to make him human. You say he's on your side. Onc't, just onc't, he had a favorite nation and they hung Him up by the hands and feet and his body hurt him and burn't him," his voice grew fainter. "Hail Mary, full of grace, the Lord is wit' thee–." His voice trailed off, he shuddered and was dead.

The hours went on. Clayton lit another pipe, heedless of what German sharpshooters might see. A heavy March mist had come down and the damp was eating into him. His whole left side was paralyzed and he felt chill creep slowly over him. He spoke aloud.

"Damned old mist–damned lucky old Irishman–Damnation." He felt a dim wonder that he was to know death but his thoughts turned as ever to England, and three faces came in sequence before him. Clara's, Dick's and Eleanor's. It was all such a mess. He'd like to have gone back and finished that conversation. It had stopped at Rochester–he had stopped living in the station at Rochester. How queer to have stopped there–Rochester had no significance. Wasn't there a play where a man was born in a station, or a handbag in a station, and he'd stopped living at– what did the Irishman say about cloaks, Eleanor said something about cloaks; too, he couldn't see any cloaks, didn't feel senti- mental–only cold and dim and mixed up. He didn't know about God– God was a good thing for curates–then there was the Y. M. C. A; God–and he always wore short sleeves, and bumpy Oxfords–but that wasn't God–that was just the man who talked about God to soldiers. And then there was O'Flaherty's God. He felt as if he knew him, but then he'd never called him God—he was fear and love, and it wasn't dignified to fear God—or even to love him except in a calm respectable way. There were so many God's it seemed—he had thought that Christianity was monotheistic, and it seemed pagan to have so many Gods.

Well, he'd find out the whole muddled business in about three minutes, and a lot of good it'd do anybody else left in the muddle.

Damned muddle—everything a muddle, everybody offside, and the referee gotten rid of—everybody trying to say that if the referee were there he'd have been on their side. He was going to go and find that old referee—find him—get hold of him, get a good hold—cling to him—cling to him—ask him—.

The Pierian Springs and the Last Straw

My Uncle George assumed, during my childhood, almost legendary proportions. His name was never mentioned except in verbal italics. His published works lay in bright, interesting binding on the library table—forbidden to my whetted curiosity until I should reach the age of corruption. When one day I broke the orange lamp into a hundred shivers and glints of glass, it was in search of closer information concerning a late arrival among the books. I spent the afternoon in bed and for weeks could not play under the table because of maternal horror of severed arteries in hands and knees. But I had gotten my first idea of Uncle George—he was a tall, angular man with crooked arms. His opinion was founded upon the shape of the handwriting in which he had written "To you, my brother, with heartiest of futile hopes that you will enjoy and approve of this: George Rombert." After this unintelligible beginning whatever interest I had in the matter waned, as would have all my ideas of the author, had he not been a constant family topic.

When I was eleven I unwillingly listened to the first comprehensible discussion of him. I was figeting on a chair in barbarous punishment when a letter arrived and I noticed my father growing stern and formidable as he read it. Instinctively I knew it concerned Uncle George—and I was right.

"What's the matter Tom?—Some one sick?" asked my mother rather anxiously.

For answer father rose and handed her the letter and some newspaper clippings it had enclosed. When she had read it twice (for her naive curiosity could never resist a preliminary skim) she plunged—

"Why should she write to you and not to me?"

Father threw himself wearily on the sofa and arranged his long limbs decoratively.

"It's getting tiresome, isn't it? This is the third time he's become—involved." I started for I distinctively heard him add under his breath "Poor damn fool!"

"It's much more than tiresome," began my mother, "It's disgusting; a great strong man with money and talent and every reason to behave and get married (she implied that these words were synonymous) playing around with serious women like a silly, conceited college boy. You'd think it was a harmless game!"

Here I put in my word. I thought that perhaps my being de trop in the conversation might lead to an early release.

"I'm here," I volunteered.

"So I see," said father in the tones he used to intimidate other young lawyers downtown; so I sat there and listened respectfully while they plumbed the iniquitous depths.

"It is a game to him," said my father; "That's all part of his theory."

My mother sighed. "Mr. Sedgewick told me yesterday that his books had done inestimable harm to the spirit in which love is held in this country."

"Mr. Sedgewick wrote him a letter," remarked my father rather dryly, "and George sent him the book of Solomon by return post—"

"Don't joke, Thomas," said mother crowding her face with eyes, "George is treacherous, his mind is unhealthy—"

"And so would mine be, had you not snatched me passionately from his clutches—and your son here will be George the second, if he feeds on this sort of conversation at his age." So the curtain fell upon my Uncle George for the first time.

Scrappy and rough-pieced information on this increasingly engrossing topic fitted gradually into my consciousness in the next five years like the parts of a picture puzzle. Here is the finished portrait from the angle of seventeen years—Uncle George was a Romeo and a mesogamist, a combination of Byron, Don Juan, and Bernard Shaw, with a touch of Havelock Ellis for good measure. He was about thirty, had been engaged seven times and drank ever so much more than was good for him. His attitude towards women was the piece-de-resistance of his character. To put it mildly he was not an idealist. He had written a series of novels, all of them bitter, each of them with some woman as the principal character. Some of the women were bad. None of them were quite good. He picked a rather wierd selection of Lauras to play muse to his whimsical Petrarch; for he could write, write well.

He was the type of author that gets dozens of letters a week from solicitors, aged men and enthusiastic young women who tell him that he is "prostituting his art" and "wasting golden literary opportunities." As a matter of fact he wasn't. It was very conceivable that he might have written better despite his unpleasant range of subject, but what he had written had a huge vogue that strangely enough, consisted not of the usual devotees of prostitute art, the eager shopgirls and sentimental salesmen to whom he was accused of pandering, but of the academic and literary circles of the country. His shrewd tenderness with nature (that is, everything but the white race), his well drawn men and the particu- larly cynical sting to his wit gave him many adherents. He was ranked in the most staid and severe of reviews as a coming man. Long psychopathic stories and dull germanized novels were predicted of him by optimistic critics. At one time he was the Thomas Hardy of America and he was several times heralded as the Balzac of his century. He was accused of having the great American novel in his coat pocket trying to peddle it from publisher to publisher. But somehow neither matter nor style had improved, people accused him of not "living." His unmarried sister and he had an apartment where she sat greying year by year with one furtive hand on the bromo-seltzer and the other on the telephone receiver of frantic feminine telephone calls. For George Rombert grew violently involved at least once a year. He filled columns in the journals of society gossip. Oddly enough most of his affairs were with debutantes—a fact which was considered particularly annoying by sheltering mothers. It seemed as though he had the most serious way of talking the most outrageous nonsense and as he was most desirable from an economic point of view, many essayed the perilous quest.

Though we had lived in the East since I had been a baby, it was always understood that home meant the prosperous Western city that still supported the roots of our family tree. When I was twenty I went back for the first time and made my only acquaintance with United George.

I had dinner in the apartment with my aunt, a very brave, gentle old lady who told me, rather proudly, I thought, that I looked like George. I was shown his pictures from babyhood, in every attitude; George at Andover, on the Y. M. C. A. committee, strange anatomy; George at Williams in the center of the Literary Magazine Picture, George as head of his fraternity. Then she handed me a scrap-book containing accounts of his exploits and all criticism of his work.

"He cares nothing at all about all this," she explained. I admired and questioned, and remember thinking as I left the apartment to seek Uncle George at his club, that between my family's depressed opinion of him and my aunts elated one my idea of him was muddled to say the least. At the Iroquois Club I was directed to the grill, and there standing in the doorway, I picked one out of the crowd, who, I was immediately sure, was he. Here is the way he looked at the time. He was tall with magnificent iron grey hair and the pale soft skin of a boy, most remarkable in a man of his mode of life. Drooping green eyes and a sneering mouth complete my picture of his physical self. He was rather drunk, for he had been at the Club all afternoon and for dinner, but he was perfectly conscious of himself and the dulling of faculties was only perceivable in a very cautious walk and a crack in his voice that sank it occasionally to a hoarse whisper. He was talking to a table of men all in various stages of inebriation, and holding them by a most peculiar and magnetic series of gestures. Right here I want to remark that this influence was not dependent so much upon a vivid physical personality but on a series of perfectly artificial mental tricks, his gestures, the peculiar range of his speaking voice, the suddenness and terseness of his remarks.

I watched him intently while my hall boy whispered to him and he walked slowly and consciously over to me to shake hands gravely and escort me to a small table. For an hour we talked of family things, of healths and deaths and births. I could not take my eyes off him. The blood-shot streakedness of his green eyes made me think of wierd color combinations in a child's paintbox. He had been looking bored for about ten minutes and my talk had been dwindling despondently down when suddenly he waved his hand as if to brush away a veil, and began to question me.

"Is that damn father of yours still defending me against your mother's tongue?"

I started, but strangely, felt no resentment.

"Because," he went on, "It's the only thing he ever did for me all his life. He's a terrible prig. I'd think it would drive you wild to have him in the house."

"Father feels very kindly toward you, sir," I said rather stiffly.

"Don't," he protested smiling. "Stick to veracity in your own family and don't bother to lie to me. I'm a totally black figure in your mind, I'm well aware. Am I not?"

"Well—you've—you've had a twenty years' history."

"Twenty years—hell—," said Uncle George. "Three years history and fifteen years aftermath."

"But your books—and all."

"Just aftermath, nothing but aftermath, my life stopped at twenty-one one night in October at sixteen minutes after ten. Do you want to hear about it? First I'll show you the heifer and then I'll take you upstairs and present you to the altar."

"I, you–if you–," I demurred feebly, for I was on fire to hear the story.

"Oh,–no trouble. I've done the story several times in books and life and around many a litered table. I have no delicacy any more–I lost that in the first smoke. This is the totally blackened heifer whom you're talking to now."

So he told me the story.

"You see it began Sophmore year–began most directly and most vividly in Christmas vacation of Sophmore year. Before that she'd always gone with a younger crowd–set, you young people call it now," he paused and clutched with mental fingers for tangible figures to express himself. "Her dancing, I guess, and beauty and the most direct, unprincipled personality I've ever come in contact with. When she wanted a boy there was no preliminary scouting among other girls for information, no sending out of tentative approaches meant to be retailed to him. There was the most direct attack by every faculty and gift that she possessed. She had no divergence of method–she just made you conscious to the highest degree that she was a girl"–he turned his eyes on me suddenly and asked:

"Is that enough–do you want a description of her eyes and hair and what she said?"

"No," I answered, "go on."

"Well, I went back to college an idealist, I built up a system of psychology in which dark ladies with alto voices and infinite possibilities floated through my days and nights. Of course we had the most frantic correspondence–each wrote ridiculous letters and sent ridiculous telegrams, told all our acquaintances about our flaming affair and–well you've been to college. All this is banal, I know. Here's an odd thing. All the time I was idealizing her to the last possibility, I was perfectly conscious that she was about the faultiest girl I'd ever met. She was selfish, conceited and uncontrolled and since these were my own faults I was doubly aware of them. Yet I never wanted to change her. Each fault was knit up with a sort of passionate energy that transcended it. Her selfishness made her play the game harder, her lack of control put me rather in awe of her and her conceit was punctuated by such delicious moments of remorse and self-denunciation that it was almost–almost dear to me–Isn't this getting ridiculous? She had the strongest effect on me. She made me want to do something for her, to get something to show her.

Every honor in college took on the semblance of a presentable trophy."

He beckoned to a waiter to my infinite misgiving, for though he seemed rather more sober than when I had arrived, he had been drinking steadily and I knew my own position would be embarrasing if he became altogether drunk.

"Then"—between sips—"we saw each other at sporadic intervals, quarreled, kissed and quarreled again. We were equals, neither was the leader. She was as interested in me as I was fascinated by her. We were both terrifically jealous but there was little occasion to show it. Each of us had small affairs on the side but merely as relaxations when the other was away. I didn't realize it but my idealism was slowly waning—or increasing into love—and rather a gentle sort of love." His face tightened. "This isn't cup sentiment." I nodded and he went on; "Well, we broke off in two hours and I was the weak one."

"Senior year I went to her school dance in New York, and there was a man there from another college of whom I became very jealous and not without cause. She and I had a few words about it and half an hour later I walked out on the street in my coat and hat, leaving behind the melancholy statement that I was through for good. So far so good. If I'd gone back to college that night or if I'd gone and gotten drunk or done almost anything wild or resentful the break would never have occurred—she'd have written next day. Here's what did happen. I walked along Fifth Avenue letting my imagination play on my sorrow, really luxuriating in it. She'd never looked better than she had that night, never; and I had never been so much in love. I worked myself up to the highest pitch of emotional imagination and moods grow real on me and then—Oh poor damn fool that I was—am—will always be—I went back. Went back! Couldn't I have known or seen—I knew her and myself—I could have plotted out for anyone else or in a cool mood, for myself just what I should have done, but my imagination made me go back, drove me. Half a thought in my brain would have sent me to Williamstown or the Manhattan bar. Another half thought sent me back to her school. When I crossed the threshold it was sixteen minutes after ten. At that minute I stopped living."

"You can imagine the rest. She was angry at me for leaving, hadn't had time to brood and when she saw me come in she resolved to punish me. I swallowed it hook and bait and temporarily lost confidence, temper, poise, every single jot of individuality or attractiveness I had. I wandered around that ballroom like a wild man trying to get a word with her and when I did I finished the job. I begged, pled, almost wept. She had no use for me from that hour. At two o'clock I walked out of that school a beaten man."

"Why the rest—it's a long nightmare—letters with all the nerve gone out of them, wild imploring letters; long silences hoping she'd care; rumors of her other affairs. At first I used to be sad when people still linked me up with her, asked me for news of her but finally when it got around that she'd thrown me over people didn't ask me about her any more, they told me of her—crumbs to a dog. I wasn't the authority any more on my own work, for that's what she was—just what I'd read into her and brought out in her. That's the story—" He broke off suddenly and rose; tottering to his feet, his voice rose and rang through the deserted grill.

"I read history with a new viewpoint since I had known Cleopatra and Messaline and Montespan,"—he started toward the door.

"Where are you going?" I asked in alarm.

"We're going upstairs to meet the lady. She's a widow now for awhile so you must say Mrs.—see—Mrs."

We went upstairs, I carefully behind with hands ready to be outstretched should he fall. I felt particularly unhappy. The hardest man in the world to handle is one who is too sober to be vacillating and too drunk to be persuaded; and I had, strange to say, an idea that my Uncle was eminently a person to be followed.

We entered a laree room. I couldn't describe it if my life depended on it. Uncle George nodded and beckoned to a woman at a bridge four across the room. She nodded and rising from the table walked slowly over. I started—naturally—

Here is my impression—a woman of thirty or a little under, dark, with intense physical magnetism and a most expressive mouth capable as I soon found out of the most remarkable change of expression by the slightest variance in facial geography. It was a mouth to be written to, but, though it could never have been called large, it could never have been crowded into a sonnet—I confess I have tried, Sonnet indeed! It contained the emotions of a drama and the history, I presume, of an epic. It was, as near as I can fathom, the eternal mouth. There were eyes also, brown, and a high warm coloring; but oh the mouth. . . .

I felt like a character in a Victorian romance. The little living groups scattered around seemed to move in small spotlights around us who were acting out a comedy "down stage." I was self-conscious about myself but purely physically so; I was merely a property; but I was very self-conscious for my Uncle. I dreaded the moment when he should lift his voice or overturn the table or kiss Mrs. Fulham bent dramatically back over his arm while the groups would start and stare. It was enormously unreal. I was introduced in a mumble and then forgotten.

"Tight again," remarked Mrs. Fulham.

My Uncle made no answer.

"Well, I'm having a heavy bridge game and we're ever so much behind. You can just have my dummy time. "Aren't you flattered?" She turned to me. "Your Uncle probably told you all about himself and me. He's behaving so badly this year. He used to be such a pathetic, innocent little boy and such a devil with the debutantes."

My Uncle broke in quickly with a rather grandiose air:

"That's sufficient I think Myra, for you."

"You're going to blame me again?" she asked in feigned astonishment. "As if I–"

"Don't–Don't," said my Uncle thickly. "Let one poor damn fool alone."

Here I found myself suddenly appreciating a sudden contrast. My Uncle's personality had dropped off him like a cloak. He was not the romantic figure of the grill, but a less sure, less attractive and somewhat contemptible individual. I had never seen personalities act like that before. Usually you either had one or you didn't. I wonder if I mean personality or temperament or perhaps that brunette alto tenor mood that lies on the borderland. . . At any rate my Uncle's mood was now that of a naughty boy to a stern aunt, almost that of a dog to his master.

"You know," said Mrs. Fulham, your Uncle is the only interesting thing in town. He's such a perfect fool."

Uncle George bowed his head and regarded the floor in a speculative manner. He smiled politely, if unhappily.

"That's your idea."

"He takes all his spite out on me."

My Uncle nodded, Mrs. Fulham's pardners called over to her that they had lost again and that the game was breaking up. She got rather angry.

"You know," she said coldly to Uncle George, "You stand there like a trained spaniel letting me say anything I want to you–Do you know what a pitiful thing you are?"

My Uncle had gone a dark red. Mrs. Fulham turned again to me.

"I've been talking to him like this for ten years–like this or not at all. He's my little lap dog. Here George, bring me my tea, write a book about me; you're snippy Georgie but interesting." Mrs. Fulham was rather carried away by the dramatic intensity of her own words and angered by George's unmovable acceptance. So she lost her head.

"You know," she said tensely, "My husband often wanted to horsewhip you but I've begged you off. He was very handy in the kennels and always said he could handle any kind of dog!"

Something had snapped. My Uncle rose, his eyes blazing. The shift of burden from her to her husband had lifted a weight from his shoulders. His eyes flashed but the words stored up for ten years came slow and measured.

"Your husband—Do you mean that crooked broker who kept you for five years. Horsewhip me! That was the prattle he may have used around the fireside to keep you under his dirty thumb. By God, I'll horsewhip your next husband myself." His voice had risen and the people were beginning to look up. A hush had fallen on the room and his words echoed from fireplace to fireplace.

"He's the damn thief that robbed me of everything in this hellish world."

He was shouting now. A few men drew near. Women shrank to the corners. Mrs. Fulham stood perfectly still. Her face had gone white but she was still sneering openly at him.

"What's this?" he picked up her hand. She tried to snatch it away but he tightened his grip and twisting the wedding ring off her finger he threw it on the floor and stamped it into a beaten button of gold.

In a minute I had his arms held. She screamed and held up her broken finger. The crowd closed around us.

In five minutes Uncle George and I were speeding homeward in a taxi. Neither of us spoke; he sat staring straight before him, his green eyes glittering in the dark. I left next morning after breakfast.

*

The story ought to end here. My Uncle George should remain with Mark Anthony and De Musset as a rather tragic semi-genius, ruined by a woman. Unfortunately the play continues into an inartistic sixth act where it topples over and descends like Uncle George himself in one of his more inebriated states, contrary to all the rules of dramatic literature. One month afterward Uncle George and Mrs. Fulham eloped in the most childish and romantic manner the night before her marriage to the Honorable Howard Bixby was to have taken place. Uncle George never drank again, nor did he ever write or in fact do anything except play a middling amount of golf and get comfortably bored with his wife.

Mother still doubts and predicts gruesome fates for his wife, Father is frankly astonished and not too pleased. In fact I rather believe he enjoyed having an author in the family, even if his books did look a bit decadent on the library table. From time to time I receive subscription lists and invitations from Uncle George. I keep them for use in my new book on Theories of Genius. You see I claim that if Dante had ever won—but a hypothetical sixth act is just as untechnical as a real one.

A Luckless Santa Claus

Miss Harmon was responsible for the whole thing. If it had not been for her foolish whim, Talbot would not have made a fool of himself, and—but I am getting ahead of my story.

It was Christmas Eve. Salvation Army Santa Clauses with highly colored noses proclaimed it as they beat upon rickety paper chimneys with tin spoons. Package laden old bachelors forgot to worry about how many slippers and dressing gowns they would have to thank people for next day, and joined in the general air of excitement that pervaded busy Manhattan.

In the parlor of a house situated on a dimly lighted residence street somewhere east of Broadway, sat the lady who, as I have said before, started the whole business. She was holding a conversation half frivolous, half sentimental, with a faultlessly dressed young man who sat with her on the sofa. All of this was quite right and proper, however, for they were engaged to be married in June.

"Harry Talbot," said Dorothy Harmon, as she rose and stood laughing at the merry young gentleman beside her, "if you aren't the most ridiculous boy I ever met, I'll eat that terrible box of candy you brought me last week!"

"Dorothy," reproved the young man, "you should receive gifts in the spirit in which they are given. That box of candy cost me much of my hard earned money."

"Your hard earned money, indeed!" scoffed Dorothy. "You know very well that you never earned a cent in your life. Golf and dancing—that is the sum total of your occupations. Why, you can't even spend money, much less earn it!"

"My dear Dorothy, I succeeded in running up some very choice bills last month, as you will find if you consult my father."

"That's not spending your money. That's wasting it. Why, I don't think you could give away twenty-five dollars in the right way to save your life."

"But why on earth," remonstrated Harry, "should I want to give away twenty-five dollars?"

"Because," explained Dorothy, "that would be real charity. It's nothing to charge a desk to your father and have it sent to me, but to give money to people you don't know is something."

"Why, any old fellow can give away money," protested Harry.

"Then," exclaimed Dorothy, "we'll see if you can. I don't believe that you could give twenty-five dollars in the course of an evening if you tried."

"Indeed, I could."

"Then try it!" And Dorothy, dashing into the hall, took down his coat and hat and placed them in his reluctant hands. "It is now half-past eight. You be here by ten o'clock."

"But, but," gasped Harry.

Dorothy was edging him towards the door.

"How much money have you?" she demanded.

Harry gloomily put his hand in his pocket and counted out a handful of bills.

"Exactly twenty-five dollars and five cents."

"Very well! Now listen! These are the conditions. You go out and give this money to anybody you care to whom you have never seen before. Don't give more than two dollars to any one person. And be back here by ten o'clock with no more than five cents in your pocket."

"But," declared Harry, still backing towards the door, "I want my twenty-five dollars."

"Harry," said Dorothy sweetly, "I am surprised!" and with that, she slammed the door in his face.

"I insist," muttered Harry, "that this is a most unusual pro- ceeding."

He walked down the steps and hesitated.

"Now," he thought, "Where shall I go?"

He considered a moment and finally started off towards Broad- way. He had gone about half a block when he saw a gentleman in a top hat approaching. Harry hesitated. Then he made up his mind, and, stepping towards the man, emitted what he intended for a pleasant laugh but what sounded more like a gurgle, and loudly vociferated, "Merry Christmas, friend!"

"The same to you," answered he of the top hat, and would have passed on, but Harry was not to be denied.

"My good fellow"—He cleared his throat. "Would you like me to give you a little money?"

"What?" yelled the man.

"You might need some money, don't you know, to—er—buy the children—a—a rag doll," he finished brilliantly.

The next moment his hat went sailing into the gutter, and when he picked it up the man was far away.

"There's five minutes wasted," muttered Harry, as, full of wrath towards Dorothy, he strode along his way. He decided to try a different method with the next people he met. He would express himself more politely.

A couple approached him,—a young lady and her escort. Harry halted directly in their path and, taking off his hat, addressed them.

"As it is Christmas, you know, and everybody gives away—er— articles, why"—

"Give him a dollar, Billy, and let's go on," said the young lady.

Billy obediently thrust a dollar into Harry's hand, and at that moment the girl gave a cry of surprise.

"Why, it's Harry Talbot," she exclaimed, "begging!"

But Harry heard no more. When he realized that he knew the girl he turned and sped like an arrow up the street, cursing has foolhardiness in taking up the affair at all.

He reached Broadway and started slowly down the gaily lighted thoroughfare, intending to give money to the street Arabs he met. All around him was the bustle of preparation. Everywhere swarmed people happy in the pleasant concert of their own generosity. Harry felt strangely out of place as he wandered aimlessly along. He was used to being catered to and bowed before, but here no one spoke to him, and one or two even had the audacity to smile at him and wish him a "Merry Christmas." He nervously accosted a passing boy.

"I say, little boy, I'm going to give you some money."

"No you ain't," said the boy sturdily. "I don't want none of your money."

Rather abashed, Harry continued down the street. He tried to present fifty cents to an inebriated man, but a policeman tapped him on the shoulder and told him to move on. He drew up beside a ragged individual and quietly whispered, "Do you wish some money?"

"I'm on," said the tramp, "what's the job?"

"Oh! there's no job!" Harry reassured him.

"Tryin' to kid me, hey?" growled the tramp resentfully. "Well, get somebody else." And he slunk off into the crowd.

Next Harry tried to squeeze ten cents into the hand of a passing bellboy, but the youth pulled open his coat and displayed a sign "No Tipping."

With the air of a thief, Harry approached an Italian bootblack, and cautiously deposited ten cents in his hand. At a safe distance he saw the boy wonderingly pocket the dime, and congratulated himself. He had but twenty-four dollars and ninety cents yet to give away! His last success gave him a plan. He stopped at a newsstand where, in full sight of the vender, he dropped a two-dollar bill and sped away in the crowd. After several minutes' hard running he came to a walk amidst the curious glances of the bundle-laden passers-by, and was mentally patting himself on the back when he heard quick breathing behind him, and the very newsie he had just left thrust into his hand the two-dollar bill and was off like a flash.

The perspiration streamed from Harry's forehead and he trudged along despondently. He got rid of twenty-five cents, however, by dropping it into a children's aid slot. He tried to get fifty cents in, but it was a small slot. His first large sum was two dollars to a Salvation Army Santa Claus, and, after this, he kept a sharp lookout for them, but it was past their closing time, and he saw no more of them on his journey.

He was now crossing Union Square, and, after another half hour's patient work, he found himself with only fifteen dollars left to give away. A wet snow was falling which turned to slush as it touched the pavements, and the light dancing pumps he wore were drenched, the water oozing out of his shoe with every step he took. He reached Cooper Square and turned into the Bowery. The number of people on the streets was fast thinning and all around him shops were closing up and their occupants going home. Some boys jeered at him, but, turning up his collar, he plodded on. In his ears rang the saying, mockingly yet kindly, "It is more blessed to give than to receive."

He turned up Third Avenue and counted his remaining money. It amounted to three dollars and seventy cents. Ahead of him he perceived through the thickening snow, two men standing under a lamp post. Here was his chance. He could divide his three dollars and seventy cents between them. He came up to them and tapped one on the shoulder. The man, a thin, ugly looking fellow, turned suspiciously.

"Won't you have some money, you fellow?" he said imperiously, for he was angry at humanity in general and Dorothy in particular. The fellow turned savagely.

"Oh!" he sneered, "you're one of these stiffs tryin' the charity gag, and then gettin' us pulled for beggin'. Come on, Jim, let's show him what we are."

And they showed him. They hit him, they mashed him, they got him down and jumped on him, they broke his hat, they tore his coat. And Harry, gasping, striking, panting, went down in the slush. He thought of the people who had that very night wished him a Merry Christmas. He was certainly having it.

*

Miss Dorothy Harmon closed her book with a snap. It was past eleven and no Harry. What was keeping him? He had probably given up and gone home long ago. With this in mind, she reached up to turn out the light, when suddenly she heard a noise outside as if someone had fallen.

Dorothy rushed to the window and pulled up the blind. There, coming up the steps on his hands and knees was a wretched caricature of a man. He was hatless, coatless, collarless, tieless, and covered with snow. It was Harry. He opened the door and walked into the parlor, leaving a trail of wet snow behind him.

"Well?" he said defiantly.

"Harry," she gasped, "can it be you?"

"Dorothy," he said solemnly, "it is me."

"What–what has happened?"

"Oh, nothing. I've just been giving away that twenty-five dollars." And Harry sat down on the sofa.

"But Harry," she faltered, "your eye is all swollen."

"Oh, my eye? Let me see. Oh, that was on the twenty-second dollar. I had some difficulty with two gentlemen. However, we afterward struck up quite an acquaintance. I had some luck after that. I dropped two dollars in a blind beggar's hat."

"You have been all evening giving away that money?"

"My dear Dorothy, I have decidedly been all evening giving away that money." He rose and brushed a lump of snow from his shoulder. "I really must be going now. I have two–er–friends outside waiting for me." He walked towards the door.

"Two friends?"

"Why–a–they are the two gentlemen I had the difficulty with. They are coming home with me to spend Christmas. They are really nice fellows, though they might seem a trifle rough at first."

Dorothy drew a quick breath. For a minute no one spoke. Then he took her in his arms.

"Dearest," she whispered, "you did this all for me."

A minute later he sprang down the steps, and arm in arm with his friends, walked off in the darkness.

"Good night, Dorothy," he called back, "and a Merry Christmas!"

Myra Meets His Family

Probably every boy who has attended an Eastern college in the last ten years has met Myra half a dozen times, for the Myras live on the Eastern colleges, as kittens live on warm milk. When Myra is young, seventeen or so, they call her a "wonderful kid"; in her prime—say, at nineteen—she is tendered the subtle compliment of being referred to by her name alone; and after that she is a "prom trotter" or "the famous coast-to-coast Myra."

You can see her practically any winter afternoon if you stroll through the Biltmore lobby. She will be standing in a group of sophomores just in from Princeton or New Haven, trying to decide whether to dance away the mellow hours at the Club de Vingt or the Plaza Red Room. Afterward one of the sophomores will take her to the theater and ask her down to the February prom—and then dive for a taxi to catch the last train back to college.

Invariably she has a somnolent mother sharing a suite with her on one of the floors above.

When Myra is about twenty-four she thinks over all the nice boys she might have married at one time or other, sighs a little and does the best she can. But no remarks, please! She has given her youth to you; she has blown fragrantly through many ballrooms to the tender tribute of many eyes; she has roused strange surges of romance in a hundred pagan young breasts; and who shall say she hasn't counted?

The particular Myra whom this story concerns will have to have a paragraph of history. I will get it over with as swiftly as possible.

When she was sixteen she lived in a big house in Cleveland and attended Derby School in Connecticut, and it was while she was still there that she started going to prep-school dances and college proms. She decided to spend the war at Smith College, but in January of her freshman year, falling violently in love with a young infantry officer, she failed all her midyear examinations and retired to Cleveland in disgrace. The young infantry officer arrived about a week later.

Just as she had about decided that she didn't love him after all he was ordered abroad, and in a great revival of sentiment she rushed down to the port of embarkation with her mother to bid him good-by. She wrote him daily for two months, and then weekly for two months, and then once more. This last letter he never got, for a machine-gun bullet ripped through his head one rainy July morning. Perhaps this was just as well, for the letter informed him that it had all been a mistake, and that something told her they would never be happy together, and so on.

The "something" wore boots and silver wings and was tall and dark. Myra was quite sure that it was the real thing at last, but as an engine went through his chest at Kelly Field in mid-August she never had a chance to find out.

Instead she came East again, a little slimmer, with a becoming pallor and new shadows under her eyes, and throughout armistice year she left the ends of cigarettes all over New York on little china trays marked "Midnight Frolic" and "Coconut Grove" and "Palais Royal." She was twenty-one now, and Cleveland people said that her mother ought to take her back home—that New York was spoiling her.

You will have to do your best with that. The story should have started long ago.

It was an afternoon in September when she broke a theater date in order to have tea with young Mrs. Arthur Elkins, once her roommate at school.

"I wish, " began Myra as they sat down exquisitely, "that I'd been a senorita or a mademoiselle or something. Good grief! What is there to do over here once you're out, except marry and retire!"

Lilah Elkins had seen this form of ennui before.

"Nothing," she replied coolly; "do it."

"I can't seem to get interested, Lilah," said Myra, bending forward earnestly. "I've played round so much that even while I'm kissing the man I just wonder how soon I'll get tired of him. I never get carried away like I used to."

"How old are you, Myra?"

"Twenty-one last spring."

"Well," said Lilah complacently, "take it from me, don't get married unless you're absolutely through playing round. It means giving up an awful lot, you know."

"Through! I'm sick and tired of my whole pointless existence. Funny, Lilah, but I do feel ancient. Up at New Haven last spring men danced with me that seemed like little boys—and once I overheard a girl say in the dressing room, 'There's Myra Harper! She's been coming up here for eight years.' Of course she was about three years off, but it did give me the calendar blues."

"You and I went to our first prom when we were sixteen—five years ago."

"Heavens!" sighed Myra. "And now some men are afraid of me. Isn't that odd? Some of the nicest boys. One man dropped me like a hotcake after coming down from Morristown for three straight weekends. Some kind friend told him I was husband hunting this year, and he was afraid of getting in too deep."

"Well, you are husband hunting, aren't you?"

"I suppose so—after a fashion." Myra paused and looked about her rather cautiously. "Have you ever met Knowleton Whitney? You know what a wiz he is on looks, and his father's worth a fortune, they say. Well, I noticed that the first time he met me he started when he heard my name and fought shy—and, Lilah darling, I'm not so ancient and homely as all that, am I?"

"You certainly are not!" laughed Lilah. "And here's my advice: Pick out the best thing in sight—the man who has all the mental, physical, social and financial qualities you want, and then go after him hammer and tongs—the way we used to. After you've got him don't say to yourself 'Well, he can't sing like Billy,' or 'I wish.he played better golf.' You can't have everything. Shut your eyes and turn off your sense of humor, and then after you're married it'll be very different and you'll be mighty glad."

"Yes," said Myra absently; "I've had that advice before."

"Drifting into romance is easy when you're eighteen," continued Lilah emphatically; "but after five years of it your capacity for it simply burns out."

"I've had such nice times," sighed Myra, "and such sweet men. To tell you the truth I have decided to go after someone."

"Who?"

"Knowleton Whitney. Believe me, I may be a bit blase, but I can still get any man I want."

"You really want him?"

"Yes—as much as I'll ever want anyone. He's smart as a whip, and shy—rather sweetly shy—and they say his family have the best-looking place in Westchester County."

Lilah sipped the last of her tea and glanced at her wrist watch.

"I've got to tear, dear."

They rose together and, sauntering out on Park Avenue, hailed taxicabs.

"I'm awfully glad, Myra; and I know you'll be glad too."

Myra skipped a little pool of water and, reaching her taxi, balanced on the running board like a ballet dancer.

" 'By, Lilah. See you soon."

"Good-by, Myra. Good luck!"

And knowing Myra as she did, Lilah felt that her last remark was distinctly superfluous.

II

That was essentially the reason that one Friday night six weeks later Knowleton Whitney paid a taxi bill of seven dollars and ten cents and with a mixture of emotions paused beside Myra on the Biltmore steps.

The outer surface of his mind was deliriously happy, but just below that was a slowly hardening fright at what he had done. He, protected since his freshman year at Harvard from the snares of fascinating fortune hunters, dragged away from several sweet young things by the acquiescent nape of his neck, had taken advantage of his family's absence in the West to become so enmeshed in the toils that it was hard to say which was toils and which was he.

The afternoon had been like a dream: November twilight along Fifth Avenue after the matinee, and he and Myra looking out at the swarming crowds from the romantic privacy of a hansom cab– quaint device–then tea at the Ritz and her white hand gleaming on the arm of a chair beside him; and suddenly quick broken words. After that had come the trip to the jeweler's and a mad dinner in some little Italian restaurant where he had written "Do you?" on the back of the bill of fare and pushed it over for her to add the ever-miraculous "You know I do!" And now at the day's end they paused on the Biltmore steps.

"Say it," breathed Myra close to his ear.

He said it. Ah, Myra, how many ghosts must have flitted across your memory then!

"You've made me so happy, dear," she said softly.

"No–you've made me happy. Don't you know–Myra–"

"I know."

"For good?"

"For good. I've got this, you see." And she raised the diamond solitaire to her lips. She knew how to do things, did Myra.

"Good night."

"Good night. Good night."

Like a gossamer fairy in shimmering rose she ran up the wide stairs and her cheeks were glowing wildly as she rang the elevator bell.

At the end of a fortnight she got a telegraph from him saying that his family had returned from the West and expected her up in Westchester County for a week's visit. Myra wired her train time, bought three new evening dresses and packed her trunk.

It was a cool November evening when she arrived, and stepping from the train in the late twilight she shivered slightly and looked eagerly round for Knowleton. The station platform swarmed for a moment with men returning from the city; there was a shouting-medley of wives and chauffeurs, and a great snorting of automobiles as they backed and turned and slid away. Then before she realized it the platform was quite deserted and not a single one of the luxurious cars remained. Knowleton must have expected her on another train.

With an almost inaudible "Damn!" she started toward the Elizabethan station to telephone, when suddenly she was accosted by a very dirty, dilapidated man who touched his ancient cap to her and addressed her in a cracked, querulous voice.

"You Miss Harper?"

"Yes," she confessed, rather startled. Was this unmentionable person by any wild chance the chauffeur?

"The chauffeur's sick," he continued in a high whine. "I'm his son.

Myra gasped.

"You mean Mr. Whitney's chauffeur?"

"Yes; he only keeps just one since the war. Great on economizin'—regelar Hoover." He stamped his feet nervously and smacked enormous gauntlets together. "Well, no use waitin' here gabbin' in the cold. Le's have your grip."

Too amazed for words and not a little dismayed, Myra followed her guide to the edge of the platform, where she looked in vain for a car. But she was not left to wonder long, for the person led her steps to a battered old flivver, wherein was deposited her grip.

"Big car's broke," he explained. "Have to use this or walk."

He opened the front door for her and nodded.

"Step in."

"I b'lieve I'll sit in back if you don't mind."

"Surest thing you know," he cackled, opening the back door. "I thought the trunk bumpin' round back there might make you nervous."

"What trunk?"

"Yourn."

"Oh, didn't Mr. Whitney–can't you make two trips?"

He shook his head obstinately.

"Wouldn't allow it. Not since the war. Up to rich people to set 'n example; that's what Mr. Whitney says. Le's have your check, please. "

As he disappeared Myra tried in vain to conjure up a picture of the chauffeur if this was his son. After a mysterious argument with the station agent he returned, gasping violently, with the trunk on his back. He deposited it in the rear seat and climbed up front beside her.

It was quite dark when they swerved out of the road and up a long dusky driveway to the Whitney place, whence lighted windows flung great blots of cheerful, yellow light over the gravel and grass and trees. Even now she could see that it was very beautiful, that its blurred outline was Georgian Colonial and that great shadowy garden parks were flung out at both sides. The car plumped to a full stop before a square stone doorway and the chauffeur's son climbed out after her and pushed open the outer door.

"Just go right in, " he cackled; and as she passed the threshold she heard him softly shut the door, closing out himself and the dark.

Myra looked round her. She was in a large somber hall paneled in old English oak and lit by dim shaded lights clinging like luminous yellow turtles at intervals along the wall. Ahead of her was a broad staircase and on both sides there were several doors, but there was no sight or sound of life, and an intense stillness seemed to rise ceaselessly from the deep crimson carpet.

She must have waited there a full minute before she began to have that unmistakable sense of someone looking at her. She forced herself to turn casually round.

A sallow little man, bald and clean shaven, trimly dressed in a frock coat and white spats, was standing a few yards away regarding her quizzically. He must have been fifty at the least, but even before he moved she had noticed a curious alertness about him–something in his pose which promised that it had been instantaneously assumed and would be instantaneously changed in a moment. His tiny hands and feet and the odd twist to his eyebrows gave him a faintly elfish expression, and she had one of those vague transient convictions that she had seen him before, many years ago.

For a minute they stared at each other in silence and then she flushed slightly and discovered a desire to swallow.

"I suppose you're Mr. Whitney." She smiled faintly and advanced a step toward him. "I'm Myra Harper."

For an instant longer he remained silent and motionless, and it flashed across Myra that he might be deaf; then suddenly he jerked into spirited life exactly like a mechanical toy started by the pressure of a button.

"Why, of course—why, naturally. I know—ah!" he exclaimed excitedly in a high-pitched elfin voice. Then raising himself on his toes in a sort of attenuated ecstasy of enthusiasm and smiling a wizened smile, he minced toward her across the dark carpet.

She blushed appropriately.

"That's awfully nice of—"

"Ah!" he went on. "You must be tired; a rickety, cindery, ghastly trip, I know. Tired and hungry and thirsty, no doubt, no doubt!" He looked round him indignantly. "The servants are frightfully inefficient in this house!"

Myra did not know what to say to this, so she made no answer. After an instant's abstraction Mr. Whitney crossed over with his furious energy and pressed a button; then almost as if he were dancing he was by her side again, making thin, disparaging gestures with his hands.

"A little minute," he assured her, "sixty seconds, scarcely more. Here!"

He rushed suddenly to the wall and with some effort lifted a great carved Louis Fourteenth chair and set it down carefully in the geometrical center of the carpet.

"Sit down—won't you? Sit down! I'll go get you something. Sixty seconds at the outside."

She demurred faintly, but he kept on repeating "Sit down!" in such an aggrieved yet hopeful tone that Myra sat down. Instantly her host disappeared.

She sat there for five minutes and a feeling of oppression fell over her. Of all the receptions she had ever received this was decidedly the oddest—for though she had read somewhere that Ludlow Whitney was considered one of the most eccentric figures in the financial world, to find a sallow, elfin little man who, when he walked, danced was rather a blow to her sense of form. Had he gone to get Knowleton! She revolved her thumbs in interminable concentric circles.

Then she started nervously at a quick cough at her elbow. It was Mr. Whitney again. In one hand he held a glass of milk and in the other a blue kitchen bowl full of those hard cubical crackers used in soup.

"Hungry from your trip! " he exclaimed compassionately. "Poor girl, poor little girl, starving!" He brought out this last word with such emphasis that some of the milk plopped gently over the side of the glass.

Myra took the refreshments submissively. She was not hungry, but it had taken him ten minutes to get them so it seemed ungracious to refuse. She sipped gingerly at the milk and ate a cracker, wondering vaguely what to say. Mr. Whitney, however, solved the problem for her by disappearing again—this time by way of the wide stairs—four steps at a hop—the back of his bald head gleaming oddly for a moment in the half dark.

Minutes passed. Myra was torn between resentment and bewilderment that she should be sitting on a high comfortless chair in the middle of this big hall munching crackers. By what code was a visiting fiancee ever thus received!

Her heart gave a jump of relief as she heard a familiar whistle on the stairs. It was Knowleton at last, and when he came in sight he gasped with astonishment.

"Myra!"

She carefully placed the bowl and glass on the carpet and rose, smiling.

"Why," he exclaimed, "they didn't tell me you were here!"

"Your father—welcomed me."

"Lordy! He must have gone upstairs and forgotten all about it. Did he insist on your eating this stuff? Why didn't you just tell him you didn't want any?"

"Why—I don't know."

"You musn't mind father, dear. He's forgetful and a little unconventional in some ways, but you'll get used to him."

He pressed a button and a butler appeared.

"Show Miss Harper to her room and have her bag carried up— and her trunk if it isn't there already." He turned to Myra. "Dear, I'm awfully sorry I didn't know you were here. How long have you been waiting?"

"Oh, only a few minutes."

It had been twenty at the least, but she saw no advantage in stressing it. Nevertheless it had given her an oddly uncomfortable feeling.

Half an hour later as she was hooking the last eye on her dinner dress there was a knock on the door.

"It's Knowleton, Myra; if you're about ready we'll go in and see mother for a minute before dinner."

She threw a final approving glance at her reflection in the mirror and turning out the light joined him in the hall. He led her down a central passage which crossed to the other wing of the house, and stopping before a closed door he pushed it open and ushered Myra into the weirdest room upon which her young eyes had ever rested.

It was a large luxurious boudoir, paneled, like the lower hall, in dark English oak and bathed by several lamps in a mellow orange glow that blurred its every outline into misty amber. In a great armchair piled high with cushions and draped with a curiously figured cloth of silk reclined a very sturdy old lady with bright white hair, heavy features, and an air about her of having been there for many years. She lay somnolently against the cushions, her eyes half closed, her great bust rising and falling under her black negligee.

But it was something else that made the room remarkable, and Myra's eyes scarcely rested on the woman, so engrossed was she in another feature of her surroundings. On the carpet, on the chairs and sofas, on the great canopied bed and on the soft Angora rug in front of the fire sat and sprawled and slept a great array of white poodle dogs. There must have been almost two dozen of them, with curly hair twisting in front of their wistful eyes and wide yellow bows flaunting from their necks. As Myra and Knowleton entered a stir went over the dogs; they raised one-and-twenty cold black noses in the air and from one-and-twenty little throats went up a great clatter of staccato barks until the room was filled with such an uproar that Myra stepped back in alarm.

But at the din the somnolent fat lady's eyes trembled open and in a low husky voice that was in itself oddly like a bark she snapped out "Hush that racket!" and the clatter instantly ceased. The two or three poodles round the fire turned their silky eyes on each other reproachfully, and lying down with little sighs faded out on the white Angora rug; the tousled ball on the lady's lap dug his nose into the crook of an elbow and went back to sleep, and except for the patches of white wool scattered about the room Myra would have thought it all a dream.

"Mother," said Knowleton after an instant's pause, "this is Myra."

From the lady's lips flooded one low husky word: "Myra?"

"She's visiting us, I told you."

Mrs. Whitney raised a large arm and passed her hand across her forehead wearily.

"Child!" she said—and Myra started, for again the voice was like a low sort of growl—"you want to marry my son Knowleton?"

Myra felt that this was putting the tonneau before the radiator, but she nodded.

"Yes, Mrs. Whitney."

"How old are you?" This very suddenly.

"I'm twenty-one, Mrs. Whitney."

"Ah—and you're from Cleveland?" This was in what was surely a series of articulate barks.

"Yes, Mrs. Whitney."

"Ah.—"

Myra was not certain whether this last ejaculation was conversation or merely a groan, so she did not answer.

"You'll excuse me if I don't appear downstairs," continued Mrs. Whitney; "but when we're in the East I seldom leave this room and my dear little doggies."

Myra nodded and a conventional health question was trembling on her lips when she caught Knowleton's warning glance and checked it.

"Well," said Mrs. Whitney with an air of finality, "you seem like a very nice girl. Come in again."

"Good night, mother," said Knowleton.

" 'Night!" barked Mrs. Whitney drowsily, and her eyes sealed gradually up as her head receded back again into the cushions.

Knowleton held open the door and Myra feeling a bit blank left the room. As they walked down the corridor she heard a burst of furious sound behind them; the noise of the closing door had again roused the poodle dogs.

When they went downstairs they found Mr. Whitney already seated at the dinner table.

"Utterly charming, completely delightful!" he exclaimed, beaming nervously. "One big family, and you the jewel of it, my dear."

Myra smiled, Knowleton frowned and Mr. Whitney tittered.

"It's been lonely here," he continued; "desolate, with only us three. We expect you to bring sunlight and warmth, the peculiar radiance and efflorescence of youth. It will be quite delightful. Do you sing?"

"Why—I have. I mean, I do, some."

He clapped his hands enthusiastically.

"Splendid! Magnificent! What do you sing? Opera? Ballads? Popular music?"

"Well, mostly popular music."

"Good; personally I prefer popular music. By the way, there's a dance to-night."

"Father, " demanded Knowleton sulkily, "did you go and invite a crowd here?"

"I had Monroe call up a few people—just some of the neighbors," he explained to Myra. "We're all very friendly hereabouts; give informal things continually. Oh, it's quite delightful."

Myra caught Knowleton's eye and gave him a sympathetic glance. It was obvious that he had wanted to be alone with her this first evening and was quite put out.

"I want them to meet Myra," continued his father. "I want them to know this delightful jewel we've added to our little household."

"Father," said Knowleton suddenly, "eventually of course Myra and I will want to live here with you and mother, but for the first two or three years I think an apartment in New York would be more the thing for us."

Crash! Mr. Whitney had raked across the tablecloth with his fingers and swept his silver to a jangling heap on the floor.

"Nonsense!" he cried furiously, pointing a tiny finger at his son. "Don't talk that utter nonsense! You'll live here, do you understand me? Here! What's a home without children?"

"But, father—"

In his excitement Mr. Whitney rose and a faint unnatural color crept into his sallow face.

"Silence!" he shrieked. "If you expect one bit of help from me you can have it under my roof—nowhere else! Is that clear? As for you my exquisite young lady," he continued, turning his wavering finger on Myra, "you'd better understand that the best thing you can do is to decide to settle down right here. This is my home, and I mean to keep it so."

He stood then for a moment on his tiptoes, bending furiously indignant glances first on one, then on the other, and then suddenly he turned and skipped from the room.

"Well," gasped Myra, turning to Knowleton in amazement "what do you know about that!"

III

Some hours later she crept into bed in a great state of restless discontent. One thing she knew—she was not going to live in this house. Knowleton would have to make his father see reason to the extent of giving them an apartment in the city. The sallow little man made her nervous, she was sure Mrs. Whitney's dogs would haunt her dreams- and there was a general casualness in the chauffeur, the butler, the maids and even the guests she had met that night, that did not in the least coincide with her ideas on the conduct of a big estate.

She had lain there an hour perhaps when she was startled from a slow reverie by a sharp cry which seemed to proceed from the adjoining room. She sat up in bed and listened, and in a minute it was repeated. It sounded exactly like the plaint of a weary child stopped summarily by the placing of a hand over its mouth. In the dark silence her bewilderment shaded gradually off into uneasiness. She waited for the cry to recur, but straining her ears she heard only the intense crowded stillness of three o'clock. She wondered where Knowleton slept, remembered that his bedroom was over in the other wing just beyond his mother's. She was alone over here—or was she?

With a little gasp she slid down into bed again and lay listening. Not since childhood had she been afraid of the dark, but the unforeseen presence of someone next door startled her and sent her imagination racing through a host of mystery stories that at one time or another had whiled away a long afternoon.

She heard the clock strike four and found she was very tired. A curtain drifted slowly down in front of her imagination, and changing her position she fell suddenly to sleep.

Next morning, walking with Knowleton under starry frosted bushes in one of the bare gardens, she grew quite light-hearted and wondered at her depression of the night before. Probably all families seemed odd when one visited them for the first time in such an intimate capacity. Yet her determination that she and Knowleton were going to live elsewhere than with the white dogs and the jumpy little man was not abated. And if the near-by Westchester County society was typified by the chilly crowd she had met at the dance—

"The family," said Knowleton, "must seem rather unusual. I've been brought up in an odd atmosphere, I suppose, but mother is really quite normal outside of her penchant for poodles in great quantities, and father in spite of his eccentricities seems to hold a secure position in Wall Street."

"Knowleton," she demanded suddenly, "who lives in the room next door to me?"

Did he start and flush slightly—or was that her imagination?

"Because," she went on deliberately, "I'm almost sure I heard someone crying in there during the night. It sounded like a child Knowleton."

"There's no one in there," he said decidedly. "It was either your imagination or something you ate. Or possibly one of the maids was sick."

Seeming to dismiss the matter without effort he changed the subject.

The day passed quickly. At lunch Mr. Whitney seemed to have forgotten his temper of the previous night; he was as nervously enthusiastic as ever; and watching him Myra again had that impression that she had seen him somewhere before. She and Knowleton paid another visit to Mrs. Whitney—and again the poodles stirred uneasily and set up a barking, to be summarily silenced by the harsh throaty voice. The conversation was short and of inquisitional flavor. It was terminated as before by the lady's drowsy eyelids and a p'an of farewell from the dogs.

In the evening she found that Mr. Whitney had insisted on organizing an informal neighborhood vaudeville. A stage had been erected in the ballroom and Myra sat beside Knowleton in the front row and watched proceedings curiously. Two slim and haughty ladies sang, a man performed some ancient card tricks, a girl gave impersonations, and then to Myra's astonishment Mr. Whitney appeared and did a rather effective buck-and-wing dance. There was something inexpressibly weird in the motion of the well-known financier flitting solemnly back and forth across the stag on his tiny feet. Yet he danced well, with an effortless grace and an unexpected suppleness, and he was rewarded with a storm of applause.

In the half dark the lady on her left suddenly spoke to her.

"Mr. Whitney is passing the word along that he wants to see you behind the scenes."

Puzzled, Myra rose and ascended the side flight of stairs that led to the raised platform. Her host was waiting for her anxiously.

"Ah," he chuckled, "splendid!"

He held out his hand, and wonderingly she took it. Before she realized his intention he had half led, half drawn her out on to the stage. The spotlight's glare bathed them, and the ripple of conversation washing the audience ceased. The faces before her were pallid splotches on the gloom and she felt her ears burning as she waited for Mr. Whitney to speak.

"Ladies and gentlemen," he began, "most of you know Miss Myra Harper. You had the honor of meeting her last night. She is a delicious girl, I assure you. I am in a position to know. She intends to become the wife of my son."

He paused and nodded and began clapping his hands. The audience immediately took up the clapping and Myra stood there in motionless horror, overcome by the most violent confusion of her life.

The piping voice went on: "Miss Harper is not only beautiful but talented. Last night she confided to me that she sang. I asked whether she preferred the opera, the ballad or the popular song, and she confessed that her taste ran to the latter. Miss Harper will now favor us with a popular song."

And then Myra was standing alone on the stage, rigid with embarrassment. She fancied that on the faces in front of her she saw critical expectation, boredom, ironic disapproval. Surely this was the height of bad form—to drop a guest unprepared into such a situation.

In the first hush she considered a word or two explaining that Mr. Whitney had been under a misapprehension—then anger came to her assistance. She tossed her head and those in front saw her lips close together sharply.

Advancing to the platform's edge she said succinctly to the orchestra leader: "Have you got 'Wave That Wishbone'?"

"Lemme see. Yes, we got it."

"All right. Let's go!"

She hurriedly reviewed the words, which she had learned quite by accident at a dull house party the previous summer. It was perhaps not the song she would have chosen for her first public appearance, but it would have to do. She smiled radiantly, nodded at the orchestra leader and began the verse in a light clear alto.

As she sang a spirit of ironic humor slowly took possession of her—a desire to give them all a run for their money. And she did. She injected an East Side snarl into every word of slang; she ragged; she shimmied, she did a tickle-toe step she had learned once in an amateur musical comedy; and in a burst of inspiration finished up in an Al Jolson position, on her knees with her arms stretched out to her audience in syncopated appeal.

Then she rose, bowed and left the stage.

For an instant there was silence, the silence of a cold tomb; then perhaps half a dozen hands joined in a faint, perfunctory applause that in a second had died completely away.

"Heavens!" thought Myra. "Was it as bad as all that? Or did I shock 'em?"

Mr. Whitney, however, seemed delighted. He was waiting for her in the wings and seizing her hand shook it enthusiastically.

"Quite wonderful!" he chuckled. "You are a delightful little actress—and you'll be a valuable addition to our little plays. Would you like to give an encore?"

"No!" said Myra shortly, and turned away.

In a shadowy corner she waited until the crowd had filed out with an angry unwillingness to face them immediately after their rejection of her effort.

When the ballroom was quite empty she walked slowly up the stairs, and there she came upon Knowleton and Mr. Whitney alone in the dark hall, evidently engaged in a heated argument.

They ceased when she appeared and looked toward her eagerly.

"Myra," said Mr. Whitney, "Knowleton wants to talk to you."

"Father," said Knowleton intensely, "I ask you—"

"Silence!" cried his father, his voice ascending testily. "You'll do your duty—now."

Knowleton cast one more appealing glance at him, but Mr. Whitney only shook his head excitedly and, turning, disappeared phantomlike up the stairs.

Knowleton stood silent a moment and finally with a look of dogged determination took her hand and led her toward a room that opened off the hall at the back. The yellow light fell through the door after them and she found herself in a dark wide chamber where she could just distinguish on the walls great square shapes which she took to be frames. Knowleton pressed a button, and immediately forty portraits sprang into life—old gallants from colonial days, ladies with floppity Gainsborough hats, fat women with ruffs and placid clasped hands.

She turned to Knowleton inquiringly, but he led her forward to a row of pictures on the side.

"Myra," he said slowly and painfully, "there's something I have to tell you. These"—he indicated the pictures with his hand—"are family portraits."

There were seven of them, three men and three women, all of them of the period just before the Civil War. The one in the middle however, was hidden by crimson-velvet curtains.

"Ironic as it may seem," continued Knowleton steadily, "that frame contains a picture of my great-grandmother."

Reaching out, he pulled a little silken cord and the curtains parted, to expose a portrait of a lady dressed as a European but with the unmistakable features of a Chinese.

"My great-grandfather, you see, was an Australian tea importer. He met his future wife in Hong-Kong."

Myra's brain was whirling. She had a sudden vision of Mr. Whitney's yellowish face, peculiar eyebrows and tiny hands and feet—she remembered ghastly tales she had heard of reversions to type—of Chinese babies—and then with a final surge of horror she thought of that sudden hushed cry in the night. She gasped, her knees seemed to crumple up and she sank slowly to the floor.

In a second Knowleton's arms were round her.

"Dearest, dearest!" he cried. "I shouldn't have told you! I shouldn't have told you!"

As he said this Myra knew definitely and unmistakably that she could never marry him, and when she realized it she cast at him a wild pitiful look, and for the first time in her life fainted dead away.

IV

When she next recovered full consciousness she was in bed. She imagined a maid had undressed her, for on turning up the reading lamp she saw that her clothes had been neatly put away. For a minute she lay there, listening idly while the hall clock struck two, and then her overwrought nerves jumped in terror as she heard again that child's cry from the room next door. The morning seemed suddenly infinitely far away. There was some shadowy secret near her—her feverish imagination pictured a Chinese child brought up there in the half dark.

In a quick panic she crept into a negligee and, throwing open the door, slipped down the corridor toward Knowleton's room. It was very dark in the other wing, but when she pushed open his door she could see by the faint hall light that his bed was empty and had not been slept in. Her terror increased. What could take him out at this hour of the night? She started for Mrs. Whitney's room, but at the thought of the dogs and her bare ankles she gave a little discouraged cry and passed by the door.

Then she suddenly heard the sound of Knowleton's voice issuing from a faint crack of light far down the corridor, and with a glow of joy she fled toward it. When she was within a foot of the door she found she could see through the crack—and after one glance all thought of entering left her.

Before an open fire, his head bowed in an attitude of great dejection, stood Knowleton, and in the corner, feet perched on the table, sat Mr. Whitney in his shirt sleeves, very quiet and calm, and pulling contentedly on a huge black pipe. Seated on the table was a part of Mrs. Whitney—that is, Mrs. Whitney without any hair. Out of the familiar great bust projected Mrs. Whitney's head, but she was bald; on her cheeks was the faint stubble of a beard, and in her mouth was a large black cigar, which she was puffing with obvious enjoyment.

"A thousand," groaned Knowleton as if in answer to a question. "Say twenty-five hundred and you'll be nearer the truth. I got a bill from the Graham Kennels to-day for those poodle dogs. They're soaking me two hundred and saying that they've got to have 'em back tomorrow."

"Well." said Mrs. Whitney in a low barytone voice, "send 'em back. We're through with 'em."

"That's a mere item," continued Knowleton glumly. "Including your salary, and Appleton's here, and that fellow who did the chauffeur, and seventy supes for two nights, and an orchestra—that's nearly twelve hundred, and then there's the rent on the costumes and that darn Chinese portrait and the bribes to the servants. Lord! There'll probably be bills for one thing or another coming in for the next month."

"Well, then," said Appleton, "for pity's sake pull yourself together and carry it through to the end. Take my word for it, that girl will be out of the house by twelve noon."

Knowleton sank into a chair and covered his face with his hands.

"Oh—"

"Brace up! It's all over. I thought for a minute there in the hall that you were going to balk at that Chinese business."

"It was the vaudeville that knocked the spots out of me," groaned Knowleton. "It was about the meanest trick ever pulled on any girl, and she was so darned game about it!"

"She had to be," said Mrs. Whitney cynically.

"Oh, Kelly, if you could have seen the girl look at me to-night just before she fainted in front of that picture. Lord, I believe she loves me! Oh, if you could have seen her!"

Outside Myra flushed crimson. She leaned closer to the door, biting her lip until she could taste the faintly bitter savor of blood.

"If there was anything I could do now," continued Knowleton— "anything in the world that would smooth it over I believe I'd do it."

Kelly crossed ponderously over, his bald shiny head ludicrous above his feminine negligee, and put his hand on Knowleton's shoulder.

"See here, my boy—your trouble is just nerves. Look at it this way: You undertook somep'n to get yourself out of an awful mess. It's a cinch the girl was after your money—now you've beat her at her own game an' saved yourself an unhappy marriage and your family a lot of suffering. Ain't that so, Appleton?"

"Absolutely!" said Appleton emphatically. "Go through with it."

"Well " said Knowleton with a dismal attempt to be righteous, "if she really loved me she wouldn't have let it all affect her this much. She's not marrying my family."

Appleton laughed.

"I thought we'd tried to make it pretty obvious that she is."

"Oh, shut up!" cried Knowleton miserably.

Myra saw Appleton wink at Kelly.

" 'At's right," he said; "she's shown she was after your money. Well, now then, there's no reason for not going through with it. See here. On one side you've proved she didn't love you and you're rid of her and free as air. She'll creep away and never say a word about it– and your family never the wiser. On the other side twenty-five hundred thrown to the bow-wows, miserable marriage, girl sure to hate you as soon as she finds out, and your family all broken up and probably disownin' you for marryin' her. One big mess, I'll tell the world."

"You're right," admitted Knowleton gloomily. "You're right, I suppose–but oh, the look in that girl's face! She's probably in there now lying awake, listening to the Chinese baby–"

Appleton rose and yawned.

"Well–" he began.

But Myra waited to hear no more. Pulling her silk kimono close about her she sped like lightning down the soft corridor, to dive headlong and breathless into her room.

"My heavens!" she cried, clenching her hands in the darkness. "My heavens!"

V

Just before dawn Myra drowsed into a jumbled dream that seemed to act on through interminable hours. She awoke about seven and lay listlessly with one blue-veined arm hanging over the side of the bed. She who had danced in the dawn at many proms was very tired.

A clock outside her door struck the hour, and with her nervous start something seemed to collapse within her–she turned over and began to weep furiously into her pillow, her tangled hair spreading like a dark aura round her head. To her, Myra Harper, had been done this cheap vulgar trick by a man she had thought shy and kind.

Lacking the courage to come to her and tell her the truth he had gone into the highways and hired men to frighten her.

Between her fevered broken sobs she tried in vain to comprehend the workings of a mind which could have conceived this in all its subtlety. Her pride refused to let her think of it as a deliberate plan of Knowleton's. It was probably an idea fostered by this little actor Appleton or by the fat Kelly with his horrible poodles. But it was all unspeakable—unthinkable. It gave her an intense sense of shame.

But when she emerged from her room at eight o'clock and disdaining breakfast, walked into the garden she was a very self-possessed young beauty, with dry cool eyes only faintly shadowed. The ground was firm and frosty with the promise of winter, and she found gray sky and dull air vaguely comforting and one with her mood. It was a day for thinking and she needed to think.

And then turning a corner suddenly she saw Knowleton seated on a stone bench, his head in his hands, in an attitude of profound dejection. He wore his clothes of the night before and-it was quite evident that he had not been to bed.

He did not hear her until she was quite close to him, and then as a dry twig snapped under her heel he looked up wearily. She saw that the night had played havoc with him—his face was deathly pale and his eyes were pink and puffed and tired. He jumped up with a look that was very like dread.

"Good morning," said Myra quietly.

"Sit down," he began nervously. "Sit down; I want to talk to you.l I've got to talk to you."

Myra nodded and taking a seat beside him on the bench clasped her knees with her hands and half closed her eyes.

"Myra, for heaven's sake have pity on me!"

She turned wondering eyes on him.

"What do you mean?"

He groaned.

"Myra, I've done a ghastly thing—to you, to me, to us. I haven't a word to say in favor of myself—I've been just rotten. I think it was a sort of madness that came over me."

"You'll have to give me a clew to what you're talking about."

"Myra—Myra"—like all large bodies his confession seemed difficult to imbue with momentum—"Myra—Mr. Whitney is not my father."

"You mean you were adopted?"

"No; I mean—Ludlow Whitney is my father, but this man you've met isn't Ludlow Whitney." "I know," said Myra coolly. "He's Warren Appleton, the actor."

Knowleton leaped to his feet. "How on earth–"

"Oh," lied Myra easily, "I recognized him the first night. I saw him five years ago in The Swiss Grapefruit."

At this Knowleton seemed to collapse utterly. He sank down limply on to the bench.

"You knew?"

"Of course! How could I help it? It simply made me wonder what it was all about."

With a great effort he tried to pull himself together.

"I'm going to tell you the whole story, Myra."

"I'm all ears."

"Well, it starts with my mother–my real one, not the woman with those idiotic dogs; she's an invalid and I'm her only child. Her one idea in life has always been for me to make a fitting match, and her idea of a fitting match centers round social position in England. Her greatest disappointment was that I wasn't a girl so I could marry a title, instead she wanted to drag me to England–marry me off to the sister of an earl or the daughter of a duke. Why, before she'd let me stay up here alone this fall she made me promise I wouldn't go to see any girl more than twice. And then I met you."

He paused for a second and continued earnestly: "You were the first girl in my life whom I ever thought of marrying. You intoxicated me, Myra. It was just as though you were making me love you by some invisible force."

"I was," murmured Myra.

"Well, that first intoxication lasted a week, and then one day a letter came from mother saying she was bringing home some wonderful English girl, Lady Helena Something-or-Other. And the same day a man told me that he'd heard I'd been caught by the most famous husband hunter in New York. Well, between these two things I went half crazy. I came into town to see you and call it off–got as far as the Biltmore entrance and didn't dare. I started wandering down Fifth Avenue like a wild man, and then I met Kelly. I told him the whole story–and within an hour we'd hatched up this ghastly plan. It was his plan–all the details. His histrionic instinct got the better of him and he had me thinking it was the kindest way out."

"Finish," commanded Myra crisply.

"Well, it went splendidly, we thought. Everything–the station meeting, the dinner scene, the scream in the night, the vaudeville– though I thought that was a little too much—until—until—Oh, Myra, when you fainted under that picture and I held you there in my arms, helpless as a baby, I knew I loved you. I was sorry then, Myra."

There was a long pause while she sat motionless, her hands still clasping her knees—then he burst out with a wild plea of passionate sincerity.

"Myra!" he cried. "If by any possible chance you can bring yourself to forgive and forget I'll marry you when you say, let my family go to the devil, and love you all my life."

For a long while she considered, and Knowleton rose and began pacing nervously up and down the aisle of bare bushes his hands in his pockets, his tired eyes pathetic now, and full of dull appeal. And then she came to a decision.

"You're perfectly sure?" she asked calmly.

"Yes."

"Very well, I'll marry you to-day."

With her words the atmosphere cleared and his troubles seemed to fall from him like a ragged cloak. An Indian summer sun drifted out from behind the gray clouds and the dry bushes rustled gently in the breeze.

"It was a bad mistake," she continued, "but if you're sure you love me now, that's the main thing. We'll go to town this morning get a license, and I'll call up my cousin, who's a minister in the First Presbyterian Church. We can go West to-night."

"Myra!" he cried jubilantly. "You're a marvel and I'm not fit to tie your shoe strings. I'm going to make up to you for this, darling girl."

And taking her supple body in his arms he covered her face with kisses.

The next two hours passed in a whirl. Myra went to the telephone and called her cousin, and then rushed upstairs to pack. When she came down a shining roadster was waiting miraculously in the drive and by ten o'clock they were bowling happily toward the City.

They stopped for a few minutes at the City Hall and again at the jeweler's, and then they were in the house of the Reverend Walter Gregory on Sixty-ninth Street, where a sanctimonious gentleman with twinkling eyes and a slight stutter received them cordially and urged them to a breakfast of bacon and eggs before the ceremony.

On the way to the station they stopped only long enough to wire Knowleton's father, and then they were sitting in their compartment on the Broadway Limited.

"Darn!" exclaimed Myra. "I forgot my bag. Left it at Cousin Walter's in the excitement."

"Never mind. We can get a whole new outfit in Chicago."

She glanced at her wrist watch.

"I've got time to telephone him to send it on."

She rose.

"Don't be long, dear."

She leaned down and kissed his forehead.

"You know I couldn't. Two minutes, honey."

Outside Myra ran swiftly along the platform and up the steel stairs to the great waiting room, where a man met her—a twinkly-eyed man with a slight stutter.

"How d-did it go, M-myra?"

"Fine! Oh, Walter, you were splendid! I almost wish you'd join the ministry so you could officiate when I do get married."

"Well—I r-rehearsed for half an hour after I g-got your telephone call."

"Wish we'd had more time. I'd have had him lease an apartment and buy furniture."

"H'm," chuckled Walter. "Wonder how far he'll go on his honeymoon."

"Oh, he'll think I'm on the train till he gets to Elizabeth." She shook her little fist at the great contour of the marble dome. "Oh, he's getting off too easy—far too easy!"

"I haven't f-figured out what the f-fellow did to you, M-myra."

"You never will, I hope."

They had reached the side drive and he hailed her a taxicab.

"You're an angel!" beamed Myra. "And I can't thank you enough."

"Well, any time I can be of use t-to you—By the way, what are you going to do with all the rings?"

Myra looked laughingly at her hand.

"That's the question," she said. "I may send them to Lady Helena Something-or-Other—and—well, I've always had a strong penchant for souvenirs. Tell the driver 'Biltmore,' Walter."

Winter Dreams

SOME OF THE CADDIES were poor as sin and lived in one-room houses with a neurasthenic cow in the front yard, but Dexter Green's father owned the second best grocery-store in Black Bear—the best one was "The Hub," patronized by the wealthy people from Sherry Island—and Dexter caddied only for pocket-money.

In the fall when the days became crisp and gray, and the long Minnesota winter shut down like the white lid of a box, Dexter's skis moved over the snow that hid the fairways of the golf course. At these times the country gave him a feeling of profound melancholy—it offended him that the links should lie in enforced fallowness, haunted by ragged sparrows for the long season. It was dreary, too, that on the tees where the gay colors fluttered in summer there were now only the desolate sand-boxes knee-deep in crusted ice. When he crossed the hills the wind blew cold as misery, and if the sun was out he tramped with his eyes squinted up against the hard dimensionless glare.

In April the winter ceased abruptly. The snow ran down into Black Bear Lake scarcely tarrying for the early golfers to brave the season with red and black balls. Without elation, without an interval of moist glory, the cold was gone.

Dexter knew that there was something dismal about this Northern spring, just as he knew there was something gorgeous about the fall. Fall made him clinch his hands and tremble and repeat idiotic sentences to himself, and make brisk abrupt gestures of command to imaginary audiences and armies. October filled him with hope which November raised to a sort of ecstatic triumph, and in this mood the fleeting brilliant impressions of the summer at Sherry Island were ready grist to his mill. He became a golf champion and defeated Mr. T. A. Hedrick in a marvellous match played a hundred times over the fairways of his imagination, a match each detail of which he changed about untiringly—sometimes he won with almost laughable ease, sometimes he came up magnificently from behind. Again, stepping from a Pierce-Arrow automobile, like Mr. Mortimer Jones, he strolled frigidly into the lounge of the Sherry Island Golf Club— or perhaps, surrounded by an admiring crowd, he gave an exhibition of fancy diving from the spring-board of the club raft. . . . Among those who watched him in open-mouthed wonder was Mr. Mortimer Jones.

And one day it came to pass that Mr. Jones—himself and not his ghost— came up to Dexter with tears in his eyes and said that Dexter was the—best caddy in the club, and wouldn't he decide not to quit if Mr. Jones made it worth his while, because every other caddy in the club lost one ball a hole for him— regularly—

"No, sir," said Dexter decisively, "I don't want to caddy any more." Then, after a pause: "I'm too old."

"You're not more than fourteen. Why the devil did you decide just this morning that you wanted to quit? You promised that next week you'd go over to the State tournament with me."

"I decided I was too old."

Dexter handed in his "A Class" badge, collected what money was due him from the caddy master, and walked home to Black Bear Village.

"The best–caddy I ever saw," shouted Mr. Mortimer Jones over a drink that afternoon. "Never lost a ball! Willing! Intelligent! Quiet! Honest! Grateful!"

The little girl who had done this was eleven–beautifully ugly as little girls are apt to be who are destined after a few years to be inexpressibly lovely and bring no end of misery to a great number of men. The spark, however, was perceptible. There was a general ungodliness in the way her lips twisted ,down at the corners when she smiled, and in the–Heaven help us!–in the almost passionate quality of her eyes. Vitality is born early in such women. It was utterly in evidence now, shining through her thin frame in a sort of glow.

She had come eagerly out on to the course at nine o'clock with a white linen nurse and five small new golf-clubs in a white canvas bag which the nurse was carrying. When Dexter first saw her she was standing by the caddy house, rather ill at ease and trying to conceal the fact by engaging her nurse in an obviously unnatural conversation graced by startling and irrelevant grimaces from herself.

"Well, it's certainly a nice day, Hilda," Dexter heard her say. She drew down the corners of her mouth, smiled, and glanced furtively around, her eyes in transit falling for an instant on Dexter.

Then to the nurse:

"Well, I guess there aren't very many people out here this morning, are there?"

The smile again–radiant, blatantly artificial–convincing.

"I don't know what we're supposed to do now," said the nurse, looking nowhere in particular.

"Oh, that's all right. I'll fix it up.

Dexter stood perfectly still, his mouth slightly ajar. He knew that if he moved forward a step his stare would be in her line of vision–if he moved backward he would lose his full view of her face. For a moment he had not realized how young she was. Now he remembered having seen her several times the year before in bloomers.

Suddenly, involuntarily, he laughed, a short abrupt laugh– then, startled by himself, he turned and began to walk quickly away.

"Boy!"

Dexter stopped.

"Boy—"

Beyond question he was addressed. Not only that, but he was treated to that absurd smile, that preposterous smile—the memory of which at least a dozen men were to carry into middle age.

"Boy, do you know where the golf teacher is?"

"He's giving a lesson."

"Well, do you know where the caddy-master is?"

"He isn't here yet this morning."

"Oh." For a moment this baffled her. She stood alternately on her right and left foot.

"We'd like to get a caddy," said the nurse. "Mrs. Mortimer Jones sent us out to play golf, and we don't know how without we get a caddy."

Here she was stopped by an ominous glance from Miss Jones, followed immediately by the smile.

"There aren't any caddies here except me," said Dexter to the nurse, "and I got to stay here in charge until the caddy-master gets here."

"Oh."

Miss Jones and her retinue now withdrew, and at a proper distance from Dexter became involved in a heated conversation, which was concluded by Miss Jones taking one of the clubs and hitting it on the ground with violence. For further emphasis she raised it again and was about to bring it down smartly upon the nurse's bosom, when the nurse seized the club and twisted it from her hands.

"You damn little mean old thing!" cried Miss Jones wildly.

Another argument ensued. Realizing that the elements of the comedy were implied in the scene, Dexter several times began to laugh, but each time restrained the laugh before it reached audibility. He could not resist the monstrous conviction that the little girl was justified in beating the nurse.

The situation was resolved by the fortuitous appearance of the caddymaster, who was appealed to immediately by the nurse.

"Miss Jones is to have a little caddy, and this one says he can't go."

"Mr. McKenna said I was to wait here till you came," said Dexter quickly.

"Well, he's here now." Miss Jones smiled cheerfully at the caddy-master. Then she dropped her bag and set off at a haughty mince toward the first tee.

"Well?" The caddy-master turned to Dexter. "What you standing there like a dummy for? Go pick up the young lady's clubs."

"I don't think I'll go out to-day," said Dexter.

"You don't–"

"I think I'll quit."

The enormity of his decision frightened him. He was a favorite caddy, and the thirty dollars a month he earned through the summer were not to be made elsewhere around the lake. But he had received a strong emotional shock, and his perturbation required a violent and immediate outlet.

It is not so simple as that, either. As so frequently would be the case in the future, Dexter was unconsciously dictated to by his winter dreams.

II

NOW, OF COURSE, the quality and the seasonability of these winter dreams varied, but the stuff of them remained. They persuaded Dexter several years later to pass up a business course at the State university–his father, prospering now, would have paid his way–for the precarious advantage of attending an older and more famous university in the East, where he was bothered by his scanty funds. But do not get the impression, because his winter dreams happened to be concerned at first with musings on the rich, that there was anything merely snobbish in the boy. He wanted not association with glittering things and glittering people–he wanted the glittering things themselves. Often he reached out for the best without knowing why he wanted it–and sometimes he ran up against the mysterious denials and prohibitions in which life indulges. It is with one of those denials and not with his career as a whole that this story deals.

He made money. It was rather amazing. After college he went to the city from which Black Bear Lake draws its wealthy patrons. When he was only twenty-three and had been there not quite two years, there were already people who liked to say: "Now there's a boy–" All about him rich men's sons were peddling bonds precariously, or investing patrimonies precariously, or plodding through the two dozen volumes of the "George Washington Commercial Course," but Dexter borrowed a thousand dollars on his college degree and his confident mouth, and bought a partnership in a laundry.

It was a small laundry when he went into it but Dexter made a specialty of learning how the English washed fine woollen golf-stockings without shrinking them, and within a year he was catering to the trade that wore knickerbockers. Men were insisting that their Shetland hose and sweaters go to his laundry just as they had insisted on a caddy who could find golfballs. A little later he was doing their wives' lingerie as well—and running five branches in different parts of the city. Before he was twenty-seven he owned the largest string of laundries in his section of the country. It was then that he sold out and went to New York. But the part of his story that concerns us goes back to the days when he was making his first big success.

When he was twenty-three Mr. Hart—one of the gray-haired men who like to say "Now there's a boy"—gave him a guest card to the Sherry Island Golf Club for a week-end. So he signed his name one day on the register, and that afternoon played golf in a foursome with Mr. Hart and Mr. Sandwood and Mr. T. A. Hedrick. He did not consider it necessary to remark that he had once carried Mr. Hart's bag over this same links, and that he knew every trap and gully with his eyes shut—but he found himself glancing at the four caddies who trailed them, trying to catch a gleam or gesture that would remind him of himself, that would lessen the gap which lay between his present and his past.

It was a curious day, slashed abruptly with fleeting, familiar impressions. One minute he had the sense of being a trespasser—in the next he was impressed by the tremendous superiority he felt toward Mr. T. A. Hedrick, who was a bore and not even a good golfer any more.

Then, because of a ball Mr. Hart lost near the fifteenth green, an enormous thing happened. While they were searching the stiff grasses of the rough there was a clear call of "Fore!" from behind a hill in their rear. And as they all turned abruptly from their search a bright new ball sliced abruptly over the hill and caught Mr. T. A. Hedrick in the abdomen.

"By Gad!" cried Mr. T. A. Hedrick, "they ought to put some of these crazy women off the course. It's getting to be outrageous."

A head and a voice came up together over the hill:

"Do you mind if we go through?"

"You hit me in the stomach!" declared Mr. Hedrick wildly.

"Did I?" The girl approached the group of men. "I'm sorry. I yelled 'Fore !'"

Her glance fell casually on each of the men—then scanned the fairway for her ball. "Did I bounce into the rough?"

It was impossible to determine whether this question was ingenuous or malicious. In a moment, however, she left no doubt, for as her partner came up over the hill she called cheerfully:

"Here I am! I'd have gone on the green except that I hit something."

As she took her stance for a short mashie shot, Dexter looked at her closely. She wore a blue gingham dress, rimmed at throat and shoulders with a white edging that accentuated her tan. The quality of exaggeration, of thinness, which had made her passionate eyes and down-turning mouth absurd at eleven, was gone now. She was arrestingly beautiful. The color in her cheeks was centered like the color in a picture—it was not a "high" color, but a sort of fluctuating and feverish warmth, so shaded that it seemed at any moment it would recede and disappear. This color and the mobility of her mouth gave a continual impression of flux, of intense life, of passionate vitality—balanced only partially by the sad luxury of her eyes.

She swung her mashie impatiently and without interest, pitching the ball into a sand-pit on the other side of the green. With a quick, insincere smile and a careless "Thank you!" she went on after it.

"That Judy Jones!" remarked Mr. Hedrick on the next tee, as they waited—some moments—for her to play on ahead. "All she needs is to be turned up and spanked for six months and then to be married off to an oldfashioned cavalry captain."

"My God, she's good-looking!" said Mr. Sandwood, who was just over thirty.

"Good-looking!" cried Mr. Hedrick contemptuously, "she always looks as if she wanted to be kissed! Turning those big cow-eyes on every calf in town!"

It was doubtful if Mr. Hedrick intended a reference to the maternal instinct.

"She'd play pretty good golf if she'd try," said Mr. Sandwood.

"She has no form," said Mr. Hedrick solemnly.

"She has a nice figure," said Mr. Sandwood.

"Better thank the Lord she doesn't drive a swifter ball," said Mr. Hart, winking at Dexter.

Later in the afternoon the sun went down with a riotous swirl of gold and varying blues and scarlets, and left the dry, rustling night of Western summer. Dexter watched from the veranda of the Golf Club, watched the even overlap of the waters in the little wind, silver molasses under the harvest-moon. Then the moon held a finger to her lips and the lake became a clear pool, pale and quiet. Dexter put on his bathing-suit and swam out to the farthest raft, where he stretched dripping on the wet canvas of the springboard.

There was a fish jumping and a star shining and the lights around the lake were gleaming. Over on a dark peninsula a piano was playing the songs of last summer and of summers before that– songs from "Chin-Chin" and "The Count of Luxemburg" and "The Chocolate Soldier"–and because the sound of a piano over a stretch of water had always seemed beautiful to Dexter he lay perfectly quiet and listened.

The tune the piano was playing at that moment had been gay and new five years before when Dexter was a sophomore at college. They had played it at a prom once when he could not afford the luxury of proms, and he had stood outside the gymnasium and listened. The sound of the tune precipitated in him a sort of ecstasy and it was with that ecstasy he viewed what happened to him now. It was a mood of intense appreciation, a sense that, for once, he was magnificently attune to life and that everything about him was radiating a brightness and a glamour he might never know again.

A low, pale oblong detached itself suddenly from the darkness of the Island, spitting forth the reverberate sound of a racing motor-boat. Two white streamers of cleft water rolled themselves out behind it and almost immediately the boat was beside him, drowning out the hot tinkle of the piano in the drone of its spray. Dexter raising himself on his arms was aware of a figure standing at the wheel, of two dark eyes regarding him over the lengthening space of water–then the boat had gone by and was sweeping in an immense and purposeless circle of spray round and round in the middle of the lake. With equal eccentricity one of the circles flattened out and headed back toward the raft.

"Who's that?" she called, shutting off her motor. She was so near now that Dexter could see her bathing-suit, which consisted apparently of pink rompers.

The nose of the boat bumped the raft, and as the latter tilted rakishly he was precipitated toward her. With different degrees of interest they recognized each other.

"Aren't you one of those men we played through this afternoon?" she demanded.

He was.

"Well, do you know how to drive a motor-boat? Because if you do I wish you'd drive this one so I can ride on the surf-board behind. My name is Judy Jones"–she favored him with an absurd smirk–rather, what tried to be a smirk, for, twist her mouth as she might, it was not grotesque, it was merely beautiful–"and I live in a house over there on the Island, and in that house there is a man waiting for me.

When he drove up at the door I drove out of the dock because he says I'm his ideal."

There was a fish jumping and a star shining and the lights around the lake were gleaming. Dexter sat beside Judy Jones and she explained how her boat was driven. Then she was in the water, swimming to the floating surfboard with a sinuous crawl. Watching her was without effort to the eye, watching a branch waving or a sea-gull flying. Her arms, burned to butternut, moved sinuously among the dull platinum ripples, elbow appearing first, casting the forearm back with a cadence of falling water, then reaching out and down, stabbing a path ahead.

They moved out into the lake; turning, Dexter saw that she was kneeling on the low rear of the now uptilted surf-board.

"Go faster," she called, "fast as it'll go."

Obediently he jammed the lever forward and the white spray mounted at the bow. When he looked around again the girl was standing up on the rushing board, her arms spread wide, her eyes lifted toward the moon.

"It's awful cold," she shouted. "What's your name?"

He told her.

"Well, why don't you come to dinner to-morrow night?"

His heart turned over like the fly-wheel of the boat, and, for the second time, her casual whim gave a new direction to his life.

III

NEXT EVENING while he waited for her to come down-stairs, Dexter peopled the soft deep summer room and the sun-porch that opened from it with the men who had already loved Judy Jones. He knew the sort of men they were—the men who when he first went to college had entered from the great prep schools with graceful clothes and the deep tan of healthy summers. He had seen that, in one sense, he was better than these men. He was newer and stronger. Yet in acknowledging to himself that he wished his children to be like them he was admitting that he was but the rough, strong stuff from which they eternally sprang.

When the time had come for him to wear good clothes, he had known who were the best tailors in America, and the best tailors in America had made him the suit he wore this evening. He had acquired that particular reserve peculiar to his university, that set it off from other universities. He recognized the value to him of such a mannerism and he had adopted it; he knew that to be careless in dress and manner required more confidence than to be careful. But carelessness was for his children. His mother's name had been Krimslich. She was a Bohemian of the peasant class and she had talked broken English to the end of her days. Her son must keep to the set patterns.

At a little after seven Judy Jones came down-stairs. She wore a blue silk afternoon dress, and he was disappointed at first that she had not put on something more elaborate. This feeling was accentuated when, after a brief greeting, she went to the door of a butler's pantry and pushing it open called: "You can serve dinner, Martha." He had rather expected that a butler would announce dinner, that there would be a cocktail. Then he put these thoughts behind him as they sat down side by side on a lounge and looked at each other.

"Father and mother won't be here," she said thoughtfully.

He remembered the last time he had seen her father, and he was glad the parents were not to be here to-night—they might wonder who he was. He had been born in Keeble, a Minnesota village fifty miles farther north, and he always gave Keeble as his home instead of Black Bear Village. Country towns were well enough to come from if they weren't inconveniently in sight and used as footstools by fashionable lakes.

They talked of his university, which she had visited frequently during the past two years, and of the near-by city which supplied Sherry Island with its patrons, and whither Dexter would return next day to his prospering laundries.

During dinner she slipped into a moody depression which gave Dexter a feeling of uneasiness. Whatever petulance she uttered in her throaty voice worried him. Whatever she smiled at—at him, at a chicken liver, at nothing—it disturbed him that her smile could have no root in mirth, or even in amusement. When the scarlet corners of her lips curved down, it was less a smile than an invitation to a kiss.

Then, after dinner, she led him out on the dark sun-porch and deliberately changed the atmosphere.

"Do you mind if I weep a little?" she said.

"I'm afraid I'm boring you," he responded quickly.

"You're not. I like you. But I've just had a terrible afternoon. There was a man I cared about, and this afternoon he told me out of a clear sky that he was poor as a church-mouse. He'd never even hinted it before. Does this sound horribly mundane?"

"Perhaps he was afraid to tell you."

"Suppose he was," she answered. "He didn't start right. You see, if I'd thought of him as poor—well, I've been mad about loads of poor men, and fully intended to marry them all. But in this case, I hadn't thought of him that way, and my interest in him wasn't strong enough to survive the shock. As if a girl calmly informed her fiancé that she was a widow. He might not object to widows, but—

"Let's start right," she interrupted herself suddenly. "Who are you, anyhow?"

For a moment Dexter hesitated. Then:

"I'm nobody," he announced. "My career is largely a matter of futures."

"Are you poor?"

"No," he said frankly, "I'm probably making more money than any man my age in the Northwest. I know that's an obnoxious remark, but you advised me to start right."

There was a pause. Then she smiled and the corners of her mouth drooped and an almost imperceptible sway brought her closer to him, looking up into his eyes. A lump rose in Dexter's throat, and he waited breathless for the experiment, facing the unpredictable compound that would form mysteriously from the elements of their lips. Then he saw—she communicated her excitement to him, lavishly, deeply, with kisses that were not a promise but a fulfillment. They aroused in him not hunger demanding renewal but surfeit that would demand more surfeit . . . kisses that were like charity, creating want by holding back nothing at all.

It did not take him many hours to decide that he had wanted Judy Jones ever since he was a proud, desirous little boy.

IV

IT BEGAN like that—and continued, with varying shades of intensity, on such a note right up to the dénouement. Dexter surrendered a part of himself to the most direct and unprincipled personality with which he had ever come in contact. Whatever Judy wanted, she went after with the full pressure of her charm. There was no divergence of method, no jockeying for position or premeditation of effects—there was a very little mental side to any of her affairs. She simply made men conscious to the highest degree of her physical loveliness. Dexter had no desire to change her. Her deficiencies were knit up with a passionate energy that transcended and justified them.

When, as Judy's head lay against his shoulder that first night, she whispered, "I don't know what's the matter with me. Last night I thought I was in love with a man and to-night I think I'm in love with you—"—it seemed to him a beautiful and romantic thing to say. It was the exquisite excitability that for the moment he controlled and owned. But a week later he was compelled to view this same quality in a different light. She took him in her roadster to a picnic supper, and after supper she disappeared, likewise in her roadster, with another man. Dexter became enormously upset and was scarcely able to be decently civil to the other people present. When she assured him that she had not kissed the other man, he knew she was lying—yet he was glad that she had taken the trouble to lie to him.

He was, as he found before the summer ended, one of a varying dozen who circulated about her. Each of them had at one time been favored above all others—about half of them still basked in the solace of occasional sentimental revivals. Whenever one showed signs of dropping out through long neglect, she granted him a brief honeyed hour, which encouraged him to tag along for a year or so longer. Judy made these forays upon the helpless and defeated without malice, indeed half unconscious that there was anything mischievous in what she did.

When a new man came to town every one dropped out—dates were automatically cancelled.

The helpless part of trying to do anything about it was that she did it all herself. She was not a girl who could be "won" in the kinetic sense—she was proof against cleverness, she was proof against charm; if any of these assailed her too strongly she would immediately resolve the affair to a physical basis, and under the magic of her physical splendor the strong as well as the brilliant played her game and not their own. She was entertained only by the gratification of her desires and by the direct exercise of her own charm. Perhaps from so much youthful love, so many youthful lovers, she had come, in self-defense, to nourish herself wholly from within.

Succeeding Dexter's first exhilaration came restlessness and dissatisfaction. The helpless ecstasy of losing himself in her was opiate rather than tonic. It was fortunate for his work during the winter that those moments of ecstasy came infrequently. Early in their acquaintance it had seemed for a while that there was a deep and spontaneous mutual attraction that first August, for example—three days of long evenings on her dusky veranda, of strange wan kisses through the late afternoon, in shadowy alcoves or behind the protecting trellises of the garden arbors, of mornings when she was fresh as a dream and almost shy at meeting him in the clarity of the rising day. There was all the ecstasy of an engagement about it, sharpened by his realization that there was no engagement. It was during those three days that, for the first time, he had asked her to marry him. She said "maybe some day," she said "kiss me," she said "I'd like to marry you," she said "I love you"—she said— nothing.

The three days were interrupted by the arrival of a New York man who visited at her house for half September. To Dexter's agony, rumor engaged them. The man was the son of the president of a great trust company. But at the end of a month it was reported that Judy was yawning. At a dance one night she sat all evening in a motor-boat with a local beau, while the New Yorker searched the club for her frantically. She told the local beau that she was bored with her visitor, and two days later he left. She was seen with him at the station, and it was reported that he looked very mournful indeed.

On this note the summer ended. Dexter was twenty-four, and he found himself increasingly in a position to do as he wished. He joined two clubs in the city and lived at one of them. Though he was by no means an integral part of the stag-lines at these clubs, he managed to be on hand at dances where Judy Jones was likely to appear. He could have gone out socially as much as he liked—he was an eligible young man, now, and popular with down-town fathers. His confessed devotion to Judy Jones had rather solidified his position. But he had no social aspirations and rather despised the dancing men who were always on tap for the Thursday or Saturday parties and who filled in at dinners with the younger married set. Already he was playing with the idea of going East to New York. He wanted to take Judy Jones with him. No disillusion as to the world in which she had grown up could cure his illusion as to her desirability.

Remember that—for only in the light of it can what he did for her be understood.

Eighteen months after he first met Judy Jones he became engaged to another girl. Her name was Irene Scheerer, and her father was one of the men who had always believed in Dexter. Irene was light-haired and sweet and honorable, and a little stout, and she had two suitors whom she pleasantly relinquished when Dexter formally asked her to marry him.

Summer, fall, winter, spring, another summer, another fall— so much he had given of his active life to the incorrigible lips of Judy Jones. She had treated him with interest, with encouragement, with malice, with indifference, with contempt. She had inflicted on him the innumerable little slights and indignities possible in such a case—as if in revenge for having ever cared for him at all. She had beckoned him and yawned at him and beckoned him again and he had responded often with bitterness and narrowed eyes. She had brought him ecstatic happiness and intolerable agony of spirit. She had caused him untold inconvenience and not a little trouble. She had insulted him, and she had ridden over him, and she had played his interest in her against his interest in his work—for fun. She had done everything to him except to criticise him—this she had not done— it seemed to him only because it might have sullied the utter indifference she manifested and sincerely felt toward him.

When autumn had come and gone again it occurred to him that he could not have Judy Jones. He had to beat this into his mind but he convinced himself at last. He lay awake at night for a while and argued it over. He told himself the trouble and the pain she had caused him, he enumerated her glaring deficiencies as a wife. Then he said to himself that he loved her, and after a while he fell asleep. For a week, lest he imagined her husky voice over the telephone or her eyes opposite him at lunch, he worked hard and late, and at night he went to his office and plotted out his years.

At the end of a week he went to a dance and cut in on her once. For almost the first time since they had met he did not ask her to sit out with him or tell her that she was lovely. It hurt him that she did not miss these things—that was all. He was not jealous when he saw that there was a new man to-night. He had been hardened against jealousy long before.

He stayed late at the dance. He sat for an hour with Irene Scheerer and talked about books and about music. He knew very little about either. But he was beginning to be master of his own time now, and he had a rather priggish notion that he—the young and already fabulously successful Dexter Green—should know more about such things.

That was in October, when he was twenty-five. In January, Dexter and Irene became engaged. It was to be announced in June, and they were to be married three months later.

The Minnesota winter prolonged itself interminably, and it was almost May when the winds came soft and the snow ran down into Black Bear Lake at last. For the first time in over a year Dexter was enjoying a certain tranquility of spirit. Judy Jones had been in Florida, and afterward in Hot Springs, and somewhere she had been engaged, and somewhere she had broken it off. At first, when Dexter had definitely given her up, it had made him sad that people still linked them together and asked for news of her, but when he began to be placed at dinner next to Irene Scheerer people didn't ask him about her any more—they told him about her. He ceased to be an authority on her.

May at last. Dexter walked the streets at night when the darkness was damp as rain, wondering that so soon, with so little done, so much of ecstasy had gone from him. May one year back had been marked by Judy's poignant, unforgivable, yet forgiven turbulence—it had been one of those rare times when he fancied she had grown to care for him. That old penny's worth of happiness he had spent for this bushel of content. He knew that Irene would be no more than a curtain spread behind him, a hand moving among gleaming tea-cups, a voice calling to children . . . fire and loveliness were gone, the magic of nights and the wonder of the varying hours and seasons . . . slender lips, down-turning, dropping to his lips and bearing him up into a heaven of eyes. . . . The thing was deep in him. He was too strong and alive for it to die lightly.

In the middle of May when the weather balanced for a few days on the thin bridge that led to deep summer he turned in one night at Irene's house. Their engagement was to be announced in a week now—no one would be surprised at it. And to-night they would sit together on the lounge at the University Club and look on for an hour at the dancers. It gave him a sense of solidity to go with her—she was so sturdily popular, so intensely "great."

He mounted the steps of the brownstone house and stepped inside.

"Irene," he called.

Mrs. Scheerer came out of the living-room to meet him.

"Dexter," she said, "Irene's gone up-stairs with a splitting headache. She wanted to go with you but I made her go to bed."

"Nothing serious, I—"

"Oh, no. She's going to play golf with you in the morning. You can spare her for just one night, can't you, Dexter?"

Her smile was kind. She and Dexter liked each other. In the living-room he talked for a moment before he said good-night.

Returning to the University Club, where he had rooms, he stood in the doorway for a moment and watched the dancers. He leaned against the door-post, nodded at a man or two—yawned.

"Hello, darling."

The familiar voice at his elbow startled him. Judy Jones had left a man and crossed the room to him—Judy Jones, a slender enamelled doll in cloth of gold: gold in a band at her head, gold in two slipper points at her dress's hem. The fragile glow of her face seemed to blossom as she smiled at him. A breeze of warmth and light blew through the room. His hands in the pockets of his dinner-jacket tightened spasmodically. He was filled with a sudden excitement.

"When did you get back?" he asked casually.

"Come here and I'll tell you about it."

She turned and he followed her. She had been away—he could have wept at the wonder of her return. She had passed through enchanted streets, doing things that were like provocative music. All mysterious happenings, all fresh and quickening hopes, had gone away with her, come back with her now.

She turned in the doorway.

"Have you a car here? If you haven't, I have."

"I have a coupé."

In then, with a rustle of golden cloth. He slammed the door. Into so many cars she had stepped—like this—like that— her back against the leather, so—her elbow resting on the door— waiting. She would have been soiled long since had there been anything to soil her—except herself—but this was her own self outpouring.

With an effort he forced himself to start the car and back into the street. This was nothing, he must remember. She had done this before, and he had put her behind him, as he would have crossed a bad account from his books.

He drove slowly down-town and, affecting abstraction, traversed the deserted streets of the business section, peopled here and there where a movie was giving out its crowd or where consumptive or pugilistic youth lounged in front of pool halls. The clink of glasses and the slap of hands on the bars issued from saloons, cloisters of glazed glass and dirty yellow light.

She was watching him closely and the silence was embarrassing, yet in this crisis he could find no casual word with which to profane the hour. At a convenient turning he began to zigzag back toward the University Club.

"Have you missed me?" she asked suddenly.

"Everybody missed you."

He wondered if she knew of Irene Scheerer. She had been back only a day—her absence had been almost contemporaneous with his engagement.

"What a remark!" Judy laughed sadly—without sadness. She looked at him searchingly. He became absorbed in the dashboard.

"You're handsomer than you used to be," she said thoughtfully. "Dexter, you have the most rememberable eyes."

He could have laughed at this, but he did not laugh. It was the sort of thing that was said to sophomores. Yet it stabbed at him.

"I'm awfully tired of everything, darling." She called every one darling, endowing the endearment with careless, individual comraderie. "I wish you'd marry me."

The directness of this confused him. He should have told her now that he was going to marry another girl, but he could not tell her. He could as easily have sworn that he had never loved her.

"I think we'd get along," she continued, on the same note, "unless probably you've forgotten me and fallen in love with another girl."

Her confidence was obviously enormous. She had said, in effect, that she found such a thing impossible to believe, that if it were true he had merely committed a childish indiscretion— and probably to show off. She would forgive him, because it was not a matter of any moment but rather something to be brushed aside lightly.

"Of course you could never love anybody but me," she continued. "I like the way you love me. Oh, Dexter, have you forgotten last year?"

"No, I haven't forgotten."

"Neither have I! "

Was she sincerely moved—or was she carried along by the wave of her own acting?

"I wish we could be like that again," she said, and he forced himself to answer:

"I don't think we can."

"I suppose not. . . . I hear you're giving Irene Scheerer a violent rush."

There was not the faintest emphasis on the name, yet Dexter was suddenly ashamed.

"Oh, take me home," cried Judy suddenly; "I don't want to go back to that idiotic dance—with those children."

Then, as he turned up the street that led to the residence district, Judy began to cry quietly to herself. He had never seen her cry before.

The dark street lightened, the dwellings of the rich loomed up around them, he stopped his coupé in front of the great white bulk of the Mortimer Joneses house, somnolent, gorgeous, drenched with the splendor of the damp moonlight. Its solidity startled him. The strong walls, the steel of the girders, the breadth and beam and pomp of it were there only to bring out the contrast with the young beauty beside him. It was sturdy to accentuate her slightness—as if to show what a breeze could be generated by a butterfly's wing.

He sat perfectly quiet, his nerves in wild clamor, afraid that if he moved he would find her irresistibly in his arms. Two tears had rolled down her wet face and trembled on her upper lip.

"I'm more beautiful than anybody else," she said brokenly, "why can't I be happy?" Her moist eyes tore at his stability—her mouth turned slowly downward with an exquisite sadness: "I'd like to marry you if you'll have me, Dexter. I suppose you think I'm not worth having, but I'll be so beautiful for you, Dexter."

A million phrases of anger, pride, passion, hatred, tenderness fought on his lips. Then a perfect wave of emotion washed over him, carrying off with it a sediment of wisdom, of convention, of doubt, of honor. This was his girl who was speaking, his own, his beautiful, his pride.

"Won't you come in?" He heard her draw in her breath sharply.

Waiting.

"All right," his voice was trembling, "I'll come in.

V

IT WAS STRANGE that neither when it was over nor a long time afterward did he regret that night. Looking at it from the perspective of ten years, the fact that Judy's flare for him endured just one month seemed of little importance. Nor did it matter that by his yielding he subjected himself to a deeper agony in the end and gave serious hurt to Irene Scheerer and to Irene's parents, who had befriended him. There was nothing sufficiently pictorial about Irene's grief to stamp itself on his mind.

Dexter was at bottom hard-minded. The attitude of the city on his action was of no importance to him, not because he was going to leave the city, but because any outside attitude on the situation seemed superficial. He was completely indifferent to popular opinion. Nor, when he had seen that it was no use, that he did not possess in himself the power to move fundamentally or to hold Judy Jones, did he bear any malice toward her. He loved her, and he would love her until the day he was too old for loving—but he could not have her. So he tasted the deep pain that is reserved only for the strong, just as he had tasted for a little while the deep happiness.

Even the ultimate falsity of the grounds upon which Judy terminated the engagement that she did not want to "take him away" from Irene—Judy, who had wanted nothing else—did not revolt him. He was beyond any revulsion or any amusement.

He went East in February with the intention of selling out his laundries and settling in New York—but the war came to America in March and changed his plans. He returned to the West, handed over the management of the business to his partner, and went into the first officers' training-camp in late April. He was one of those young thousands who greeted the war with a certain amount of relief, welcoming the liberation from webs of tangled emotion.

VI

THIS STORY is not his biography, remember, although things creep into it which have nothing to do with those dreams he had when he was young. We are almost done with them and with him now. There is only one more incident to be related here, and it happens seven years farther on.

It took place in New York, where he had done well—so well that there were no barriers too high for him. He was thirty-two years old, and, except for one flying trip immediately after the war, he had not been West in seven years. A man named Devlin from Detroit came into his office to see him in a business way, and then and there this incident occurred, and closed out, so to speak, this particular side of his life.

"So you're from the Middle West," said the man Devlin with careless curiosity. "That's funny—I thought men like you were probably born and raised on Wall Street. You know—wife of one of my best friends in Detroit came from your city. I was an usher at the wedding."

Dexter waited with no apprehension of what was coming.

"Judy Simms," said Devlin with no particular interest; "Judy Jones she was once."

"Yes, I knew her." A dull impatience spread over him. He had heard, of course, that she was married—perhaps deliberately he had heard no more.

"Awfully nice girl," brooded Devlin meaninglessly, "I'm sort of sorry for her."

"Why?" Something in Dexter was alert, receptive, at once.

"Oh, Lud Simms has gone to pieces in a way. I don't mean he ill-uses her, but he drinks and runs around."

"Doesn't she run around?"

"No. Stays at home with her kids."

"Oh."

"She's a little too old for him," said Devlin.

"Too old!" cried Dexter. "Why, man, she's only twenty-seven."

He was possessed with a wild notion of rushing out into the streets and taking a train to Detroit. He rose to his feet spasmodically.

"I guess you're busy," Devlin apologized quickly. "I didn't realize–"

"No, I'm not busy," said Dexter, steadying his voice. "I'm not busy at all. Not busy at all. Did you say she was– twenty-seven? No, I said she was twenty-seven."

"Yes, you did," agreed Devlin dryly.

"Go on, then. Go on."

"What do you mean?"

"About Judy Jones."

Devlin looked at him helplessly.

"Well, that's, I told you all there is to it. He treats her like the devil. Oh, they're not going to get divorced or anything. When he's particularly outrageous she forgives him. In fact, I'm inclined to think she loves him. She was a pretty girl when she first came to Detroit."

A pretty girl! The phrase struck Dexter as ludicrous

"Isn't she–a pretty girl, any more?"

"Oh, she's all right."

"Look here," said Dexter, sitting down suddenly, "I don't understand. You say she was a 'pretty girl' and now you say she's 'all right.' I don't understand what you mean–Judy Jones wasn't a pretty girl, at all. She was a great beauty. Why, I knew her, I knew her. She was–"

Devlin laughed pleasantly.

"I'm not trying to start a row," he said. "I think Judy's a nice girl and I like her. I can't understand how a man like Lud Simms could fall madly in love with her, but he did." Then he added: "Most of the women like her."

Dexter looked closely at Devlin, thinking wildly that there must be a reason for this, some insensitivity in the man or some private malice.

"Lots of women fade just like that," Devlin snapped his fingers. "You must have seen it happen. Perhaps I've forgotten how pretty she was at her wedding. I've seen her so much since then, you see. She has nice eyes."

A sort of dulness settled down upon Dexter. For the first time in his life he felt like getting very drunk. He knew that he was laughing loudly at something Devlin had said, but he did not know what it was or why it was funny. When, in a few minutes, Devlin went he lay down on his lounge and looked out the window at the

New York sky-line into which the sun was sinking in dull lovely shades of pink and gold.

He had thought that having nothing else to lose he was invulnerable at last–but he knew that he had just lost something more, as surely as if he had married Judy Jones and seen her fade away before his eyes.

The dream was gone. Something had been taken from him. In a sort of panic he pushed the palms of his hands into his eyes and tried to bring up a picture of the waters lapping on Sherry Island and the moonlit veranda, and gingham on the golf-links and the dry sun and the gold color of her neck's soft down. And her mouth damp to his kisses and her eyes plaintive with melancholy and her freshness like new fine linen in the morning. Why, these things were no longer in the world! They had existed and they existed no longer.

For the first time in years the tears were streaming down his face. But they were for himself now. He did not care about mouth and eyes and moving hands. He wanted to care, and he could not care. For he had gone away and he could never go back any more. The gates were closed, the sun was gone down, and there was no beauty but the gray beauty of steel that withstands all time. Even the grief he could have borne was left behind in the country of illusion, of youth, of the richness of life, where his winter dreams had flourished.

"Long ago," he said, "long ago, there was something in me, but now that thing is gone. Now that thing is gone, that thing is gone. I cannot cry. I cannot care. That thing will come back no more."

Two for a Cent

When the rain was over, the sky became yellow in the west and the air was cool. Close to the street, which was of red dirt and lined with cheap bungalows dating from 1910, a little boy was riding a big bicycle along the sidewalk. His plan afforded a monotonous fascination. He rode each time for about a hundred yards, dismounted, turned the bicycle around so that it adjoined a stone step and getting on again, not without toil or heat, retraced his course. At one end this was bounded by a colored girl of fourteen holding an anemic baby, and at the other by a scarred, ill-nourished kitten, squatting dismally on the curb. These four were the only souls in sight.

The little boy had accomplished an indefinite number of trips oblivious alike to the melancholy advances of the kitten at one end and to the admiring vacuousness of the colored girl at the other when he swerved dangerously to avoid a man who had turned the corner into the street and recovered his balance only after a moment of exaggerated panic.

But if the incident was a matter of gravity to the boy, it attracted scarcely an instant's notice from the newcomer, who turned suddenly from the sidewalk and stared with obvious and peculiar interest at the house before which he was standing. It was the oldest house in the street, built with clapboards and a shingled roof. It was a house—in the barest sense of the word: the sort of house that a child would draw on a blackboard. It was of a period, but of no design, and its exterior had obviously been made only as a decent cloak for what was within. It antedated the stucco bungalows by about thirty years and except for the bungalows, which were reproducing their species with prodigious avidity as though by some monstrous affiliation with the guinea-pig, it was the most common type of house in the country. For thirty years such dwellings had satisfied the canons of the middle class; they had satisfied its financial canons by being cheap, they had satisfied its aesthetic canons by being hideous. It was a house built by a race whose more energetic complement hoped either to move up or move on, and it was the more remarkable that its instability had survived so many summers and retained its pristine hideousness and discomfort so obviously unimpaired.

The man was about as old as the house, that is to say, about forty-five. But unlike the house, he was neither hideous nor cheap. His clothes were too good to have been made outside of a metropolis—moreover, they were so good that it was impossible to tell in which metropolis they were made. His name was Abercrombie and the most important event of his life had taken place in the house before which he was standing. He had been born there.

It was one of the last places in the world where he should have been born. He had thought so within a very few years after the event and he thought so now—an ugly home in a third-rate Southern town where his father had owned a partnership in a grocery store. Since then Abercrombie had played golf with the President of the United States and sat between two duchesses at dinner. He had been bored with the President, he had been bored and not a little embarrassed with the duchesses—nevertheless, the two incidents had pleased him and still sat softly upon his naive vanity. It delighted him that he had gone far.

He had looked fixedly at the house for several minutes before he perceived that no one lived there. Where the shutters were not closed it was because there were no shutters to be closed and in these vacancies, blind vacuous expanses of gray window looked unseeingly down at him. The grass had grown wantonly long in the yard and faint green mustaches were sprouting facetiously in the wide cracks of the walk. But it was evident that the property had been recently occupied for upon the porch lay half a dozen newspapers rolled into cylinders for quick delivery and as yet turned only to a faint resentful yellow.

They were not nearly so yellow as the sky when Abercrombie walked up on the porch and sat down upon an immemorial bench, for the sky was every shade of yellow, the color of tan, the color of gold, the color of peaches. Across the street and beyond a vacant lot rose a rampart of vivid red brick houses and it seemed to Abercrombie that the picture they rounded out was beautiful—the warm earthy brick and the sky fresh after the rain, changing and gray as a dream. All his life when he had wanted to rest his mind he had called up into it the image those two things had made for him when the air was clear just at this hour. So Abercrombie sat there thinking about his young days.

Ten minutes later another man turned the corner of the street, a different sort of man, both in the texture of his clothes and the texture of his soul. He was forty-six years old and he was a shabby drudge, married to a woman, who, as a girl, had known better days. This latter fact, in the republic, may be set down in the red italics of misery.

His name was Hemmick—Henry W. or George D. or John F.—the stock that produced him had had little imagination left to waste either upon his name or his design. He was a clerk in a factory which made ice for the long Southern Summer. He was responsible to the man who owned the patent for canning ice, who, in his turn was responsible only to God. Never in his life had Henry W. Hemmick discovered a new way to advertise canned ice nor had it transpired that by taking a diligent correspondence course in ice canning he had secretly been preparing himself for a partnership. Never had he rushed home to his wife, crying: "You can have that servant now, Nell, 1 have been made General Superintendent." You will have to take him as you take Abercrombie, for what he is and will always be. This is a story of the dead years.

When the second man reached the house he turned in and began to mount the tipsy steps, noticed Abercrombie, the stranger, with a tired surprise, and nodded to him.

"Good evening," he said.

Abercrombie voiced his agreement with the sentiment.

"Cool"—The newcomer covered his forefinger with his handkerchief and sent the swatched digit on a complete circuit of his collar band. "Have you rented this?" he asked.

"No, indeed, I'm just—resting. Sorry if I've intruded—I saw the house was vacant—"

"Oh, you're not intruding!" said Hemmick hastily. "I don't reckon anybody could intrude in this old barn. I got out two months ago. They're not ever goin' to rent it any more. I got a little girl about this high—" he held his hand parallel to the ground and at an indeterminate distance"—and she's mighty fond of an old doll that got left here when we moved. Began hollerin' for me to come over and look it up."

"You used to live here?" inquired Abercrombie with interest.

"Lived here eighteen years. Came here'n I was married, raised four children in this house. Yes, sir. I know this old fellow." He struck the door-post with the flat of his hand. "I know every leak in her roof and every loose board in her old floor."

Abercrombie had been good to look at for so many years that he knew if he kept a certain attentive expression on his face his companion would continue to talk—indefinitely.

"You from up North?" inquired Hemmick politely, choosing with habituated precision the one spot where the anemic wooden railing would support his weight. "I thought so," he resumed at Abercrombie's nod. "Don't take long to tell a Yankee."

"I'm from New York."

"So?" The man shook his head with inappropriate gravity. "Never have got up there, myself. Started to go a couple of times, before I was married, but never did get to go."

He made a second excursion with his finger and handkerchief and then, as though having come suddenly to a cordial decision, he replaced the handkerchief in one of his bumpy pockets and extended the hand toward his companion.

"My name's Hemmick."

"Glad to know you." Abercrombie took the hand without rising. "Abercrombie's mine."

"I'm mighty glad to know you, Mr. Abercrombie."

Then for a moment they both hesitated, their two faces assumed oddly similar expressions, their eyebrows drew together, their eyes looked far away. Each was straining to force into activity some minute cell long sealed and forgotten in his brain. Each made a little noise in his throat, looked away, looked back, laughed. Abercrombie spoke first.

"We've met."

"I know," agreed Hemmick, "but whereabouts? That's what's got me. You from New York you say?"

"Yes, but I was born and raised in this town. Lived in this house till I left here when I was about seventeen. As a matter of fact, I remember you—you were a couple of years older."

Again Hemmick considered.

"Well," he said vaguely, "I sort of remember, too. I begin to remember— I got your name all right and I guess maybe it was your daddy had this house before I rented it. But all I can recollect about you is, that there was a boy named Abercrombie and he went away."

In a few moments they were talking easily. It amused them both to have come from the same house—amused Abercrombie especially, for he was a vain man, rather absorbed, that evening, in his own early poverty. Though he was not given to immature impulses, he found it necessary somehow to make it clear in a few sentences that five years after he had gone away from the house and the town he had been able to send for his father and mother to join him in New York.

Hemmick listened with that exaggerated attention which men who have not prospered generally render to men who have. He would have continued to listen had Abercrombie become more expansive, for he was beginning faintly to associate him with an Abercrombie who had figured in the newspapers for several years at the head of shipping boards and financial committees. But Abercrombie, after a moment, made the conversation less personal.

"I didn't realize you had so much heat here. I guess I've forgotten a lot in twenty-five years."

"Why, this is a cool day," boasted Hemmick, "this is cool. I was just sort of overheated from walking when I came up."

"It's too hot," insisted Abercrombie with a restless movement; then he added abruptly, "I don't like it here. It means nothing to me—nothing—I've wondered if it did, you know; that's why I came down. And I've decided.

"You see," he continued hesitantly, "up to recently the North was still full of professional Southerners, some real, some by sentiment, but all given to flowery monologues on the beauty of their old family plantations and all jumping up and howling when the band played 'Dixie.' You know what I mean"—he turned to Hemmick—"it got to be a sort of a national joke. Oh, I was in the game, too, I suppose. I used to stand up and perspire and cheer, and I've given young men positions for no particular reason except that they claimed to come from South Carolina or Virginia—" again he broke off and became suddenly abrupt—"but I'm through, I've been here six hours and I'm through!"

"Too hot for you?" inquired Hemmick, with mild surprise.

"Yes! I've felt the heat and I've seen the men—those two or three dozen loafers standing in front of the stores on Jackson Street—in thatched straw hats"—then he added, with a touch of humor, "they're what my son calls 'slash-pocket, belted-back boys.' Do you know the ones I mean?"

"Jelly-beans," Hemmick nodded gravely, "we call 'em Jelly-beans. No-account lot of boys all right. They got signs up in front of most of the stores asking 'em not to stand there."

"They ought to!" asserted Abercrombie, with a touch of irascibility. "That's my picture of the South now, you know—a skinny, dark-haired young man with a gun on his hip and a stomach full of corn liquor or Dope Dola, leaning up against a drug store waiting for the next lynching."

Hemmick objected, though with apology in his voice.

"You got to remember, Mr. Abercrombie, that we haven't had the money down here since the war—"

Abercrombie waved this impatiently aside.

"Oh, I've heard all that," he said, "and I'm tired of it. And I've heard the South lambasted till I'm tired of that, too. It's not taking France and Germany fifty years to get on their feet, and their war made your war look like a little fracas up an alley. And it's not your fault and it's not anybody's fault. It's just that this is too damn hot to be a white man's country and it always will be. I'd like to see 'em pack two or three of these states full of darkies and drop 'em out of the Union."

Hemmick nodded, thoughtfully, though without thought. He had never thought; for over twenty years he had seldom ever held opinions, save the opinions of the local press or of some majority made articulate through passion. There was a certain luxury in thinking that he had never been able to afford. When cases were set before him he either accepted them outright if they were comprehensible to him or rejected them if they required a modicum of concentration. Yet he was not a stupid man. He was poor and busy and tired and there were no ideas at large in his community, even had he been capable of grasping them. The idea that he did not think would have been equally incomprehensible to him. He was a closed book, half full of badly printed, uncorrelated trash.

Just now, his reaction to Abercrombie's assertion was exceedingly simple. Since the remarks proceeded from a man who was a Southerner by birth, who was successful—moreover, who was confident and decisive and persuasive and suave—he was inclined to accept them without suspicion or resentment. He took one of Abercrombie's cigars and pulling on it, still with a stern imitation of profundity upon his tired face, watched the color glide out of the sky and the gray veils come down. The little boy and his bicycle, the baby, the nursemaid, the forlorn kitten, all had departed. In the stucco bungalows pianos gave out hot weary notes that inspired the crickets to competitive sound, and squeaky Graphophones filled in the intervals with patches of whining ragtime until the impression was created that each living room in the street opened directly out into the darkness.

"What I want to find out," Abercrombie was saying with a frown, "is why I didn't have sense enough to know that this was a worthless town. It was entirely an accident that I left here, an utterly blind chance, and as it happened, the very train that took me away was full of luck for me. The man I sat beside gave me my start in life." His tone became resentful. "But I thought this was all right. I'd have stayed except that I'd gotten into a scrape down at the high school—I got expelled and my daddy told me he didn't want me at home any more. Why didn't I know the place wasn't any good? Why didn't I see?"

"Well, you'd probably never known anything better?" suggested Hemmick mildly.

"That wasn't any excuse," insisted Abercrombie. "If I'd been any good I'd have known. As a matter of fact—as—a—matter—of—fact," he repeated slowly, "I think that at heart I was the sort of boy who'd have lived and died here happily and never known there was anything better." He turned to Hemmick with a look almost of distress. "It worries me to think that my— that what's happened to me can be ascribed to chance. But that's the sort of boy I think I was. I didn't start off with the Dick Whittington idea—I started off by accident."

After this confession, he stared out into the twilight with a dejected expression that Hemmick could not understand. It was impossible for the latter to share any sense of the importance of such a distinction—in fact from a man of Abercrombie's position it struck him as unnecessarily trivial. Still, he felt that some manifestation of acquiescence was only polite.

"Well," he offered, "it's just that some boys get the bee to get up and go North and some boys don't. I happened to have the bee to go North. But I didn't. That's the difference between you and me."

Abercrombie turned to him intently.

"You did?" he asked, with unexpected interest. "You wanted to get out?"

"At one time." At Abercrombie's eagerness Hemmick began to attach a new importance to the subject. "At one time," he repeated, as though the singleness of the occasion was a thing he had often mused upon.

"How old were you?"

"Oh—'bout twenty."

"What put it into your head?"

"Well, let me see—" Hemmick considered. "—I don't know whether I remember sure enough but it seems to me that when I was down to the University—I was there two years—one of the professors told me that a smart boy ought to go North. He said business wasn't going to amount to much down here for the next fifty years. And I guessed he was right. My father died about then, so I got a job as runner in the bank here, and I didn't have much interest in anything except saving up enough money to go North. I was bound I'd go."

"Why didn't you? Why didn't you?" insisted Abercrombie in an aggrieved tone.

"Well," Hemmick hesitated. "Well, I right near did but—things didn't work out and I didn't get to go. It was a funny sort of business. It all started about the smallest thing you can think of. It all started about a penny."

"A penny?"

"That's what did it—one little penny. That's why I didn't go 'way from here and all, like I intended."

"Tell me about it, man!" exclaimed his companion. He looked at his watch impatiently. "I'd like to hear the story."

Hemmick sat for a moment, distorting his mouth around the cigar.

"Well, to begin with," he said, at length, "I'm going to ask you if you remember a thing that happened here about twenty-five years ago. A fellow named Hoyt, the cashier of the Cotton National Bank, disappeared one night with about thirty thousand dollars in cash. Say, man, they didn't talk about anything else down here at the time. The whole town was shaken up about it, and I reckin you can imagine the disturbance it caused down at all the banks and especially at the Cotton National."

"I remember."

"Well, they caught him, and they got most of the money back, and by and by the excitement died down, except in the bank where the thing had happened. Down there it seemed as if they'd never get used to it. Mr. Deems, the First Vice-President, who'd always been pretty kind and decent, got to be a changed man. He was suspicious of the clerks, the tellers, the janitor, the watchman, most of the officers, and yes, by Golly, I guess he got so he kept an eye on the President himself.

"I don't mean he was just watchful—he was downright hipped on the subject. He'd come up and ask you funny questions when you were going about your business. He'd walk into the teller's cage on tip-toe and watch him without saying anything. If there was any mistake of any kind in the bookkeeping, he'd not only fire a clerk or so, but he'd raise such a riot that he made you want to push him into a vault and slam the door on him.

"He was just about running the bank then, and he'd affected the other officers, and—oh, you can imagine the havoc a thing like that could work on any sort of an organization. Everybody was so nervous that they made mistakes whether they were careful or not. Clerks were staying downtown until eleven at night trying to account for a lost nickel. It was a thin year, anyhow, and everything financial was pretty rickety, so one thing worked on another until the crowd of us were as near craziness as anybody can be and carry on the banking business at all.

"I was a runner—and all through the heat of one God-forsaken Summer I ran. I ran and I got mighty little money for it, and that was the time I hated that bank and this town, and all I wanted was to get out and go North. I was getting ten dollars a week, and I'd decided that when I'd saved fifty out of it I was going down to the depot and buy me a ticket to Cincinnati. I had an uncle in the banking business there, and he said he'd give me an opportunity with him. But he never offered to pay my way, and I guess he thought if I was worth having I'd manage to get up there by myself. Well, maybe I wasn't worth having because, anyhow, I never did.

"One morning on the hottest day of the hottest July I ever knew—and you know what that means down here—I left the bank to call on a man named Harlan and collect some money that'd come due on a note. Harlan had the cash waiting for me all right, and when I counted it I found it amounted to three hundred dollars and eighty-six cents, the change being in brand-new coin that Harlan had drawn from another bank that morning. I put the three one-hundred-dollar bills in my wallet and the change in my watch pocket, signed a receipt and left. I was going straight back to the bank.

"Outside the heat was terrible. It was enough to make you dizzy, and I hadn't been feeling right for a couple of days, so, while I waited in the shade for a street car, I was congratulating myself that in a month or so I'd be out of this and up where it was some cooler. And then as I stood there it occurred to me all of a sudden that outside of the money which I'd just collected, which, of course, I couldn't touch, I didn't have a cent in my pocket. I'd have to walk back to the bank, and it was about fifteen blocks away. You see, on the night before, I'd found that my change came to just a dollar, and I'd traded it for a bill at the corner store and added it to the roll in the bottom of my trunk. So there was no help for it—I took off my coat and I stuck my handkerchief into my collar and struck off through the suffocating heat for the bank.

"Fifteen blocks—you can imagine what that was like, and I was sick when I started. From away up by Juniper Street—you remember where that is; the new Mieger Hospital's there now—all the way down to Jackson. After about six blocks I began to stop and rest whenever I found a patch of shade wide enough to hold me, and as I got pretty near I could just keep going by thinking of the big glass of iced tea my mother'd have waiting beside my plate at lunch. But after that I began getting too sick to even want the iced tea— I wanted to get rid of that money and then lie down and die.

"When I was still about two blocks away from the bank I put my hand into my watch pocket and pulled out that change; was sort of jingling it in my hand; making myself believe that I was so close that it was convenient to have it ready. I happened to glance into my hand, and all of a sudden I stopped up short and reached down quick into my watch pocket. The pocket was empty. There was a little hole in the bottom, and my hand held only a half dollar, a quarter, and a dime. I had lost one cent.

"Well, sir, I can't tell you, I can't express to you the feeling of discouragement that this gave me. One penny, mind you—but think: just the week before a runner had lost his job because he was a little bit shy twice. It was only carelessness; but there you were! They were all in a panic that they might get fired themselves, and the best thing to do was to fire some one else—first.

"So you can see that it was up to me to appear with that penny.

"Where I got the energy to care as much about it as I did is more than I can understand. I was sick and hot and weak as a kitten, but it never occurred to me that I could do anything except find or replace that penny, and immediately I began casting about for a way to do it. I looked into a couple of stores, hoping I'd see some one I knew, but while there were a few fellows loafing in front, just as you saw them today, there wasn't one that I felt like going up to and saying: 'Here! You got a penny?' I thought of a couple of offices where I could have gotten it without much trouble, but they were some distance off, and besides being pretty dizzy, I hated to go out of my route when I was carrying bank money, because it looked kind of strange.

"So what should I do but commence walking back along the street toward the Union Depot where I last remembered having the penny. It was a brand-new penny, and I thought maybe I'd see it shining where it dropped. So I kept walking, looking pretty carefully at the sidewalk and thinking what I'd better do. I laughed a little, because I felt sort of silly for worrying about a penny, but I didn't enjoy laughing, and it really didn't seem silly to me at all.

"Well, by and by I got back to the Union Depot without having either seen the old penny or having thought what was the best way to get another. I hated to go all the way home, 'cause we lived a long distance out; but what else was I to do? So I found a piece of shade close to the depot, and stood there considering, thinking first one thing and then another, and not getting anywhere at all. One little penny, just one—something almost any man in sight would have given me; something even the nigger baggage-smashers were jingling around in their pockets... I must have stood there about five minutes. I remember there was a line of about a dozen men in front of an army recruiting station they'd just opened, and a couple of them began to yell: 'Join the Army!' at me. That woke me up, and I moved on back toward the bank, getting worried now, getting mixed up and sicker and sicker and knowing a million ways to find a penny and not one that seemed convenient or right. I was exaggerating the importance of losing it, and I was exaggerating the difficulty of finding another, but you just have to believe that it seemed about as important to me just then as though it were a hundred dollars.

"Then I saw a couple of men talking in front of Moody's soda place, and recognized one of them—Mr. Burling—who'd been a friend of my father's. That was relief, I can tell you. Before I knew it I was chattering to him so quick that he couldn't follow what I was getting at.

"'Now,' he said, 'you know I'm a little deaf and can't understand when you talk that fast! What is it you want, Henry? Tell me from the beginning.'

"'Have you got any change with you?' I asked him just as loud as I dared. 'I just want—' Then I stopped short; a man a few feet away had turned around and was looking at us. It was Mr. Deems, the First Vice-President of the Cotton National Bank."

Hemmick paused, and it was still light enough for Abercrombie to see that he was shaking his head to and fro in a puzzled way. When he spoke his voice held a quality of pained surprise, a quality that it might have carried over twenty years.

"I never could understand what it was that came over me then. I must have been sort of crazy with the heat—that's all I can decide. Instead of just saying, 'Howdy' to Mr. Deems, in a natural way, and telling Mr. Burling I wanted to borrow a nickel for tobacco, because I'd left my purse at home, I turned away quick as a flash and began walking up the street at a great rate, feeling like a criminal who had come near being caught.

"Before I'd gone a block I was sorry. I could almost hear the conversation that must've been taking place between those two men:

"'What do you reckon's the matter with that young man?' Mr. Burling would say without meaning any harm. 'Came up to me all excited and wanted to know if I had any money, and then he saw you and rushed away like he was crazy.'

"And I could almost see Mr. Deems' big eyes get narrow with suspicion and watch him twist up his trousers and come strolling along after me. I was in a real panic now, and no mistake. Suddenly I saw a one-horse surrey going by, and recognized Bill Kennedy, a friend of mine, driving it. I yelled at him, but he didn't hear me. Then I yelled again, but he didn't pay any attention, so I started after him at a run, swaying from side to side, I guess, like I was drunk, and calling his name every few minutes. He looked around once, but he didn't see me; he kept right on going and turned out of sight at the next comer. I stopped then because I was too weak to go any farther. I was just about to sit down on the curb and rest when I looked around, and the first thing I saw was Mr. Deems walking after me as fast as he could come. There wasn't any of my imagination about it this time—the look in his eyes showed he wanted to know what was the matter with me!

"Well, that's about all I remember clearly until about twenty minutes later, when I was at home trying to unlock my trunk with fingers that were trembling like a tuning fork. Before I could get it open, Mr. Deems and a policeman came in. I began talking all at once about not being a thief and trying to tell them what had happened, but I guess I was sort of hysterical, and the more I said the worse matters were. When I managed to get the story out it seemed sort of crazy, even to me—and it was true—it was true, true as I've told you—every word!—that one penny that I lost somewhere down by the station—" Hemmick broke off and began laughing grotesquely—as though the excitement that had come over him as he finished his tale was a weakness of which he was ashamed. When he resumed it was with an affectation of nonchalance.

"I'm not going into the details of what happened because nothing much did—at least not on the scale you judge events by up North. It cost me my job, and I changed a good name for a bad one. Somebody tattled and somebody lied, and the impression got around that I'd lost a lot of the bank's money and had been tryin' to cover it up.

"I had an awful time getting a job after that. Finally I got a statement out of the bank that contradicted the wildest of the stories that had started, but the people who were still interested said it was just because the bank didn't want any fuss or scandal—and the rest had forgotten: that is they'd forgotten what had happened, but they remembered that somehow I just wasn't a young fellow to be trusted—"

Hemmick paused and laughed again, still without enjoyment, but bitterly, uncomprehendingly, and with a profound helplessness.

"So, you see, that's why I didn't go to Cincinnati," he said slowly; "my mother was alive then, and this was a pretty bad blow to her. She had an idea—one of those old-fashioned Southern ideas that stick in people's heads down here—that somehow I ought to stay here in town and prove myself honest. She had it on her mind, and she wouldn't hear of my going. She said that the day I went'd be the day she'd die. So I sort of had to stay till I'd got back my—my reputation."

"How long did that take?" asked Abercrombie quietly.

"About—ten years."

"Oh—"

"Ten years," repeated Hemmick, staring out into the gathering darkness. "This is a little town, you see: I say ten years because it was about ten years when the last reference to it came to my ears. But I was married long before that; had a kid. Cincinnati was out of my mind by that time."

"Of course," agreed Abercrombie.

They were both silent for a moment—then Hemmick added apologetically:

"That was sort of a long story, and I don't know if it could have interested you much. But you asked me—"

"It did interest me," answered Abercrombie politely. "It interested me tremendously. It interested me much more than I thought it would."

It occurred to Hemmick that he himself had never realized what a curious, rounded tale it was. He saw dimly now that what had seemed to him only a fragment, a grotesque interlude, was really significant, complete. It was an interesting story; it was the story upon which turned the failure of his life. Abercrombie's voice broke in upon his thoughts.

"You see, it's so different from my story," Abercrombie was saying. "It was an accident that you stayed—and it was an accident that I went away. You deserve more actual—actual credit, if there is such a thing in the world, for your intention of getting out and getting on. You see, I'd more or less gone wrong at seventeen. I was—well, what you call a Jelly-bean. All I wanted was to take it easy through life—and one day I just happened to see a sign up above my head that had on it: 'Special rate to Atlanta, three dollars and forty-two cents.' So I took out my change and counted it—"

Hemmick nodded. Still absorbed in his own story, he had forgotten the importance, the comparative magnificence of Abercrombie. Then suddenly he found himself listening sharply:

"I had just three dollars and forty-one cents in my pocket. But, you see, I was standing in line with a lot of other young fellows down by the Union Depot about to enlist in the army for three years. And I saw that extra penny on the walk not three feet away. I saw it because it was brand new and shining in the sun like gold."

The Alabama night had settled over the street, and as the blue drew down upon the dust the outlines of the two men had become less distinct, so that it was not easy for any one who passed along the walk to tell that one of these men was of the few and the other of no importance. All the detail was gone—Abercrombie's fine gold wrist watch, his collar, that he ordered by the dozen from London, the dignity that sat upon him in his chair—all faded and were engulfed with Hemmick's awkward suit and preposterous humped shoes into that pervasive depth of night that, like death, made nothing matter, nothing differentiate, nothing remain. And a little later on a passerby saw only the two glowing disks about the size of a penny that marked the rise and fall of their cigars.

The Mystery of the Raymond Mortgage

When I first saw John Syrel of the New York Daily News, he was standing before an open window of my house gazing out on the city. It was about six o'clock and the lights were just going on. All down 33rd Street was a long line of gayly illuminated buildings. He was not a tall man, but thanks to the erectness of his posture, and the suppleness of his movement, it would take no athlete to tell that he was of fine build. He was twenty-three years old when I first saw him, and was already a reporter on the News. He was not a handsome man; his face was clean-shaven, and his chin showed him to be of strong character. His eyes and hair were brown.

As I entered the room he turned around slowly and addressed me in a slow, drawling tone: "I think I have the honor of speaking to Mr. Egan, chief of police." I assented, and he went on: "My name is John Syrel and my business,–to tell you frankly, is to learn all I can about that case of the Raymond mortgage."

I started to speak but he silenced me with a wave of his hand. "Though I belong to the staff of the Daily News," he continued, "I am not here as an agent of the paper,"

"I am not here," I interrupted coldly, "to tell every newspaper reporter or adventurer about private affairs. James, show this man out."

Syrel turned without a word and I heard his steps echo up the driveway.

However, this was not destined to be the last time I ever saw Syrel, as events will show.

The morning after I first saw John Syrel, I proceeded to the scene of the crime to which he had alluded. On the train I picked up a newspaper and read the following account of the crime and theft, which had followed it:

"EXTRA"

"Great Crime Committed in Suburbs of City"

"Mayor Proceeding to Scenes of Crime"

On the morning of July 1st, a crime and serious theft were committed on the outskirts of the city. Miss Raymond was killed and the body of a servant was found outside of the house. Mr. Raymond of Santuka Lake was awakened on Tuesday morning by a scream and two revolver shots which proceeded from his wife's room. He tried to open the door but it would not open. He was almost certain the door was locked from the inside, when suddenly it swung open disclosing a room in frightful disorder. On the center of the floor was a revolver and on his wife's bed was a blood stain in the shape of a hand. His wife was missing, but on a closer search he found his daughter under the bed, stone dead. The window was broken in two places. Miss Raymond had a bullet wound on her body and her head was fearfully cut. The body of a servant was found outside with a bullet hole through this head. Mrs. Raymond has not been found.

The room was upset. The bureau drawers were out as if the murderer had been looking for something. Chief of Police Egan is on the scene of the crime, etc., etc.

Just then the conductor called out "Santuka!" The train came to a stop, and getting out of the car I walked up to the house. On the porch I met Gregson, who was supposed to be the ablest detective in the force. He gave me a plan of the house which he said he would like to have me look at before we went in.

"The body of the servant," he said, "is that of John Standish. He has been with family 12 years and was a perfectly honest man. He was only 32 years old."

"The bullet which killed him was not found?" I asked.

"No," he answered; and then, "Well, you had better come in and see for yourself. By the way, there was a fellow hanging around here, who was trying to see the body. When I refused to let him in, he went around to where the servant was shot and I saw him go down on his knees on the grass and begin to search. A few minutes later he stood up and leaned against a tree. Then he came up to the house and asked to see the body again. I said he could if he would go away afterwards. He assented, and when he got inside the room he went down on his knees and under the bed and hunted around. Then he went over to the window and examined the broken pane carefully. After that he declared himself satisfied and went down towards the hotel."

After I had examined the room to my satisfaction, I found that I might as well try to see through a millstone as to try to fathom this mystery. As I finished my investigation I met Gregson in the laboratory.

"I suppose you heard about the mortgage," said he, as we went down stairs. I answered in the negative, and he told me that a valuable mortgage had disappeared from the room in which Miss Raymond was killed. The night before Mr. Raymond had placed the mortgage in a drawer and it had disappeared."

On my way to town that night I met Syrel again, and he bowed cordially to me. I began to feel ashamed of myself for sending him out of my house. As I went into the car the only vacant seat was next to him. I sat down and apologized for my rudeness of the day before. He took it lightly and, there being nothing to say, we sat in silence. At last I ventured a remark.

"What do you think of the case?"

"I don't think anything of it as yet. I haven't had time yet."

Nothing daunted I began again. "Did you learn anything?"

Syrel dug his hand into his pocket and produced a bullet. I examined it.

"Where did you find it?" I asked.

"In the yard," he answered briefly.

At this I again relapsed into my seat. When we reached the city, night was coming on. My first day's investigation was not very successful.

My next day's investigation was no more successful than the first. My friend Syrel was not at home. The maid came into Mr. Raymond's room while I was there and gave notice that she was going to leave. "Mr. Raymond," she said, "there was queer noises outside my window last night. I'd like to stay, sir, but it grates on my nerves." Beyond this nothing happened, and I came home worn out. On the morning of the next day I was awakened by the maid who had a telegram in her hand. I opened it and found it was from Gregson. "Come at once," it said "startling development." I dressed hurriedly and took the first car to Santuka. When I reached the Santuka station, Gregson was waiting for me in a runabout. As soon as I got into the carriage Gregson told me what had happened.

"Someone was in the house last night. You know Mr. Raymond asked me to sleep there. Well, to continue, last night, about one, I began to be very thirsty. I went into the hall to get a drink from the faucet there, and as I was passing from my room (I sleep in Miss Raymond's room) into the hall I heard somebody in Mrs. Raymond's room. Wondering why Mr. Raymond was up at that time of night I went into the sitting room to investigate. I opened the door of Mrs. Raymond's room. The body of Miss Raymond was lying on the sofa. A man was kneeling beside it. His face was away from me, but I could tell by his figure that he was not Mr. Raymond. As I looked he got up softly and I saw him open a bureau. He took something out and put it into his pocket. As he turned around he saw me, and I saw that he was a young man. With a cry of rage he sprang at me, and having no weapon I retreated. He snatched up a heavy Indian club and swung it over my head. I gave a cry which must have alarmed the house, for I know nothing more till I saw Mr. Raymond bending over me."

"How did this man look," I asked. "Would you know him if you saw him again?"

"I think not," he answered, "I only saw his profile."

"The only explanation I can give is this," said I. "The murderer was in Miss

Raymond's room and when she came in he overpowered her and inflicted the gash. He then made for Mrs. Raymond's room and carried her off after having first shot Miss Raymond, who attempted to rise. Outside the house he met Standish, who attempted to stop him and was shot."

Gregson smiled. "That solution is impossible," he said.

As we reached the house I saw John Syrel, who beckoned me aside. "If you come with me," he said, "you will learn something that may be valuable to you." I excused myself to Gregson and followed Syrel. As we reached the walk he began to talk.

"Let us suppose that the murderer or murderess escaped from the house. Where would they go? Naturally they wanted to get away. Where did they go? Now, there are two railroad stations near by, Santuka and Lidgeville. I have ascertained that they did not go by Santuka. So did Gregson. I supposed, therefore, that they went by Lidgeville. Gregson didn't; that's the difference. A straight line is the shortest distance between two points. I followed a straight line between here and Lidgeville. At first there was nothing. About two miles farther on I saw some footprints in a marshy hollow. They consisted of three footprints. I took an impression. Here it is. You see this one is a woman's. I have compared it with one of Mrs. Raymond's boots. They are identical. The others are mates. They belong to a man. I compared the bullet I found, where Standish was killed, with one of the remaining cartridges in the revolver that was found in Mrs. Raymond's room. They were mates. Only one shot had been fired and as I had found one bullet, I concluded that either Mrs. or Miss Raymond had fired the shot. I preferred to think Mrs. Raymond fired it because she had fled. Summing these things up and also taking into consideration that Mrs. Raymond must have had some cause to try to kill Standish, I concluded that John Standish killed Miss Raymond through the window of her mother's room, Friday night. I also conclude Mrs. Raymond after ascertaining that her daughter was dead, shot Standish through the window and killed him. Horrified at what she had done she hid behind the door when Mr. Raymond came in. Then she ran down the back stairs. Going outside she stumbled upon the revolver Standish had used and picking it up took it with her. Somewhere between here and Lidgeville she met the owner of these footprints, either by accident or design and walked with him to the station where they took the early train for Chicago. The station master did not see the man. He says that only a woman bought a ticket, so I concluded that the young man didn't go. Now you must tell me what Gregson told you."

"How did you know all this," exclaimed I astonshed. And then I told him about the midnight visitor. He did not appear to be much astonished, and he said "I guess that the young man is our friend of the footprints. Now you had better go get a brace of revolvers and pack your suitcase if you wish to go with me to find this young man and Mrs. Raymond, whom I think is with him.

Greatly surprised at what I had heard I took the first train back to town. I bought a pair of fine Colt revolvers, a dark lantern, and two changes of clothing. We went over to Lidgeville and found that a young man had left on the six o'clock train for Ithaca. On reaching Ithaca we found that he had changed trains and was now half way to Princeton, New Jersey. It was five o'clock, but we took a fast train and expected to overtake him half way between Ithaca and Princeton. What was our chagrin when on reaching the slow train, to find he had gotten off at Indianous and was now probably safe. Thoroughly disappointed we took the train for Indianous. The ticket seller said that a young man in a light gray suit had taken a bus to the Raswell Hotel. We found the bus which the station master said he had taken, in the street. We went up to the driver and he admitted that he had started for the Raswell Hotel in his cab.

"But," said the old fellow, "when I reached there, the fellow had clean disappeared, an' I never got his fare."

Syrel groaned; it was plain that we had lost the young man. We took the next train for New York and telegraphed to Mr. Raymond that we would be down Monday. Sunday night, however, I was called to the phone and recognized Syrel's voice. He directed me to come at once to five hundred thirty-four Chestnut Street. I met him on the doorstep.

"What have you heard?" I asked.

"I have an agent in Indianous," he replied, "in the shape of an Arab boy whom I employ for 10 cents a day. I told him to spot the woman and today I got a telegram from him (I left him money to send one), saying to come at once. So come on."

We took the train for Indianous. "Smidy," the young Arab, met us at the station.

"You see, sur, it's dis way. You says, 'Spot de guy wid dat hack,' and I says I would. Dat night a young dude comes out of er house on Pine Street and give the cabman a $10 bill. An den he went back into the house and a minute after he comes out wid a woman, an' den day went down here a little way an' goes into a house farther down the street, I'll show you de place."

We followed Smidy down the street until we arrived at a corner house. The ground floor was occupied by a cigar store, but the second floor was evidently for rent. As we stood there a face appeared at the window and, seeing us, hastily retreated. Syrel pulled a picture from his pocket. "It's she," he exclaimed, and calling us to follow he dashed into a little side door. We heard voices upstairs, a shuffle of feet and a noise as if a door had been shut.

"Up the stairs," shouted Syrel, and we followed him, taking two steps at a bound. As we reached the top landing we were met by a young man.

"What right have you to enter this house?" he demanded.

"The right of the law," replied Syrel.

"I didn't do it" broke out the young man. "It was this way. Agnes Raymond loved me–she did not love Standish–he shot her; and God did not let her murder go unrevenged. It was well Mrs. Raymond killed him, for his blood would have been on my hands. I went back to see Agnes before she was buried. A man came in. I knocked him down. I didn't know until a moment ago that Mrs. Raymond had killed him.

"I forgot Mrs. Raymond" screamed Syrel, "where is she?"

"She is out of your power forever," said the young man.

Syrel brushed past him and, with Smidy and I following, burst open the door of the room at the head of the stairs. We rushed in.

On the floor lay a woman, and as soon as I touched her heart I knew she was beyond the doctor's skill.

"She has taken poison," I said. Syre looked around, the young man had gone. And we stood there aghast in the presence of death.

Reade, Substitute Right Half

"Hold! Hold! Hold!" The slogan thundered up the field to where the battered, crimson warders trotted wearily into their places again. The blues' attack this time came straight at center and was good for a gain of seven yards.

"Second down, three," yelled the referee, and again the attack came straight at center. This time there was no withstanding the rush and the huge Hilton fullback crushed through the crimson line again and shaking off his many tacklers, staggered on toward the Warrentown goal.

The midget Warrentown quarter-back ran nimbly up the field and, dodging the interference, shot in straight at the fullback's knees throwing him to the ground. The teams sprang back into line again, but Hearst, the crimson right tackle, lay still upon the ground. The right half was shifted to tackle and Berl, the captain, trotted over to the sidelines to ask the advice of the coaches.

"Who have we got for half, sir?" he inquired of the head coach.

"Suppose you try Reade," answered the coach, and calling to one of the figures on the pile of straw, which served as a seat for the substitutes, he beckoned to him. Pulling off his sweater, a light haired stripling trotted over to the coach.

"Pretty light," said Berl as he surveyed the form before him.

"I guess that's all we have, though," answered the coach. Reade was plainly nervous as he shifted his weight from one foot to the other and fidgeted with the end of his jersey.

"Oh, I guess he'll do," said Berl. "Come on kid," and they trotted off on the field.

The teams quickly lined up and the Hilton quarter gave the signal "6-8-7G." The play came between guard and tackle, but before the full-back could get started a lithe form shot out from the Warrentown line and brought him heavily to the ground.

"Good work, Reade," said Berl, as Reade trotted back into his place, and blushing at the compliment he crouched low in the line and waited for the play. The center snapped the ball to quarter, who, turning, was about to give it to the half. The ball slipped from his grasp and he reached for it, but too late. Reade had slipped in between the end and tackle and dropped on the ball.

"Good one, Reade," shouted Mridle, the Warrentown quarter, as he came racing up, crying signals as he ran. Signal "48-10G-37,"

It was Reade around left end, but the pass was bad and the quarter dropped the ball. Reade scooped it up on a run and raced around left end. In the delay which had been caused by the fumble Reade's interference had been broken up and he must shift for himself; even as he rounded the end he was thrown with a thud by the blue full-back. He had gained but a yard. "Never mind, Reade," said the quarter, "my fault." The ball was snapped, but again the pass was bad and a Hilton line man fell on the ball.

Then began a steady march up the field toward the Warrentown goal. Time and time again Reade slipped through the Hilton line and nailed the runner before he could get started. But slowly Hilton pushed down the field toward the Warrentown goal. When the Blues were on the Crimson's ten-yard line their quarter-back made his only error of judgment during the game. He gave the signal for a forward pass. The ball was shot to the full-back, who turned to throw it to the right half. As the pigskin left his hand, Reade leaped upward and caught the ball. He stumbled for a moment, but, soon getting his balance, started out for the Hilton goal with a long string of Crimson and Blue men spread out behind him. He had a start of about five yards on his nearest opponent, but this distance was decreased to three before he had passed his own forty-five-yard line. He turned his head and looked back. His pursuer was breathing heavily and Reade saw what was coming. He was going to try a diving tackle. As the man's body shot out straight for him he stepped out of the way and the man fell harmlessly past him, missing him by a foot.

From there to the goal line it was easy running, and as Reade laid the pigskin on the ground and rolled happily over beside it he could just hear another slogan echo down the field: "One point—two points—three points—four points—five points. Reade! Reade! Reade!"

A Debt of Honor

"Prayle!"

"Here."

"Martin!"

"Absent."

"Sanderson!"

"Here."

"Carlton, for sentry duty!"

"Sick."

"Any volunteers to take his place?"

"Me, me," said Jack Sanderson, eagerly.

"All right," said the captain and went on with the roll.

It was a very cold night. Jack never quite knew how it came about. He had been wounded in the hand the day before and his gray jacket was stained a bright red where he had been hit by a stray ball. And "number six" was such a long post. From way up by the general's tent to way down by the lake. He could feel a faintness stealing over him. He was very tired and it was getting very dark—very dark.

They found him there, sound alseep, in the morning, worn out by the fatigue of the march and the fight which had followed it. There was nothing the matter with him save the wounds, which were slight, and military rules were very strict. To the last day of his life Jack always remembered the sorrow in his captain's voice as he read aloud the dismal order.

Camp Bowling Green, C. S. A.

Jan. 15, 1863, U. S.

For falling asleep while in a position of trust at a sentry post, private John Sanderson is hereby condemned to be shot at sunrise on Jan, 16, 1863.

By order of

Robert E. Lee,

Lieutenant General Commanding.

Jack never forgot the dismal night and the march which followed it. They tied a hankerchief over his head and led him a little apart to a wall which bounded one side of the camp. Never had life seemed so sweet.

General Lee in his tent thought long and seriously upon the matter.

"He is so awfully young and of good family too; but camp discipline must be enforced. Still it was not much of an offense for such a punishment. The lad was over tired and wounded. By George, he shall go free if I risk my reputation. Sergeant, order private John Sanderson to be brought before me."

"Very well, sir," and saluting, the orderly left the tent.

Jack was brought in, supported by two soldiers, for a reaction had set in after his narrow escape from death.

"Sir," said General Lee sternly, "on account of your extreme youth you will get off with a reprimand but see that it never happens again, for, if it should, I shall not be so lenient."

"General," answered Jack drawing himself up to his full height, "The Confederate States of America shall never have cause to regret that I was not shot." And Jack was led away, still trembling, but happy in the knowledge of a new found life.

*

Six weeks after with Lee's army near Chancellorsville. The success of Fredricksburg had made possible this advance of the Confederate arms. The firing had just commenced when a courier rode up to General Jackson.

"Colonel Barrows says sir, that the enemy have possession of a small frame house on the outskirts of the woods and it overlooks our earthworks. Has he your permission to take it by assault?"

"My compliments to Colonel Barrows and say that I cannot spare more than twenty men but that he is welcome to charge with that number," answered the General.

"Yes, sir," and the orderly setting spurs to his horse rode away.

Five minutes later a column of men from the 3rd Virginia burst out from the woods and ran toward the house. A galling fire broke out from the Federal lines and many a brave man fell, among whom was their leader, a young lieutenant. Jack Sanderson sprang to the front and waving his gun encouraged the men onward. Half way between the Confederate lines and the house was a small mound, and behind this the men threw themselves to get a minute's respite.

A minute later a figure sprang up and ran toward the house, and before the Union troops saw him he was half way across the bullet-swept clearing. Then the federal fire was directed at him. He staggered for a moment and placed his hand to his forehead. On he ran and reaching the house he quickly opened the door and went inside. A minute later a pillar of flame shot out of the windows of the house and almost immediately afterwards the Federal occupants were in full flight. A long cheer rolled along the Confederate lines and then the word was given to charge and they charged sweeping all before them. That night the searchers wended their way to the half burned house. There on the floor, beside the mattress he had set on fire, lay the body of him who had once been John Sanderson, private, third Virginia. He had paid his debt.

The Room with the Green Blinds

I

It was ominous looking enough in broad daylight, with its dull, brown walls, and musty windows. The garden, if it might be called so, was simply a mass of overgrown weeds, and the walk was falling to pieces, the bricks crumbling from the touch of time. Inside it was no better. Rickety old three-legged chairs covered with a substance that had once been plush, were not exactly hospitable looking objects. And yet this house was part of the legacy my grandfather had left mc. In his will had been this clause: "The house, as it now stands, and all that is inside it, shall go to my grandson, Robert Calvin Raymond, on his coming to the age of twenty-one years. I furthermore desire that he shall not open the room at the end of the corridor, on the second floor until Carmatle falls. He may fix up three rooms of the house as modern as he wishes, but let the others remain unchanged. He may keep but one servant."

To a poor young man with no outlook in life, and no money, but a paltry eight hundred a year, this seemed a windfall when counted with the twenty-five thousand dollars that went with it. I resolved to fix up my new home, and so started South to Macon, Ga., near which my grandfather's house was situated. All the evening on the Pullman I had thought about that clause, "He shall not open the room at the end of the corridor on the second floor until Carmatle falls." Who was Carmatle? And what did it mean when it said, "When Carmatle falls?" In vain I supposed and guessed and thought; I could make no sense of it.

When I finally arrived at the house, I lighted one of a box of candles which I had brought with me and walked up the creaking stairs to the third floor and down a long, narrow corridor covered with cobwebs and bugs of all sorts till I finally came to a massive oaken door which barred my further progress. On the door I could just make out with the aid of the candle the initials J. W. B. in red paint. The door was barred on the outside by heavy iron bars, effectually barricaded against anybody entering or going out. Suddenly, without even a warning flicker my candle went out, and I found myself in complete darkness. Though I am not troubled with weak nerves, I confess I was somewhat startled by this, for there was not a breath of air stirring. I relit the candle and walked out of the corridor down to the room of the three-legged chairs. As it was now almost nine o'clock and as I was tired after my day of traveling, I soon fell off to sleep.

How long I slept I do not know. I awoke suddenly and sat bolt upright on the lounge. For far down the downstairs hall I heard approaching footsteps, and a second later saw the reflection of a candle on the wall outside my door. I made no noise but as the steps came closer I crept softly to my feet. Another sound and the intruder was directly outside and I had a look at him. The flickering flame of the candle shone on a strong, handsome face, fine brown eyes and a determined chin. A stained grey Confederate uniform covered a magnificent form and here and there a blood stain made him more weird as he stood looking straight ahead with a glazed stare. His clean shaven face seemed strangely familiar to me, and some instinct made me connect him with the closed door on the right wing.

I came to myself with a start and crouched to leap at him, but some noise I made must have alarmed him, for the candle was suddenly extinguished and I brought up against a chair, nursing a bruised shin. I spent the rest of the night trying to connect the clause in my uncle's will with this midnight prowler.

When morning came, things began to look clearer, and I resolved to find out whether I had been dreaming or whether I had had a Confederate officer for a guest. I went into the hall and searched for any sign which might lead to a revelation of the mystery. Sure enough, just outside my door was a tallow stain. About ten yards further on was another, and I found myself following a trail of spots along the hall, and upstairs toward the left wing of the house. About twenty feet from the door of the forbidden room they stopped; neither was there any trace of anyone having gone further. I walked up to the door and tried it to make sure that no one could possibly go in or out. Then I descended and, sauntering out, went around to the east wing to see how it looked from the outside. The room had three windows, each of which was covered with a green blind, and with three iron bars. To make sure of this I went around to the barn, a tumbly old structure, and, by dint of much exertion, succeeded in extracting a ladder from a heap of debris behind it. I placed this against the house, and climbing up, tested each bar carefully. There was no deception. They were firmly set in the concrete sill.

Therefore, there could be but one explanation, the man concealed there must have a third way of getting out, some sort of secret passageway. With this thought in mind I searched the house from garret to cellar, but not a sign could I see of any secret entrance. Then I sat down to think it over.

In the first place there was somebody concealed in the room in the east wing. I had no doubt of that, who was in the habit of making midnight visits to the front hall. Who was Carmatle? It was an unusual name, and I felt if I could find its possessor I could unravel this affair.

Aha! now I had it. Carmatle, the governor of Georgia; why had I not thought of that before? I resolved that that afternoon I would start for Atlanta to see him.

II

"Mr. Carmattyle, I believe?"

"At your service."

"Governor, it's rather a personal matter I have come to see you about and I may have made a mistake in identity. Do you know anything about 'J. W. B.' or did you ever know a man with those initials?"

The governor paled.

"Young man, tell me where you heard those initials and what brought you here?"

In as few words as possible I related to him my story, beginning with the will and ending with my theories regarding it.

When I had finished, the governor rose to his feet.

"I see it all; I see it all. Now with your permission I shall spend a night with you in your house in company with a friend of mine who is in the secret service. If I am right, concealed in that house is—well," he broke off. "I had better not say now, for it may be only a remarkable coincidence. Meet me at the station in half an hour, and you had better bring a revolver.

Six o'clock found us at the manor and the governor and I with the detective he had brought along, a fellow by the name of Butler, proceeded at once to the room.

After half an hour's labor we succeeded in finding no such thing as a passageway, secret or otherwise. Being tired I sat down to rest and in doing so my hand touched a ledge projecting from the wall. Instantly a portion of the wall swung open, disclosing an opening about three feet square. Instantly the governor, with the agility of a cat, was through it and his form disappeared from view. We grasped the situation and followed him. I found myself crawling along on hard stone in black darkness. Suddenly a shot resounded, and another. Then the passageway came to an end. We were in a room magnificently hung with oriental draperies, the walls covered with medieval armor and ancient swords, shields and battle axes. A red lamp on the table threw a lurid glare over all and cast a red glow on a body which lay at the foot of a Turkish divan. It was the Confederate officer, shot through the heart, for the life blood was fast staining his grey uniform red. The governor was standing near the body, a smoking revolver in his hand.

"Gentlemen," said he, "let me present to you John Wilkes Booth, the slayer of Albraham Lincoln."

III

"Mr. Carmatle, you will explain this I hope."

"Certainly," and drawing up a chair the governor began:

"My son and I served in Forest's cavalry during the Civil War, and being on a scouting expedition did not hear of Lee's surrender at Appomatox until about three months afterwards. As we were riding southward along the Cumberland pike we met a man riding down the road. Having struck up an acquaintance, as travelers do, we camped together, the next morning the man was gone, together with my son's old horse and my son's old uniform, leaving his new horse and new civilian suit instead. We did not know what to make of this, but never suspected who this man was. My son and I separated and I never saw him again. He was bound for his aunt's in Western Maryland and one morning he was shot by some Union soldiers in a barn where he had tried to snatch a minute's rest on the way. The story was given out to the public that it was Booth that was shot but I knew and the government knew that my innocent son had been shot by mistake and that John Wilkes Booth, the man who had taken his horse and clothes had escaped. For four years I hunted Booth, but until I heard you mention the initials J. W. B. I had heard no word of him. As it was, when I found him he shot first. I think that his visit to the hall in the Confederate uniform was simply to frighten you away. The fact that your grandfather was a Southern sympathizer probably had protected him all these years. So now, gentlemen, you have heard my story. It rests with you whether this gets no farther than us three here and the government, or whether I shall be proclaimed a murderer and brought to trial."

"You are as innocent as Booth is guilty," said I. "My lips shall be forever sealed."

And we both pressed forward and took him by the hand.

Pain and the Scientist

Walter Hamilton Bartney moved to Middleton because it was quiet and offered him an opportunity of studying law, which he should have done long ago. He chose a quiet house rather out in the suburbs of the village, for as he reasoned to himself, "Middleton is a suburb and remarkably quiet at that. Therefore a suburb of a suburb must be the very depth of solitude, and that is what I want." So Bartney chose a small house in the suburbs and settled down. There was a vacant lot on his left, and on his right Skiggs, the famous Christian Scientist. It is because of Skiggs that this story was written.

Bartney, like the very agreeable young man he was, decided that it would be only neighborly to pay Skiggs a visit, not that he was very much interested in the personality of Mr. Skiggs, but because he had never seen a real Christian Scientist and he felt that his life would be empty without the sight of one.

However, he chose a most unlucky time for his visit. It was one night, dark as pitch that, feeling restless, he set off as the clock struck ten to investigate and become acquainted. He strode out of his lot and along the path that went by name of a road, feeling his way between bushes and rocks and keeping his eye on the solitary light that burned in Mr. Skiggs' house.

"It would be blamed unlucky for me if he should take a notion to turn out that light," he muttered through his clenched teeth. "I'd be lost. I'd just have to sit down and wait until morning."

He approached the house, felt around cautiously, and, reaching for what he thought was a step, uttered an exclamation of pain, for a large stone had rolled down over his leg and pinned him to the earth. He grunted, swore, and tried to move the rock, but he was held powerless by the huge stone, and his efforts were unavailing.

"Hello!" he shouted. "Mr. Skiggs!"

There was no answer.

"Help, in there," he cried again, "Help!"

A light was lit upstairs and a head, topped with a conical shaped night-cap, poked itself out of the window like an animated jack-in-the-box.

"Who's there?" said the night-cap in a high-pitched querulous voice. "Who's there? Speak, or I fire."

"Don't fire! It's me—Bartney, your neighbor. I've had an accident, a nasty ankle wrench, and there's a stone on top of me."

"Bartney?" queried the night cap, nodding pensively. "Who's Bartney?"

Bartney swore inwardly.

"I'm your neighbor. I live next door. This stone is very heavy. If you would come down here—"

"How do I know you're Bartney, whoever he is?" demanded the night cap. "How do I know you won't get me out there and blackjack me?"

"For heaven's sake," cried Bartney, "look and see. Turn a searchlight on me, and see if I'm not pinned down."

"I have no searchlight," came the voice from above.

"Then you'll have to take a chance. I can't stay here all night."

"Then go away. I am not stopping you," said the night cap with a decisive squeak in his voice.

"Mr. Skiggs," said Bartney in desperation, "I am in mortal agony and—"

"You are not in mortal agony," announced Mr. Skiggs.

"What? Do you still think I'm trying to entice you out here to murder you?"

"I repeat, you are not in mortal agony. I am convinced now that you really think you are hurt, but I assure you, you are not."

"He's crazy," thought Bartney.

"I shall endeavor to prove to you that you are not, thus causing you more relief than I would if I lifted the stone. I am very moderate. I will treat you now at the rate of three dollars an hour."

"An hour?" shouted Bartney fiercely. "You come down here and roll this stone off me, or I'll skin you alive!"

"Even against your will," went on Mr. Skiggs. "I feel called upon to treat you, for it is a duty to everyone to help the injured, or rather those who fancy themselves injured. Now, clear your mind of all sensation, and we will begin the treatment."

"Come down here, you mean, low-browed fanatic!" yelled Bartney, forgetting his pain in a paroxysm of rage. "Come down here, and I'll drive every bit of Christian Science out of your head."

"To begin with," began the shrill falsetto from the window, "there is no pain–absolutely none. Do you begin to have an inkling of that?"

"No," shouted Bartney. "You, you–" his voice was lost in a gurgle of impotent rage.

"Now, all is mind. Mind is everything. Matter is nothing–absolutely nothing. You are well. You fancy you are hurt, but you are not."

"You lie," shrieked Bartney.

Unheeding, Mr. Skiggs went on.

"Thus, if there is no pain, it can not act on your mind. A sensation is not physical. If you had no brain, there would be no pain, for what you call pain acts on the brain. You see?"

"Oh-h," cried Bartney, "if you saw what a bottomless well of punishment you were digging for yourself, you'd cut out that monkey business."

"Therefore, as so-called pain is a mental sensation, your ankle doesn't hurt you. Your brain may imagine it does, but all sensation goes to the brain. You are very foolish when you complain of hurt–"

Bartney's patience wore out. He drew in his breath, and let out a yell that echoed and re-echoed through the night air. He repeated it again and again, and at length he heard the sound of footsteps coming up the road.

"Hello!" came a voice.

Bartney breathed a prayer of thanksgiving.

"Come here! I've had an accident," he called, and a minute later the night watchman's brawny arms had rolled the stone off him, and he staggered to his feet.

"Good night," called the Christian Scientist sweetly. "I hope I have made some impression on you."

"You certainly have," called back Bartney as he limped off, his hand on the watchman's shoulder, "one I won't forget."

Two days later, as Bartney sat with his foot on a pillow he pulled an unfamiliar envelope out of his mail and opened it. It read:

WILLIAM BARTNEY.

To HEPEZIA SKIGGS, DR.

Treatment by Christian Science–$3.00. Payment by check or money order.

The weeks wore on. Bartney was up and around. Out in his yard he started a flower garden and became a floral enthusiast. Every day he planted, and the next day he would weed what he had planted. But it gave him something to do, for law was tiresome at times.

One bright summer's day, he left his house and strolled towards the garden, where the day before he had planted in despair some "store bought" pansies. He perceived to his surprise a long, thin, slippery-looking figure bending over, picking his new acquisitions. With quiet tread he approached, and, as the invader turned around, he said severely:

"What are you doing, sir?"

"I was plucking-er-a few posies–"

The long, thin, slippery looking figure got no further. Though the face had been strange to Bartney, the voice, a thin, querelous falsetto, was one he would never forget. He advanced slowly, eyeing the owner of that voice, as the wolf eyes his prey.

"Well, Mr. Skiggs, how is it I find you on my property?"

Mr. Skiggs appeared unaccountably shy and looked the other way.

"I repeat," said Bartney, "that I find you here on my property–and in my power."

"Yes, sir," said Mr. Skiggs, squirming in alarm.

Bartney grabbed him by the collar, and shook him as a terrier does a rat.

"You conceited imp of Christian Science! You miserable hypocrite! What?" he demanded fiercely, as Skiggs emitted a cry of protest. "You yell. How dare you? Don't you know there is no such thing as pain? Come on, now, give me some of that Christian Science. Say 'mind is everything'. Say it!"

Mr. Skiggs, in the midst of his jerky course, said quaveringly, "Mind is everyth-thing."

"Pain is nothing," urged his tormenter grimly.

"P-Pain is nothing," repeated Mr. Skiggs feelingly.

The shaking continued.

"Remember, Skiggs, this is all for the good of the cause. I hope you're taking it to heart. Remember, such is life, therefore life is such. Do you see?"

He left off shaking, and proceeded to entice Skiggs around by a grip on his collar, the scientist meanwhile kicking and struggling violently.

"Now," said Bartney, "I want you to assure me that you feel no pain. Go on, do it!"

"I f-feel—ouch," he exclaimed as he passed over a large stone is his course, "n-no pain."

"Now," said Bartney, "I want two dollars for the hours' Christian Science treatment I have given you. Out with it."

Skiggs hesitated, but the look of Bartney's eyes and a tightening of Bartney's grip convinced him, and he unwillingly tendered a bill. Bartney tore it to pieces and distributed the fragments to the wind.

"Now, you may go."

Skiggs, when his collar was released, took to his heels, and his flying footsteps crossed the boundary line in less time than you would imagine.

"Good-bye, Mr. Skiggs," called Bartney pleasantly. "Any other time you want a treatment come over. The price is always the same. I see you know one thing I didn't have to teach you. There's no such thing as pain, when somebody else is the goat."

The Trail of the Duke

It was a hot July night. Inside, through screen, window and door fled the bugs and gathered around the lights like so many humans at a carnival, buzzing, thugging, whirring. From out the night into the houses came the sweltering late summer heat, over-powering and enervating, bursting against the walls and enveloping all mankind like a huge smothering blanket. In the drug stores, the clerks, tired and grumbling handed out ice cream to hundreds of thirsty but misled civilians, while in the corners buzzed the electric fans in a whirring mockery of coolness. In the flats that line upper New York, pianos (sweating ebony perspiration) ground out rag-time tunes of last winter and here and there a wan woman sang the air in a hot soprano. In the tenements, shirt-sleeves gleamed like beacon lights in steady rows along the streets in tiers of from four to eight according to the number of stories of the house. In a word, it was a typical, hot New York summer night.

In his house on upper Fifth Avenue, young Dodson Garland lay on a divan in the billiard room and consumed oceans of mint juleps, as he grumbled at the polo that had kept him in town, the cigarettes, the butler, and occasionally breaking the Second Commandment. The butler ran back and forth with large consignments of juleps and soda and finally, on one of his dramatic entrances, Garland turned towards him and for the first time that evening perceived that the butler was a human being, not a living bottle-tray.

"Hello, Allen," he said, rather surprised that he had made such a discovery. "Are you hot?"

Allen made an expressive gesture with his handkerchief, tried to smile but only succeeded in a feeble, smothery grin.

"Allen," said Garland struck by an inspiration, "what shall I do tonight?" Allen again essayed the grin but, failing once more, sank into a hot, undignified silence.

"Get out of here," exclaimed Garland petulantly, "and bring me another julep and a plate of ice."

"Now," thought the young man, "What shall I do? I can go to the theatre and melt. I can go to a roof-garden and be sung to by a would-be prima donna, or—or go calling." "Go calling," in Garland's vocabulary meant but one thing: to see Mirabel. Mirabel Walmsley was his fiancee since some three months, and was in the city to receive some nobleman or other who was to visit her father. The lucky youth yawned, rolled over, yawned again and rose to a sitting position where he yawned a third time and then got to his feet.

"I'll walk up and see Mirabel. I need a little exercise." And with this final decision he went to his room where he dressed, sweated and dressed, for half an hour. At the end of that time, he emerged from his residence, immaculate, and strolled up Fifth Avenue to Broadway. The city was all outside. As he walked along the white way, he passed groups and groups clad in linen and lingerie, laughing, talking, smoking, smiling, all hot, all uncomfortable.

He reached Mirabel's house and then suddenly stopped on the door step.

"Heavens," he thought, "I forgot all about it. The Duke of Dunsinlane or Artrellane or some lane or other was to arrive today to see Mirabel's papa. Isn't that awful? And I haven't seen Mirabel for three days." He sighed, faltered, and finally walked up the steps and rang the bell. Hardly had he stepped inside the door, when the vision of his dreams came running into the hall in a state of great excitement and perturbation.

"Oh, Doddy!" she burst out, "I'm in an awful situation. "The Duke went out of the house an hour ago. None of the maids saw him go. He just wandered out. You must find him. He's probably lost—lost and nobody knows him." Mirabel wrung her hands in entrancing despair. "Oh, I shall die if he's lost—and it so hot. He'll have a sunstroke surely or a—moonstroke. Go and find him. We've telephoned the police, but it won't do any good. Hurry up! Do! oh, Doddy, I'm so nervous."

"Doddy" put his hands in his pockets, sighed, put his hat on his head and sighed again. Then he turned towards the door. Mirabel, her face anxious, followed him.

"Bring him right up here if you find him. Oh Doddy you're a life-saver." The life-saver sighed again and walked quickly through the portal. On the door-step he paused.

"Well, of all outrageous things! To hunt for a French Duke in New York. This is outrageous. Where shall I go? What will I do." He paused at the door-step and then, following the crowd, strode toward Broadway. "Now let me see. I must have a plan of action. I can't go up and ask everybody I meet if he's the Duke of—, well of, well—I can't remember his name. I don't know what he looks like. He probably can't talk English. Oh, curses on the nobility."

He strode aimlessly, hot and muddled. He wished he had asked Mirabel the Duke's name and personal appearance, but it was now too late. He would not convict himself of such a blunder. Reaching Broadway he suddenly bethought himself of a plan of action.

"I'll try the restaurants." He started down towards Sherry's and had gone but half a block when he had an inspiration. The Duke's picture was in some evening paper, and his name, too.

He bought a paper and sought for the picture with no result. He tried again and again. On his seventh paper he found it: "The Duke of Matterlane Visits American Millionaire."

The Duke, a man with side whiskers and eye-glasses stared menacingly at him from the paper. Garland heaved a sigh of relief, took a long look at the likeness and stuck the paper into his pocket.

"Now to business," he muttered, wiping his drenched brow, "Duke or die."

Five minutes later he entered Sherry's, where he sat down and ordered ginger ale.

There was the usual summer night crowd, listless, flushed, and sunburned. There was the usual champagne and ice that seemed hotter than the room; but there was no Duke. He sighed, rose, and visited Delmonico's, Martin's, at each place consuming a glass of ginger ale.

"I'll have to cut out the drinking," he thought, "or I'll be inebriated by the time I find his royal nuisance."

On his weary trail, he visited more restaurants and more hotels, ever searching; sometimes thinking he saw an oasis and finding it only a mirage. He had consumed so much ginger ale that he felt a swaying sea-sickness as he walked; yet he plodded on, hotter and hotter, uncomfortable, and, as Alice in Wonderland would have said, uncomfortabler. His mind was grimly and tenaciously set on the Duke's face. As he walked along, from hotel to cafe, from cafe to restaurant, the Duke's whiskers remained glued firmly to the insides of his brains. It was half past eight by the City Hall clock when he started on his quest. It was now quarter past ten, hotter, sultrier and stuffier than ever. He had visited every important place of refreshment. He tried the drug stores. He went to four theatres and had the Duke paged, at a large bribe. His money was getting low, his spirits were lower still; but his temperature soared majestically and triumphantly aloft.

Finally, passing through an alley which had been recommended to him as a short cut, he saw before him a man lighting a cigarette. By the flickering match he noticed the whiskers. He stopped dead in his tracks, afraid that it might not be the Duke. The man lit another cigarette. Sure enough, the sideburns, eyeglasses and the whole face proved the question without a doubt.

Garland walked towards the man. The man looked back at him and started to walk in the opposite direction. Garland started to run; the man looked over his shoulder and started to run also. Garland slowed down. The man slowed down. They emerged upon Broadway in the same relative position and the man started north. Forty feet behind, in stolid determination, walked Garland without his hat. He had left it in the alley.

For eight blocks they continued, the man behind being the pacemaker. Then the Duke spoke quietly to a policeman and when Garland, lost in an obsession of pursuit, was grabbed by the arm by a blue-coated Gorgas, he saw ahead of him the Duke start to run. In a frenzy he struck at the policeman and stunned him. He ran on and in three blocks he had made up what he had lost. For five more blocks the Duke continued, glancing now and then over his shoulder. On the sixth block he stopped. Garland approached him with steady step. He of the side whiskers was standing under a lamp post. Garland came up and put his hand on his shoulder.

"Your Grace."

"What's dat?" said the Duke, with an unmistakable east-side accent. Garland was staggered.

"I'll grace you," continued the side burns aggressively. "I saw you was a swell and I'd a dropped you bad only I'm just out of jail myself. Now listen here. I'll give you two seconds to get scarce. Go on, beat it."

Garland beat it. Crestfallen and broken-hearted he walked away and set off for Mirabel's. He would at least make a decent ending to a miserable quest. A half an hour later he rang the bell, his clothes hanging on him like a wet bathing suit.

Mirabel came to the door cool and fascinating.

"Oh Doddy," she exclaimed. "Thank you so much. Dukey," and she held up a small white poodle which she had in her arms, "came back ten minutes after you left. He had just followed the mail man."

Garland sat down on the step.

"But the Duke of Matterlane?"

"Oh," said Mirabel, "he comes tomorrow. You must come right over and meet him."

"Im afraid I can't," said Garland, rising feebly, "previous engagement." He paused, smiled faintly and set off across the sultry moon-lit pavement.

Shadow Laurels

Pitou—Coming, coming—Hold tight! (The knocking stops. Pitou unlatches the door and it swings open. A man in a top hat and opera cloak enters. Jaques Chandelle is perhaps thirty-seven, tall and well groomed. His eyes are clear and penetrating, his chin, clean shaven, is sharp and decisive. His manner is that of a man accustomed only to success but ready and willing to work hard in any emergency. He speaks French with an odd accent as of one who knew the language well in early years but whose accent had grown toneless through long years away from France.)

Pitou—Good afternoon, Monsieur.

Chandelle—(looking about him curiously) Are you perhaps Monsieur Pitou?

Pitou—Yes, Monsieur.

Chandelle—Ah! I was told that one would always find you in at this hour. (He takes off his overcoat and lays it carefully on a chair) I was told also that you could help me.

Pitou—(puzzled) I could help you?

Chandelle—(Sitting down wearily on a wooden chair near the table) Yes, I'm a—a stranger in the city—now. I'm trying to trace someone—someone who has been dead many years. I've been informed that you're the oldest inhabitant (he smiles faintly).

Pitou—(rather pleased) Perhaps—and yet there are older than I, ah yes, older than I. (He sits down across the table from Chandelle.)

Chandelle—And so I came for you. (He bends earnestly over the table toward Pitou.) Monsieur Pitou, I am trying to trace my father.

Pitou—Yes.

Chandelle—He died in this district about twenty years ago.

Pitou—Monsieur's father was murdered?

Chandelle—Good God, no! What makes you think that?

Pitou—I thought perhaps in this district twenty years ago, an aristocrat—

Chandelle—My father was no aristocrat. As I remember, his last position was that of waiter in some forgotten cafe. (Pitou glances at Chandelle's clothes and looks mystified.) Here I'll explain. I left France twenty-eight years ago to go to the States with my uncle. We went over in an immigrant ship, if you know what that is.

Pitou—Yes; I know.

Chandelle—My parents remained in France. The last I remember of my father was that he was a little man with a black beard, terribly lazy—the only good I ever remember his doing was to teach me to read and write. Where he picked up that accomplishment I don't know. Five years after we reached America we ran across some newly landed French from this part of the city, who said that both my parents were dead. Soon after that my uncle died and I was far too busy to worry over parents whom I had half forgotten anyway. (He pauses.) Well to cut it short I prospered and—

Pitou—(deferentially) Monsieur is rich—'tis strange—'tis very strange.

Chandelle—Pitou, it probably appears strange to you that I should burst in on you now at this time of life, looking for traces of a father who went completely out of my life over twenty years ago.

Pitou—Oh—I understood you to say he was dead.

Chandelle—Yes he's dead, but (hesitates) Pitou, I wonder if you can understand if I tell you why I am here.

Pitou—Yes, perhaps.

Chandelle—(very earnestly) Monsieur Pitou, in America the men I see now, the women I know all had fathers, fathers to be ashamed of, fathers to be proud of, fathers in gilt frames, and fathers in the family closet, Civil War fathers, and Ellis Island fathers. Some even had grandfathers.

Pitou—I had a grandfather. I remember.

Chandelle—(interrupting) I want to see people who knew him, who had talked with him. I want to find out his intelligence, his life, his record. (Impetuously) I want to sense him—I want to know him—

Pitou—(interrupting) What was his name?

Chandelle—Chandelle, Jean Chandelle.

Pitou—(quietly) I knew him.

Chandelle—You knew him?

Pitou—He came here often to drink—that was long ago when this place was the rendezvous of half the district.

Chandelle—(excitedly) Here? He used to come here? To this room? Good Lord, the very house he lived in was torn down ten years ago. In two days' search you are the first soul I've found who knew him. Tell me of him—everything—be frank.

Pitou—Many come and go in forty years (shakes his head.) There are many names and many faces—Jean Chandelle—ah, of course, Jean Chandelle. Yes, yes; the chief fact I can remember about your father was that he was a—a—

Chandelle—Yes.

Pitou—A terrible drunkard.

Chandelle—A drunkard—I expected as much. (He looks a trifle downcast, but makes a half-hearted attempt not to show it.)

Pitou—(Rambling on through a sea of reminiscence) I remember one Sunday night in July—hot night—baking—your father—let's see—your father tried to knife Pierre Courru for drinking his mug of sherry.

Chandelle—Ah!

Pitou—And then—ah, yes, (excitedly standing up) I see it again. Your father is playing vingt-et-un and they say he is cheating so he breaks Clavine's chin with a chair and throws a bottle at someone and Lafouquet sticks a knife into his lung. He never got over that. That was—was two years before he died.

Chandelle—So he cheated and was murdered. My God, I've crossed the ocean to discover that.

Pitou—No—no—I never believed he cheated. They were laying for him—

Chandelle—(burying his face in his hands) Is that all (he shrugs his shoulders; his voice is a trifle broken) I scarcely expected a—saint but—well: so he was a rotler.

Pitou—(Laying his hand on Chandelle's shoulder) There Monsieur, I have talked too much. Those were rough days. Knives were drawn at anything. Your father—but hold—do you want to meet three friends of his, his best friends. They can tell you much more than I.

Chandelle—(gloomily) His friends?

Pitou—(reminiscent again) There were four of them. Three come here yet—will be here this afternoon—your father was the fourth and they would sit at this table and talk and drink. They talked nonsense—everyone said; the wine room poked fun at them—called them les "Academicians Ridicules." Night after night would they sit there. They would slouch in at eight and stagger out at twelve—

(The door swings open and three men enter. The first, Lamarque, is a tall man, lean and with a thin straggly beard. The second, Destage, is short and fat, white bearded and bald. The third, Francois Meridien is slender, with black hair streaked with grey and a small moustache. His face is pitifully weak, his eyes small, his chin sloping. He is very nervous. They all glance with dumb curiosity at Chandelle.)

Pitou—(including all three with a sweep of his arm) Here they are, Monsieur, they can tell you more than I. (Turning to the others) Messieurs, this gentleman desires to know about—

Chandelle—(rising hastily and interrupting Pitou) About a friend of my father's. Pitou tells me you knew him. I believe his name was—Chandelle.

(The three men start and Francois begins to laugh nervously.)

Lamarque—(after a pause) Chandelle?

Francois—Jean Chandelle? So he had another friend besides us?

Destage—You will pardon me, Monsieur: that name—no one but us had mentioned it for twenty-two years.

Lamarque—(trying to be dignified, but looking a trifle ridiculous) And with us it is mentioned with reverence and awe.

Destage—Lamarque exaggerates a little perhaps. (Very seriously) He was very dear to us. (Again Francois laughs nervously.)

Lamarque—But what is it that Monsieur wishes to know? (Chandelle motions them to sit down. They take places at the big table and Destage produces a pipe and begins to fill it.)

Francois—Why, we're four again!

Lamarque—Idiot!

Chandelle—Here, Pitou! Wine for everyone. (Pitou nods and shuffles out) Now, Messieurs, tell me of Chandelle. Tell me of his personality.

(Lamarque looks blankly at Destage.)

Destage—Well, he was—was attractive—

Lamarque—Not to everyone.

Destage—But to us. Some thought him a sneak. (Chandelle winces) He was a wonderful talker—when he wished, he could amuse the whole wine room. But he preferred to talk to us. (Pitou enters with a bottle and glasses. He pours and leaves the bottle on the table. Then he goes out.)

Lamarque—He was educated. God knows how.

Francois—(draining his glass and pouring out more.) He knew everything, he could tell anything—he used to tell me poetry. Oh, what poetry! And I would listen and dream—

Destage—And he could make verses and sing them with his guitar.

Lamarque—And he would tell us about men and women of history—about Charlotte Corday and Fouquet and Moliere and St. Louis and Mamine, the strangler, and Charlemagne and Mme. Dubarry and Machiavelli and John Law and Francois Villon—

Destage—Villon! (enthusiastically) He loved Villon. He would talk for hours of him.

Francois—(Pouring more wine) And then he would get very drunk and say "Let us fight" and he would stand on the table and say that everyone in the wine shop was a pig and a son of pigs. La! He would grab a chair or a table and Sacre Vie Dieu! but those were hard nights for us.

Lamarque—Then he would take his hat and guitar and go into the streets to sing. He would sing about the moon.

Francois—And the roses and the ivory towers of Babylon and about the ancient ladies of the court and about "the silent chords that flow from the ocean to the moon. "

Destage—That's why he made no money. He was bright and clever—when we worked, he worked feverishly hard, but he was always drunk, night and day.

Lamarque—Often he lived on liquor alone for weeks at a time.

Destage—He was much in jail toward the end.

Chandelle—(calling) Pitou! More wine!

Francois—(excitedly) And me! He used to like me best. He used to say that I was a child and he would train me. He died before he began. (Pitou enters with another bottle of wine; Francois seizes it eagerly and pours himself a glass.)

Destage—And then that cursed Lafouquet—stuck him with a knife.

Francois—But I fixed Lafouquet. He stood on the Seine bridge drunk and—

Lamarque—Shut up, you fool you—

Francois—I pushed him and he sank—down—down—and that night Chandelle came in a dream and thanked me.

Chandelle—(shuddering) How long—for how many years did you come here.

Destage—Six or seven. (Gloomily) Had to end—had to end.

Chandelle—And he's forgotten. He left nothing. He'll never be thought of again.

Destage—Remembered! Bah! Posterity is as much a charlatan as the most prejudiced tragic critic that ever boot-licked an actor. (He turns his glass nervously round and round) You don't realize—I'm afraid—how we feel about Jean Chandelle, Francois and Lamarque and I—he was more than a genius to be admired—

Francois—(hoarsely) Don't you see, he stood for us as well as for himself.

Lamarque—(rising excitedly and walking up and down.) There we were—four men—three of us poor dreamers—artistically educated, practically illiterate (he turns savagely to Chandelle and speaks almost menacingly) Do you realize that I can neither read nor write. Do you realize that back of Francois there, despite his fine phrases, there is a character weak as water, a mind as shallow as—

(Francois starts up angrily.)

Lamarque—Sit down (Francois sits down muttering.)

Francois—(after a pause) But, Monsieur, you must know—I leave the gift of—of—(helplessly) I can't name it—appreciation, artistic, aesthetic sense—call it what you will. Weak—yes, why not? Here I am, with no chance, the world against me. I lie—I steal perhaps—I am drunk—I—

(Destage fills up Francois glass with wine.)

Destage—Here! Drink that and shut up! You are boring the gentleman. There is his weak side—poor infant.

(Chandelle who has listened to the last, keenly turns his chair toward Destage.)

Chandelle—But you say my father was more to you than a personal friend; in what way?

Lamarque—Can't you see?

Francois—I—I—he helped—(Destage pours out more wine and gives it to him.)

Destage—You see he—how shall I say it?—he expressed us. If you can imagine a mind like mine, potently lyrical, sensitive without being cultivated. If you can imagine what a balm, what a medicine, what an all in all was summed up for me in my conversations with him. It was everything to me. I would struggle pathetically for a phrase to express a million yearnings and he would say it in a word.

Lamarque—Monsieur is bored? (Chandelle shakes his head and opening his case selects a cigarette and lights it)

Lamarque—Here, sir, are three rats, the product of a sewer—destined by nature to live and die in the filthy ruts where they were born. But these three rats in one thing are not of the sewer—they have eyes. Nothing to keep them from remaining in the sewer but their eyes, nothing to help them if they go out but their eyes—and now here comes the light. And it came and passed and left us rats again—vile rats—and one, when he lost the light, went blind.

Francois—(muttering to himself)—

Blind! Blind! Blind!
Then he ran alone, when the light had passed;
The sun had set and the night fell fast;
The rat lay down in the sewer at last,
Blind!

(A beam of the sunset has come to rest on the glass of wine that Francois holds in his hand. The wine glitters and sparkles. Francois looks at it, starts, and drops the glass. The wine runs over the table.)

Destage—(animatedly) Fifteen—twenty years ago he sat where you sat, small, heavy-bearded, black eyed—always sleepy looking.

Francois—(his eyes closed—his voice trailing off) Always sleepy, sleepy, slee—

Chandelle—(dreamily) He was a poet unsinging, crowned with wreaths of ashes. (His voice rings with just a shade of triumph.)

Francois—(talking in his sleep) Ah, well Chandelle, are you witty to-night, or melancholy or stupid or drunk.

Chandelle—Messieurs—it grows late. I must be off. Drink, all of you (enthusiastically) Drink until you cannot talk or walk or see. (He throws a bill on the table.)

Destage—Young Monsieur?

(Chandelle dons his coat and hat. Pitou enters with more wine. He fills the glasses.)

Lamarque–Drink with us, Monsieur.

Francois–(asleep) Toast, Chandelle, toast.

Chandelle–(taking a glass and raising it aloft). Toast (His face is a little red and his hand unsteady. He appears infinitely more gallic than when he entered the wine shop.)

Chandelle–I drink to one who might have been all, who was nothing–who might have sung; who only listened–who might have seen the sun; who but watched a dying ember–who drank of gall and wore a wreath of shadow laurels–

(The others have risen, even Francois who totters wildly forward.)

Francois–Jean, Jean, don't go–don't–till I, Francois–you can't leave me–I'll be all alone–alone–alone (his voice rises higher and higher) My God, man, can't you see, you have no right to die–You are my soul. (He stands for a moment, then sprawls across the table. Far away in the twilight a violin sighs plaintively. The last beam of the sun rests on Francois' head. Chandelle opens the door and goes out.)

Destage–The old days go by, and the old loves and the old spirit. "Ou sont les neiges d'antan? " I guess. (Pauses unsteadily and then continues.) I've gone far enough without him.

Lamarque–(dreamily) Far enough.

Destage–Your hand Jaques! (They clasp hands).

Francois–(wildly) Here–I, too–you won't leave me (feebly) I want–just one more glass–one more–

(The light fades and disappears.)

(CURTAIN.)

The Ordeal

The hot four o'clock sun beat down familiarly upon the wide stretch of Maryland country, burning up the long valleys, powdering the winding road into fine dust and glaring on the ugly slated roof of the monastery. Into the gardens it poured hot, dry, lazy, bringing with it, perhaps, some quiet feeling of content, unromantic and cheerful. The walls, the trees, the sanded walks, seemed to radiate back into the fair cloudless sky the sweltering late summer heat and yet they laughed and baked happily. The hour brought some odd sensation of comfort to the farmer in a nearby field, drying his brow for a moment by his thirsty horse, and to the lay-brother opening boxes behind the monastery kitchen.

The man walked up and down on the bank above the creek. He had been walking for half an hour. The lay-brother looked at him quizzically as he passed and murmured an invocation. It was always hard, this hour before taking first vows. Eighteen years before one, the world just behind. The lay-brother had seen many in this same situation, some white and nervous, some grim and determined, some despairing. Then, when the bell tolled five, there were the vows and usually the novice felt better. It was this hour in the country when the world seemed gloriously apparent and the monastery vaguely impotent. The lay-brother shook his head in sympathy and passed on.

The man's eyes were bent upon his prayer-book. He was very young, twenty at the most, and his dark hair in disorder gave him an even more boyish expression. A light flush lay on his calm face and his lips moved incessantly. He was not nervous. It seemed to him as if he had always known he was to become a priest. Two years before, he had felt the vague stirring, the transcendent sense of seeing heaven in everything, that warned him softly, kindly that the spring of his life was coming. He had given himself every opportunity to resist. He had gone a year to college, four months abroad, and both experiences only increased within him the knowledge of his destiny. There was little hesitation. He had at first feared self-committal with a thousand nameless terrors. He thought he loved the world. Panicky, he struggled, but surer and surer he felt that the last word had been said. He had his vocation—and then, because he was no coward, he decided to become a priest.

Through the long month of his probation he alternated between deep, almost delirious, joy and the same vague terror at his own love of life and his realization of all he sacrificed. As a favorite child he had been reared in pride and confidence in his ability, in faith in his destiny. Careers were open to him, pleasure, travel, the law, the diplomatic service. When, three months before, he had walked into the library at home and told his father that he was going to become a Jesuit priest, there was a family scene and letters on all sides from friends and relatives. They told him he was ruining a promising young life because of a sentimental notion of self sacrifice, a boyish dream. For a month he listened to the bitter melodrama of the commonplace, finding his only rest in prayer, knowing his salvation and trusting in it. After all, his worst battle had been with himself. He grieved at his father's disappointment and his mother's tears, but he knew that time would set them right.

And now in half an hour he would take the vows which pledged him forever to a life of service. Eighteen years of study—eighteen years where his every thought, every idea would be dictated to him, where his individuality, his physical ego would be effaced and he would come forth strong and firm to work and work and work. He felt strangely calm, happier in fact than he had been for days and months. Something in the fierce, pulsing heat of the sun likened itself to his own heart, strong in its decision, virile and doing its own share in the work, the greatest work. He was elated that he had been chosen, he from so many unquestionably singled out, unceasingly called for. And he had answered.

The words of the prayers seemed to run like a stream into his thoughts, lifting him up peacefully, serenely; and a smile lingered around his eyes. Everything seemed so easy; surely all life was a prayer. Up and down he walked. Then of a sudden something happened. Afterwards he could never describe it except by saying that some undercurrent had crept into his prayer, something unsought, alien. He read on for a moment and then it seemed to take the form of music. He raised his eyes with a start—far down the dusty road a group of negro hands were walking along singing, and the song was an old song that he knew:

"We hope ter meet you in heavan whar we'll
Part no mo',
Whar we'll part no mo'.
Gawd a'moughty bless you twel we
Me-et agin."

Something flashed into his mind that had not been there before. He felt a sort of resentment toward those who had burst in upon him at this time, not because they were simple and primitive, but because they had vaguely disturbed him. That song was old in his life. His nurse had hummed it through the dreamy days of his childhood. Often in the hot summer afternoons he had played it softly on his banjo. It reminded him of so many things: months at the seashore on the hot beach with the gloomy ocean rolling around him, playing with sand castles with his cousin; summer evenings on the big lawn at home when he chased fireflys and the breeze carried the tune over the night to him from the negro-quarters. Later, with new words, it had served as a serenade—and now-well, he had done with that part of life, and yet he seemed to see a girl with kind eyes, old in a great sorrow, waiting, ever waiting. He seemed to hear voices calling, children's voices. Then around him swirled the city, busy with the hum of men; and there was a family that would never be, beckoning him.

Other music ran now as undercurrent to his thoughts: wild, incoherent music, illusive and wailing, like the shriek of a hundred violins, yet clear and chord-like. Art, beauty, love and life passed in a panorama before him, exotic with the hot perfumes of world-passion. He saw struggles and wars, banners waving somewhere, voices giving hail to a king—and looking at him through it all were the sweet sad eyes of the girl who was now a woman.

Again the music changed; the air was low and sad. He seemed to front a howling crowd who accused him. The smoke rose again around the body of John Wycliffe, a monk knelt at a prie-dieu and laughed because the poor had not bread, Alexander VI pressed once more the poisoned ring into his brother's hand, and the black robed figures of the inquisition scowled and whispered. Three great men said there was no God, a million voices seemed to cry, "Why! Why! must we believe?" Then as in a chrystal he seemed to hear Huxley, Nietzsche, Zola, Kant cry, "I will not"—He saw Voltaire and Shaw wild with cold passion. The voices pleaded "Why?" and the girl's sad eyes gazed at him with infinite longing.

He was in a void above the world—the ensemble, everything called him now. He could not pray. Over and over again he said senselessly, meaninglessly, "God have mercy, God have mercy." For a minute, an eternity, he trembled in the void and then—something snapped. They were still there, but the girl's eyes were all wrong, the lines around her mouth were cold and chiselled and her passion seemed dead and earthy.

He prayed, and gradually the cloud grew clearer, the images appeared vague and shadowy. His heart seemed to stop for an instant and then—he was standing by the bank and a bell was tolling five. The reverend superior came down the steps and toward him.

"It is time to go in." The man turned instantly.

"Yes, Father, I am coming."

II

The novices filed silently into the chapel and knelt in prayer. The blessed Sacrament in the gleaming monstrance was exposed among the flaming candles on the altar. The air was rich and heavy with incense. The man knelt with the others. A first chord of the magnificat, sung by the concealed choir above, startled him; he looked up. The late afternoon sun shone through the stained glass window of St.

Francis Xavier on his left and fell in red tracery on the cassock of the man in front of him. Three ordained priests knelt on the altar. Above them a huge candle burned. He watched it abstractedly. To the right of him a novice was telling his beads with trembling fingers. The man looked at him. He was about twenty-six with fair hair and green-grey eyes that darted nervously around the chapel. They caught each other's eye and the elder glanced quickly at the altar candle as if to draw attention to it. The man followed his eye and as he looked he felt his scalp creep and tingle. The same unsummoned instinct filled him that had frightened him half an hour ago on the bank. His breath came quicker. How hot the chapel was. It was too hot; and the candle was wrong—wrong—everything suddenly blurred. The man on his left caught him.

"Hold up," he whispered, "they'll postpone you. Are you better? Can you go through with it?"

He nodded vaguely and turned to the candle. Yes, there was no mistake. Something was there, something played in the tiny flame, curled in the minute wreath of smoke. Some evil presence was in the chapel, on the very altar of God. He felt a chill creeping over him, though he knew the room was warm. His soul seemed paralyzed, but he kept his eyes riveted on the candle. He knew that he must watch it. There was no one else to do it. He must not take his eyes from it. The line of novices rose and he mechanically reached his feet.

"Per omnia saecula, saeculorum. Amen."

Then he felt suddenly that something corporeal was missing—his last earthly support. He realized what it was. The man on his left had gone out overwrought and shaken. Then it began. Something before had attacked the roots of his faith; had matched his world-sense against his God-sense, had brought, he had thought, every power to bear against him; but this was different. Nothing was denied, nothing was offered. It could best be described by saying that a great weight seemed to press down upon his innermost soul, a weight that had no essence, mental or physical. A whole spiritual realm evil in its every expression engulfed him. He could not think, he could not pray. As in a dream he heard the voices of the men beside him singing, but they were far away, farther away from him than anything had ever been before. He existed on a plane where there was no prayer, no grace; where he realized only that the forces around him were of hell and where the single candle contained the essence of evil. He felt himself alone pitted against an infinity of temptation. He could bring no parallel to it in his own experience or any other.

One fact he knew: one man had succumbed to this weight and he must not—must not. He must look at the candle and look and look until the power that filled it and forced him into this plane died forever for him. It was now or not at all.

He seemed to have no body and even what he had thought was his innermost self was dead. It was something deeper that was he, something that he had never felt before. Then the forces gathered for one final attack. The way that the other novice had taken was open to him. He drew his breath quickly and waited and then the shock came. The eternity and infinity of all good seemed crushed, washed away in an eternity and infinity of evil. He seemed carried helplessly along, tossed this way and that—as in a black limitless ocean where there is no light and the waves grow larger and larger and the sky darker and darker. The waves were dashing him toward a chasm, a maelstrom everlastingly evil, and blindly, unseeingly, desperately he looked at the candle, looked at the flame which seemed like the one black star in the sky of despair. Then suddenly he became aware of a new presence. It seemed to come from the left, seemed consummated and expressed in warm, red tracery somewhere. Then he knew. It was the stained window of St. Francis Xavier. He gripped at it spiritually, clung to it and with aching heart called silently for God.

"Tantum ergo Sacramentum
Veneremur cernui."

The words of the hymn gathered strength like a triumphant paean of glory, the incense filled his brain, his very soul, a gate clanged somewhere and the candle on the altar went out.

"Ego vos absolvo a peccatis tuis in nomine patris, filii, spiritus sancti. Amen."

The file of novices started toward the altar. The stained lights from the windows mingled with the candle glow and the eucharist in its golden halo seemed to the man very mystical and sweet. It was very calm. The subdeacon held the Book for him. He placed his right hand upon it.

"In the name of the Father and the Son and of the Holy Ghost—"

The Débutante (A One-Act Play)

SCENE I:—A large and dainty bedroom in the Connage house—a girl's room; pink walls and curtains and a pink bedspread on a cream-colored bed. Pink and cream are the motifs of the room, but the only article of furniture in full view is a luxurious dressing table with a glass top and a three-sided mirror. On the walls we have an expensive print of "Cherry Ripe," a few polite dogs by Landseer, and "The Young King of the Black Isles" by Maxfield Parrish.

Great disorder consisting of the following items: (1) seven or eight empty cardboard boxes, with tissue paper tongues handing panting from their mouths; (2) an assortment of street dresses mingled with their sisters of the evening, all upon the table, all evidently new; (3) a roll of tulle, which has lost its dignity and wound itself tortuously around everything in sight; and (4) upon the two small chairs, a collection of lingerie that beggars description. One would enjoy seeing the bill called forth by the finery displayed and one is possessed by a desire to see the princess for whose benefit—Look! There's someone!—Disappointment! This is only a maid looking for something—she lifts a heap from a chair—Not there; another heap, the dressing table, the chiffonier drawers. She brings to light several beautiful chemises and an amazing pajama, but this does not satisfy her—she goes out.

An indistinguishable mumble from the next room.

Now, we are getting warm. This is Mrs. Connage, ample, dignified, rouged to the dowager point and quite worn out. Her lips move significantly as she looks for it. Her search is less thorough than the maid's, but there is a touch of fury in it that quite makes up for its sketchiness. She stumbles on the tulle and her "damn" is quite audible. She retires empty-handed.

More chatter outside and a girl's voice, a very spoiled voice, says: "Of all the stupid people"—

After a pause a third seeker enters, not she of the spoiled voice but a younger edition. This is Cecelia Connage, sixteen, pretty, shrewd and constitutionally good-humored. She is dressed for the evening in a gown the obvious simplicity of which probably bores her. She goes to the nearest pile, selects a small pink garment and holds it up appraisingly.

CECELIA: Pink?

ROSALIND: Yes!

CECELIA: Very snappy?

ROSALIND: Yes!

CECELIA: I've got it!

(She sees herself in the mirror of the dressing table and commences to tickle-toe on the carpet.)

ROSALIND: (Outside.) What are you doing—trying it on?

(Cecelia ceases and goes out, carrying the garment at the right shoulder. From the other door, enters Alec Connage, about twenty-three, healthy and quite sure of the cut of his dress clothes. He comes to the center of the room and in a huge voice shouts:)

Mamma!

(There is a chorus of protest from next door and encouraged he starts toward it, but is repelled by another chorus.)

ALEC: So that's where you all are! Amory Blaine is here.

CECELIA: (Quickly.) Take him down stairs.

ALEC: Oh, he is down stairs.

MRS. CONNAGE: Well, you can show him where his room is. Tell him I'm sorry that I can't meet him now.

ALEC: He's heard a lot about you all. I wish you'd hurry. Father's telling him all about the war and he's restless. He's sort of temperamental.

(This last suffices to draw Cecelia into the room.)

CECELIA: (Seating herself high upon lingerie.) How do you mean temperamental?

ALEC: Oh, he writes stuff.

CECELIA: Does he play the piano?

ALEC: I don't know. He's sort of ghostly, too—makes you scared to death sometimes—you know, all that artistic business.

CECELIA: (Speculatively.) Drink?

ALEC: Yes—nothing queer about him.

CECELIA: Money?

ALEC: Good Lord—ask him. No, I don't think so. Still he was at Princeton when I was at New Haven. He must have some.

MRS. CONNAGE: (Enter Mrs. Connage.) Alec, of course, we're glad to have any friend of yours, but you must admit this is an inconvenient time, and he'll be a little neglected. This is Rosalind's week, you see. When a girl comes out she needs all the attention.

ROSALIND: (Outside.) Well, then prove it by coming here and hooking me.

(Exit Mrs. Connage.)

ALEC: Rosalind hasn't changed a bit.

CECELIA: (In a lower tone.) She's awfully spoiled.

ALEC: Well, she'll meet her match tonight.

CECELIA: Who—Mr. Amory Blaine?

(Alec nods.)

Well Rosalind has still to meet the man she can't out-distance. Honestly, Alec, she treats men terribly. She abuses them and cuts them and breaks dates with them and yawns in their faces—and they come back for more.

ALEC: They love it.

CECELIA: They hate it. She's a—she's a sort of vampire, I think—and she can make girls do what she wants usually—only she hates girls.

ALEC: Personality runs in our family.

CECELIA: (Resignedly.) I guess it ran out before it got to me.

ALEC: Does Rosalind behave herself?

CECELIA: Not particularly well. Oh, she's average—smokes sometimes, drinks punch, frequently kissed—Oh, yes—common knowledge—one of the effects of the war, you know.

(Emerges—Mrs. Connage.)

MRS. CONNAGE: Rosalind's almost finished and I can go down and meet your friend.

(Exeunt Alec and his mother.)

ROSALIND: (Outside.) Oh, Mother—

CECELIA: Mother's gone down.

(Rosalind enters, dressed—except for her flowing hair. Rosalind is unquestionably beautiful. A radiant skin with two spots of vanishing color, and a face with one of those eternal mouths, which only one out of every fifty beauties possesses.

It is sensual, slightly, but small and beautifully shaped. If Rosalind had less intelligence her "spoiled" expression might be called a pout, but she seems to have sprung into growth without that immaturity that "pout" suggests. She is wonderfully built, one notices immediately, slender and athletic, yet lacking under-development. Her voice, scarcely musical, has the ghost of an alto quality and is full of vivid instant personality.)

ROSALIND: Honestly, there are only two costumes in the world I really enjoy being in—(combing her hair at the dressing table) a hoop-skirt dress with pantaloons or a bathing suit. I'm quite charming in both of them.

CECELIA: Are you glad you're coming out?

ROSALIND: Delighted.

CECELIA: (Cynically.) So you can get married and live on Long Island with the fast younger married set? You want life to be a chain of flirtation, with a man for every link.

ROSALIND: Want it to be one!—you mean I've found it one.

CECELIA: Ha!

ROSALIND: Cecelia, darling, you don't know what a trial it is to be—like me—I've got to keep my face like steel in the street to keep men from winking at me. If I laugh hard from a front row at the theater, the comedian plays to me for the rest of the evening. If I drop my voice, my eyes, my handkerchief at a dance my partner calls me up on the phone every day for a week.

CECELIA: It must be an awful strain.

ROSALIND: The unfortunate part is that the only men who interest me at all are the totally ineligible ones. Ah—if I were poor, I'd go on the stage. That's where my type belongs.

CECELIA: Yes, you might as well get paid for the amount of acting you do.

ROSALIND: Sometimes when I've felt particularly radiant I've thought—why should this be wasted on one man—?

CECELIA: Often when you're particularly sulky, I've wondered why it should all be wasted on just one family.

(Getting up.) I think I'll go down and meet Mr. Amory Blaine. I like temperamental men.

ROSALIND: My dear girl, there aren't any. Men don't know how to be really angry or really happy—and the ones that do go to pieces.

CECELIA: Well, I'm glad I don't have all your worries. I'm engaged.

ROSALIND: (With a scornful smile.) Engaged? Why you little lunatic. If mother heard you talking like that she'd send you off to boarding school where you belong.

CECELIA: You won't tell her, though, because I know things I could tell—and you're too selfish.

ROSALIND: (A little annoyed.) Run along, little girl!—Who are you engaged to, the iceman?—the man that keeps the candy store?

CECELIA: Cheap wit—good-bye, darling, I'll see you later.

ROSALIND: Oh, be sure and do that—you're such a help.

(Exit Cecelia. Rosalind finishes her hair and rises, humming. She goes up to the mirror and starts to dance in front of it, on the soft carpet. She watches not her feet, but her eyes—never casually but always intently, even when she smiles.)

(The door suddenly opens and then slams behind a good-looking young man, with a straight, romantic profile, who sees her and melts to instant confusion.)

HE: Oh, I'm sorry, I thought–

SHE: (Smiling radiantly.) Oh, you're Amory Blaine, aren't you?

HE: (Regarding her closely.) And you're Rosalind?

SHE: I'm going to call you Amory–oh, come in–it's all right–Mother'll be right in–(under her breath) unfortunately.

HE: (Gazing around.) This is sort of a new wrinkle for me.

SHE: This is No Man's Land.

HE: This is where you–you– (embarrassment.)

SHE: Yes–all those things.

(She crosses to the bureau.) See, here's my rouge–eye pencils.

HE: I didn't know you were that way.

SHE: What did you expect?

HE: I thought you'd be sort of–sort of–sexless; you know, swim and play golf.

SHE: Oh, I do–but not in business hours.

HE: Business?

SHE: Six to two–strictly.

HE: I'd like to have some stock in the corporation.

SHE: Oh, it's not a corporation–it's just "Rosalind, Unlimited. " Fifty-one shares, name, good will and everything goes at $25,000 a year.

HE: (Disapprovingly.) Sort of a chilly proposition.

SHE: Well, Amory, you don't mind–do you? When I meet a man that doesn't bore me to death after two weeks, perhaps it'll be different.

HE: Odd, you have the same point of view on men that I have on women.

SHE: I'm not really feminine, you know–in my mind.

HE: (Interested.) Go on.

SHE: No, you–you go on–you've made me talk about myself. That's against the rules.

HE: Rules?

SHE: My own rules–but you–oh, Amory, I hear you're brilliant. The family expects so much of you.

HE: How encouraging.

SHE: Alec said you'd taught him to think. Did you? I don't believe anyone could.

HE: No. I'm really quite dull.

(He evidently doesn't intend this to be taken quite seriously.)

SHE: Liar.

HE: I'm—I'm religious—I'm literary. I've—I've even written poems.

SHE: Vers libre—splendid. (She declaims.)

Trees are green,
The birds are singing in the trees,
The girl sips her poison,
The bird flies away; the girl dies.

HE: (Laughing.) No, not that kind.

SHE: (Suddenly.) I like you.

HE: Don't.

SHE: Modest, too—

HE: I'm afraid of you. I'm always afraid of a girl—until I've kissed her.

SHE: (Emphatically.) My dear boy, the war is over.

HE: So I'll always be afraid of you.

SHE: (Rather sadly.) I suppose you will.

(A slight pause on both their parts.)

HE: (After due consideration.) Listen. This is a frightful thing to ask.

SHE: (Knowing what's coming.) After five minutes.

HE: But will you—kiss me?—Or are you afraid?

SHE: I'm never afraid—but your reasons are so poor.

HE: Rosalind, I really want to kiss you.

SHE: So do I.

(They kiss—definitely and thoroughly.)

HE: (After a breathless second.) Well, your curiosity is satisfied.

SHE: IS yours?

HE: No, it's only aroused.

(He looks it.)

SHE: (Dreamily.) I've kissed dozens of men. I suppose I'll kiss dozens more.

HE: (Abstractedly.) Yes, I suppose you could—like that.

SHE: Most people like the way I kiss.

HE: (Remembering himself.) Good Lord, yes. Kiss me once more, Rosalind.

SHE: No—my curiosity is generally satisfied at one.

HE: (Discouraged.) Is that a rule?

SHE: I make rules to fit the cases.

HE: You and I are somewhat alike—except that I'm years older in experience.

SHE: How old are you?

HE: Twenty-three. You?

SHE: Nineteen—just.

HE: I suppose you're the product of a fashionable school.

SHE: No—I'm fairly raw material. I was expelled from Spence—I've forgotten why.

HE: What's your general trend?

SHE: Oh, I'm bright, quite selfish, emotional when aroused, fond of admiration—

HE: (Suddenly.) I don't want to fall in love with you—

SHE: (Raising her eyebrows.) Nobody asked you to.

HE: (Continuing calmly)—But I probably will. I love your mouth.

SHE: Hush—please don't fall in love with my mouth—hair, eyes, shoulders, slippers—but not my mouth. Everybody falls in love with my mouth.

HE: It's quite beautiful.

SHE: It's too small.

HE: No, it isn't—let's see.

(He kisses her again with the same thoroughness.)

SHE: (Rather moved.) Say something sweet!

HE: (Frightened.) Lord help me.

SHE: (Drawing away.) Well, don't—if it's so hard.

HE: Shall we pretend? So soon?

SHE: We haven't the same standards of time as other people.

HE: Already it's—other people.

SHE: Let's pretend.

HE: No—I can't—it's sentimental.

SHE: You're not sentimental?

HE: No, I'm romantic—a sentimental person thinks things will last—a romantic person hopes against hope that they won't. Sentiment is emotional.

SHE: And you're not? (with her eyes half closed.) You probably flatter yourself that that's a superior attitude.

HE: Well—Oh, Rosalind, Rosalind, don't argue—kiss me again.

SHE: (Quite chilly now.) No—I have no desire to kiss you.

HE: (Openly taken aback.) You wanted to kiss me a minute ago.

SHE: This is now.

HE: I'd better go.

SHE: I suppose so.

(He goes toward the door.)

SHE: Oh!

(He turns.)

SHE: (Laughing.) Score: Home Team, 100—Opponents, Zero.

(He starts back.)

(Quickly.) Rain—no game!

(He goes out.)

(She goes quickly to the chiffonier, takes out a cigarette case and hides it in the side drawer of a desk. Her mother enters—note book in hand.)

MRS. CONNAGE: Good—I've been wanting to speak to you alone before we go downstairs.

ROSALIND: Heavens, you frighten me.

MRS. CONNAGE: Rosalind, you've been a very expensive proposition.

ROSALIND: (Resignedly.) Yes.

MRS. CONNAGE: And you know your father hasn't what he once had.

ROSALIND: (Making a wry face.) Oh please don't talk about money.

MRS. CONNAGE: You can't do anything without it. This is our last year in this house—and unless things change, Cecelia won't have the advantages you've had.

ROSALIND: (Impatiently.) Well—what is it?

MRS. CONNAGE: So I ask you to please mind me in several things I've put down in my note book. The first one is: Don't disappear with young men. There may be a time when it's valuable, but at present I want you on the dance floor where I can find you. There are certain men I want to have you meet and I don't like finding you in some corner of the conservatory exchanging silliness with anyone—or listening to it.

ROSALIND: (Sarcastically.) Yes, listening to it is better.

MRS. CONNAGE: And don't waste a lot of time with the college set—little boys nineteen and twenty years old. I don't mind a prom or a football game, but staying away from advantageous parties to eat in little cafes downtown with Tom, Dick and Harry—

ROSALIND: (Offering her code, which is, by the way, quite as high as her mother's.) Mother, it's done—one can't run everything now the way one did in the early nineties.

MRS. CONNAGE: (Paying no attention.) There are several bachelor friends of your father's that I want you to meet tonight—youngish men.

ROSALIND: (Nodding wisely.) About forty-five?

MRS. CONNAGE: (Sharply.) Why not?

ROSALIND: Oh, quite all right—they know life and are so adorably tired looking—(shakes her head) but they will dance.

MRS. CONNAGE: I haven't met Mr. Blaine—but I don't think you'll care for him. He doesn't sound like a money maker.

ROSALIND: Mother, I never think about money.

MRS. CONNAGE: You never keep it long enough to think about it.

ROSALIND: (Sighs.) Yes, I suppose some day I'll marry a ton of it—out of sheer boredom.

MRS. CONNAGE: (Referring to note book.) I had a wire from Hartford. Dawson Ryder is coming up. Now, there's a young man I like, and he's floating in money. It seems to me that since you seem tired of Howard Gillespie, you might give Mr. Ryder some encouragement. This is the third time he's been up in a month.

ROSALIND: How did you know I was tired of Howard Gillespie?

MRS. CONNAGE: The poor boy looks so miserable every time he comes.

ROSALIND: That was one of those romantic pre-battle affairs. They're all wrong.

MRS. CONNAGE: (Her say said.) At any rate, make us proud of you tonight.

ROSALIND: Don't you think I'm beautiful?

MRS. CONNAGE: You know you are.

(From downstairs is heard the shriek of a violin being tuned, the rattle of a drum. Mrs. Connage turns quickly to her daughter.)

MRS. CONNAGE: Come.

ROSALIND: One minute.

(Her mother leaves. Rosalind goes to the glass, where she gazes at herself with great satisfaction. She kisses her hand and touches her mirrored mouth with it. Then she turns out the lights and leaves the room.

Silence for a moment. A few chords from the piano, the discreet message of faint drums, the rustle of new silk, all blend on the staircase outside and drift in through the partly opened door. Bundled figures pass in the lighted hall. The laughter heard below becomes doubled and multiplied. Then some one comes in from the side, switches on the lights and closes the door. It is Cecelia. She goes to the chiffonier, looks in the drawers, hesitates—then to the desk whence she takes the cigarette case and selects one. She lights it and puffing and blowing walks toward the mirror.)

CECELIA: (In tremendously sophisticated accents.) Oh, yes, coming out is such a farce nowadays, you know. One really plays around so much before one is seventeen, that it's positively anticlimax.

(Shaking hands with a visionary, middle-aged nobleman.)

Yes, your grace—I b'lieve I've heard my sister speak of you. Have a puff— they're good. They're—they're Coronas. You don't smoke? What a pity! The King doesn't allow it, I suppose. Yes, I'll dance.

(So she dances around the room to a tune from downstairs. Her arms outstretched to an imaginary partner. The cigarette waving in her hand. Darkness comes quickly down and the lights stay low until—)

SCENE II

(Draperies cut off the stage to a corner of a den downstairs, filled by a very comfortable leather lounge. A small light is on each side above and in the middle; over the couch hangs a painting of a very old, very dignified gentleman, period 1860. Outside, the music is heard in a fox trot.

Rosalind is seated on the lounge and on her left is Howard Gillespie, a shallow youth of about twenty-four. He is obviously very unhappy and she quite bored.)

GILLESPIE: (Feebly.) What do you mean I've changed? I feel the same toward you.

ROSALIND: But you don't look the same to me.

GILLESPIE: Three weeks ago you used to say that you liked me because I was so blase, so indifferent—I still am.

ROSALIND: But not about me. I used to like you because you had brown eyes and thin legs.

GILLESPIE: (Helplessly.) They're still thin and brown.

ROSALIND: I used to think you were never jealous. Now you follow me with your eyes wherever I go.

GILLESPIE: I love you.

ROSALIND: (Coldly.) I know it.

GILLESPIE: And you haven't kissed me for two weeks. I had an idea that after a girl was kissed she was—was—won.

ROSALIND: Those days are over. I have to be won all over again every time you see me.

GILLESPIE: Are you serious?

ROSALIND: About as usual. There used to be two kinds of kisses: First when girls were kissed and deserted, second when they were engaged. Now there's a third kind where the man is kissed and deserted. If Mr. Jones of the nineties bragged he'd kissed a girl everyone knew he was through with her. If Mr. Jones of 1919 brags the same, everyone knows it's because he can't kiss her any more. Given a decent start any girl can beat a man nowadays.

GILLESPIE: Then why do you play with men?

ROSALIND: (Leaning forward confidentially.) For that first moment, when he's interested. There is a moment–Oh, just before the first kiss, a whispered word–something that makes it worth while.

GILLESPIE: And then?

ROSALIND: Then after that you make him talk about himself. Pretty soon he thinks of nothing but being alone with you.–He sulks, he won't fight, he doesn't want to play–Victory.

(Enter Dawson Ryder, twenty-six, handsome, rather cold, wealthy, faithful to his own, a bore perhaps, but steady and sure of success.)

RYDER: I believe this is my dance, Rosalind.

ROSALIND: Very well, Dawson. Mr. Ryder, this is Mr. Gillespie. (They shake hands and Gillespie leaves tremendously downcast.)

RYDER: Your party is certainly a success.

ROSALIND: Is it–I haven't seen it lately. I'm weary–Do you mind sitting out?

RYDER: Mind–I'm delighted. You know I loath this "rushing" idea. See a girl yesterday, today, tomorrow.

ROSALIND: Dawson!

RYDER: What?

ROSALIND: I wonder if you know you love me.

RYDER: (Startled.) What–Oh–I say, you're remarkable.

ROSALIND: Because, you know, I'm an awful proposition. Anyone who marries me would have his hands full. I'm mean–mighty mean.

RYDER: Oh, I wouldn't say that.

ROSALIND: Oh, yes I am–especially to the people nearest me.

(She rises.)

Come, let's go. I have changed my mind and I want to dance. Mother is probably having a fit.

(They start out.)

Does one shimmy in Hartford?

(Exeunt.)

(Enter Alec and Cecelia.)

CECELIA: Just my luck to get my own brother for an intermission.

ALEC: (Gloomingly.) I'll go if you want me to.

CECELIA: Good heavens, no—who would I begin the next dance with?

(Sighs.)

There's no color in a dance since the French officers went back.

ALEC: I hope Amory doesn't fall in love with Rosalind.

CECELIA: Why, I had an idea you wanted him to.

ALEC: I did, but since seeing these girls—I don't know. I'm awfully attached to Amory. He's sensitive and I don't want him to break his heart over somebody who doesn't care about him.

CECELIA: He's very good looking.

ALEC: She won't marry him, but a girl doesn't have to marry a man to break his heart.

CECELIA: What does it? I wish I knew the secret.

ALEC: Why, you cold-blooded little kitty. It's lucky for some that the Lord gave you a pug nose.

(Enter Mrs. Connage.)

MRS. CONNAGE: Where on earth is Rosalind?

ALEC: (Brilliantly.) Of course, you've come to the best people to find out. She'd naturally be with us.

MRS. CONNAGE: Her father has marshalled eight bachelor millionaires to meet her.

ALEC: You might form a squad and march through the halls.

MRS. CONNAGE: I'm perfectly serious—for all I know she may be at the Cocoanut Grove with some football player on the night of her debut. You look left and I'll—

ALEC: (Flippantly.) Hadn't you better send the butler through the cellar?

MRS. CONNAGE: (Perfectly serious.) Oh, you don't think she'd be there!

CECELIA: He's only joking, Mother.

ALEC: Mother had a picture of her tapping a keg of beer with some high hurdler.

MRS. CONNAGE: Let's look right away.

(They go out. Enter Rosalind with Gillespie.)

GILLESPIE: Rosalind—Once more I ask you. Don't you care a blessed thing about me?

(Enter Amory.)

AMORY: My dance.

ROSALIND: Mr. Gillespie, this is Mr. Blaine.

GILLESPIE: I've met Mr. Blaine. From Dayton, aren't you?

AMORY: Yes.

GILLESPIE: (Desperately.) I've been there. It's rather awful.

AMORY: (Spicily.) I don't know. I always felt that I'd rather be provincial hot-tamale than soup without seasoning.

GILLESPIE: What?

AMORY: Oh, no offense.

(Gillespie bows and leaves.)

ROSALIND: He's too much people.

AMORY: I was in love with a people once.

ROSALIND: So?

AMORY: Oh yes, some fool—nothing at all to her, except what I read into her.

ROSALIND: What happened?

AMORY: Finally I convinced her that she was smarter than I was—then she threw me over. Said I was impractical, you know.

ROSALIND: What do you mean, impractical?

AMORY: Oh—drive a car, but can't change a tire.

ROSALIND: What are you going to do?

AMORY: Write—I'm going to start here in New York.

ROSALIND: Greenwich Village.

AMORY: Good heavens, no—I said write—not drink.

ROSALIND: I like business men. Clever men are usually so homely.

AMORY: I feel as if I'd known you ages.

ROSALIND: Oh, are you going to commence the "pyramid" story?

AMORY: No—I was going to make it French. I was Louis 14th and you were one of my—my—(Changing his tone.) Suppose—we fell in love.

ROSALIND: I've suggested pretending.

AMORY: If we did, it would be very big.

ROSALIND: Why?

AMORY: Because selfish people are in a way terribly capable of great loves.

ROSALIND: Pretend. (Turning her lips up.) (Very deliberately they kiss.)

AMORY: I can't say sweet things. But you are beautiful.

ROSALIND: Not that.

AMORY: What then?

ROSALIND: (Sadly.) Oh, nothing—only I want sentiment, real sentiment—and I never find it.

AMORY: I never find anything else in the world—and I loathe it.

ROSALIND: It's so hard to find a male to gratify one's artistic taste. (Someone has opened a door and the music of a waltz surges into the room. Rosalind rises.)

ROSALIND: Listen, they're playing "Kiss Me Again. " (He looks at her.)

AMORY: Well?

ROSALIND: Well?

AMORY: (Softly—the battle lost.) I love you.

ROSALIND: I love you. (They kiss.)

AMORY: Oh, God, what have I done?

ROSALIND: Nothing. Oh, don't talk. Kiss me again.

AMORY: I don't know why or how, but I love you—from the moment I saw you.

ROSALIND: Me, too—I—I—want to belong to you. (Her brother strolls in, starts and then in a loud voice says, "Oh, excuse me, " and goes.)

ROSALIND: (Her lips scarcely stirring.) Don't let me go—I don't care who knows.

AMORY: Say it.

ROSALIND: I love you. (They part.)

ROSALIND: Oh—I am very youthful, thank God—and rather beautiful, thank God—and happy, thank God, thank God—(She pauses and then in an odd burst of frankness adds.) Poor Amory! (He kisses her again.)

CURTAIN.

The Smilers

We all have that exasperated moment!

There are times when you almost tell the harmless old lady next door what you really think of her face—that it ought to be on a night-nurse in a house for the blind; when you'd like to ask the man you've been waiting ten minutes for if he isn't all overheated from racing the postman down the block; when you nearly say to the waiter that if they deducted a cent from the bill for every degree the soup was below tepid the hotel would owe you half a dollar; when—and this is the infallible earmark of true exasperation—a smile affects you as an oil-baron's undershirt affects a cow's husband.

But the moment passes. Scars may remain on your dog or your collar or your telephone receiver, but your soul has slid gently back into its place between the lower edge of your heart and the upper edge of your stomach, and all is at peace.

But the imp who turns on the shower-bath of exasperation apparently made it so hot one time in Sylvester Stockton's early youth that he never dared dash in and turn it off—in consequence no first old man in an amateur production of a Victorian comedy was ever more pricked and prodded by the daily phenomena of life than was Sylvester at thirty.

Accusing eyes behind spectacles—suggestion of a stiff neck—this will have to do for his description, since he is not the hero of this story. He is the plot. He is the factor that makes it one story instead of three stories. He makes remarks at the beginning and end.

The late afternoon sun was loitering pleasantly along Fifth Avenue when Sylvester, who had just come out of that hideous public library where he had been consulting some ghastly book, told his impossible chauffeur (it is true that I am following his movements through his own spectacles) that he wouldn't need his stupid, incompetent services any longer. Swinging his cane (which he found too short) in his left hand (which he should have cut off long ago since it was constantly offending him), he began walking slowly down the Avenue.

When Sylvester walked at night he frequently glanced behind and on both sides to see if anyone was sneaking up on him. This had become a constant mannerism. For this reason he was unable to pretend that he didn't see Betty Tearle sitting in her machine in front of Tiffany's.

Back in his early twenties he had been in love with Betty Tearle. But he had depressed her. He had misanthropically dissected every meal, motor trip and musical comedy that they attended together, and on the few occasions when she had tried to be especially nice to him—from a mother's point of view he had been rather desirable—he had suspected hidden motives and fallen into a deeper gloom than ever. Then one day she told him that she would go mad if he ever again parked his pessimism in her sun-parlour.

And ever since then she had seemed to be smiling—uselessly, insultingly, charmingly smiling.

"Hello, Sylvo," she called.

"Why—how do, Betty." He wished she wouldn't call him Sylvo—it sounded like a—like a darn monkey or something.

"How goes it?" she asked cheerfully. "Not very well, I suppose."

"Oh, yes," he answered stiffly, "I manage."

"Taking in the happy crowd?"

"Heavens, yes." He looked around him. "Betty, why are they happy? What are they smiling at? What do they find to smile at?"

Betty flashed him a glance of radiant amusement.

"The women may smile because they have pretty teeth, Sylvo."

"You smile," continued Sylvester cynically, "because you're comfortably married and have two children. You imagine you're happy, so you suppose everyone else is."

Betty nodded.

"You may have hit it, Sylvo—" The chauffeur glanced around and she nodded at him. "Good-bye."

Sylvo watched with a pang of envy which turned suddenly to exasperation as he saw she had turned and smiled at him once more. Then her car was out of sight in the traffic, and with a voluminous sigh he galvanized his cane into life and continued his stroll.

At the next corner he stopped in at a cigar store and there he ran into Waldron Crosby. Back in the days when Sylvester had been a prize pigeon in the eyes of debutantes he had also been a game partridge from the point of view of promoters. Crosby, then a young bond salesman, had given him much safe and sane advice and saved him many dollars. Sylvester liked Crosby as much as he could like anyone. Most people did like Crosby.

"Hello, you old bag of nerves," cried Crosby genially, "come and have a big gloom-dispelling Corona."

Sylvester regarded the cases anxiously. He knew he wasn't going to like what he bought.

"Still out at Larchmont, Waldron?" he asked.

"Right-o."

"How's your wife?"

"Never better."

"Well," said Sylvester suspiciously, "you brokers always look as if you're smiling at something up your sleeve. It must be a hilarious profession."

Crosby considered.

"Well," he admitted, "it varies—like the moon and the price of soft drinks—but it has its moments."

"Waldron," said Sylvester earnestly, "you're a friend of mine—please do me the favour of not smiling when I leave you. It seems like a—like a mockery."

A broad grin suffused Crosby's countenance.

"Why, you crabbed old son-of-a-gun!"

But Sylvester with an irate grunt had turned on his heel and disappeared.

He strolled on. The sun finished its promenade and began calling in the few stray beams it had left among the westward streets. The Avenue darkened with black bees from the department stores; the traffic swelled in to an interlaced jam; the buses were packed four deep like platforms above the thick crowd; but Sylvester, to whom the daily shift and change of the city was a matter only of sordid monotony, walked on, taking only quick sideward glances through his frowning spectacles.

He reached his hotel and was elevated to his four-room suite on the twelfth floor.

"If I dine downstairs," he thought, "the orchestra will play either 'Smile, Smile, Smile' or 'The Smiles That You Gave To Me'. But then if I go to the Club I'll meet all the cheerful people I know, and if I go somewhere else where there's no music, I won't get anything fit to eat."

He decided to have dinner in his rooms.

An hour later, after disparaging some broth, a squab and a salad, he tossed fifty cents to the room-waiter, and then held up his hand warningly.

"Just oblige me by not smiling when you say 'thanks'?"

He was too late. The waiter had grinned.

"Now, will you please tell me," asked Sylvester peevishly, "what on earth you have to smile about?"

The waiter considered. Not being a reader of the magazines he was not sure what was characteristic of waiters, yet he supposed something characteristic was expected of him.

"Well, mister," he answered, glancing at the ceiling with all the ingenuousness he could muster in his narrow, sallow countenance, "it's just something my face does when it sees four bits comin'."

Sylvester waved him away.

"Waiters are happy because they've never had anything better," he thought. "They haven't enough imagination to want anything."

At nine o'clock from sheer boredom he sought his expressionless bed.

II

As Sylvester left the cigar store, Waldron Crosby followed him out, and turning off Fifth Avenue down a cross street entered a brokerage office. A plump man with nervous hands rose and hailed him.

"Hello, Waldron."

"Hello, Potter—I just dropped in to hear the worst."

The plump man frowned.

"We've just got the news," he said.

"Well, what is it? Another drop?"

"Closed at seventy-eight. Sorry, old boy."

"Whew!"

"Hit pretty hard?"

"Cleaned out!"

The plump man shook his head, indicating that life was too much for him, and turned away.

Crosby sat there for a moment without moving. Then he rose, walked into Potter's private office and picked up the phone.

"Gi'me Larchmont 838."

In a moment he had his connection.

"Mrs. Crosby there?"

A man's voice answered him.

"Yes; this you, Crosby? This is Doctor Shipman."

"Dr. Shipman?" Crosby's voice showed sudden anxiety.

"Yes—I've been trying to reach you all afternoon. The situation's changed and we expect the child tonight."

"Tonight?"

"Yes. Everything's OK. But you'd better come right out."

"I will. Good-bye."

He hung up the receiver and started out the door, but paused as an idea struck him. He returned, and this time called a Manhattan number.

"Hello, Donny, this is Crosby."

"Hello, there, old boy. You just caught me; I was going—"

"Say, Donny, I want a job right away, quick."

"For whom?"

"For me."

"Why, what's the—"

"Never mind. Tell you later. Got one for me?"

"Why, Waldron, there's not a blessed thing here except a clerkship. Perhaps next—"

"What salary goes with the clerkship?"

"Forty—say forty-five a week."

"I've got you. I start tomorrow."

"All right. But say, old man—"

"Sorry, Donny, but I've got to run."

Crosby hurried from the brokerage office with a wave and a smile at Potter. In the street he took out a handful of small change and after surveying it critically hailed a taxi.

"Grand Central—quick!" he told the driver.

III

At six o'clock Betty Tearle signed the letter, put it into an envelope and wrote her husband's name upon it. She went into his room and after a moment's hesitation set a black cushion on the bed and laid the white letter on it so that it could not fail to attract his attention when he came in. Then with a quick glance around the room she walked into the hall and upstairs to the nursery.

"Clare," she called softly.

"Oh, Mummy!" Clare left her doll's house and scurried to her mother.

"Where's Billy, Clare?"

Billy appeared eagerly from under the bed.

"Got anything for me?" he inquired politely.

His mother's laugh ended in a little catch and she caught both her children to her and kissed them passionately. She found that she was crying quietly and their flushed little faces seemed cool against the sudden fever racing though her blood.

"Take care of Clare—always—Billy darling—"

Billy was puzzled and rather awed.

"You're crying," he accused gravely.

"I know—I know I am—"

Clare gave a few tentative sniffles, hesitated, and then clung to her mother in a storm of weeping.

"I d-don't feel good, Mummy—I don't feel good."

Betty soothed her quietly.

"We won't cry any more, Clare dear—either of us."

But as she rose to leave the room her glance at Billy bore a mute appeal, too vain, she knew, to be registered on his childish consciousness.

Half an hour later as she carried her travelling bag to a taxicab at the door she raised her hand to her face in mute admission that a veil served no longer to hide her from the world.

"But I've chosen," she thought dully.

As the car turned the corner she wept again, resisting a temptation to give up and go back.

"Oh, my God!?" she whispered. "What am I doing? What have I done? What have I done?"

IV

When Jerry, the sallow, narrow-faced waiter, left Sylvester's rooms he reported to the head-waiter, and then checked out for the day.

He took the subway south and alighting at William Street walked a few blocks and entered a billiard parlour.

An hour later he emerged with a cigarette drooping from his bloodless lips, and stood on the sidewalk as if hesitating before making a decision. He set off eastward.

As he reached a certain corner his gait suddenly increased and then quite as suddenly slackened. He seemed to want to pass by, yet some magnetic attraction was apparently exerted on him, for with a sudden face-about he turned in at the door of a cheap restaurant—half cabaret, half chop-suey parlour—where a miscellaneous assortment gathered nightly.

Jerry found his way to a table situated in the darkest and most obscure corner. Seating himself with a contempt for his surroundings that betokened familiarity rather than superiority he ordered a glass of claret.

The evening had begun. A fat woman at the piano was expelling the last jauntiness from a hackneyed foxtrot, and a lean, dispirited male was assisting her with lean, dispirited notes from a violin. The attention of the patrons was directed at a dancer wearing soiled stockings and done largely in peroxide and rouge who was about to step upon a small platform, meanwhile exchanging pleasantries with a fat, eager person at the table beside her who was trying to capture her hand.

Over in the corner Jerry watched the two by the platform and, as he gazed, the ceiling seemed to fade out, the walls growing into tall buildings and the platform becoming the top of a Fifth Avenue bus on a breezy spring night three years ago. The fat, eager person disappeared, the short skirt of the dancer rolled down and the rouge faded from her cheeks—and he was beside her again in an old delirious ride, with the lights blinking kindly at them from the tall buildings beside and the voices of the street merging into a pleasant somnolent murmur around them.

"Jerry," said the girl on top of the bus, "I've said that when you were gettin' seventy-five I'd take a chance with you. But, Jerry, I can't wait for ever."

Jerry watched several street numbers sail by before he answered.

"I don't know what's the matter," he said helplessly, "they won't raise me. If I can locate a new job—"

"You better hurry, Jerry," said the girl; "I'm gettin' sick of just livin' along. If I can't get married I got a couple of chances to work in a cabaret—get on the stage maybe."

"You keep out of that," said Jerry quickly. "There ain't no need, if you just wait about another month or two."

"I can't wait for ever, Jerry," repeated the girl. "I'm tired of stayin' poor alone."

"It won't be so long," said Jerry clenching his free hand, "I can make it somewhere, if you'll just wait."

But the bus was fading out and the ceiling was taking shape and the murmur of the April streets was fading into the rasping whine of the violin—for that was all three years before and now he was sitting here.

The girl glanced up on the platform and exchanged a metallic impersonal smile with the dispirited violinist, and Jerry shrank farther back in his corner watching her with burning intensity.

"Your hands belong to anybody that wants them now," he cried silently and bitterly. "I wasn't man enough to keep you out of that—not man enough, by God, by God!"

But the girl by the door still toyed with the fat man's clutching fingers as she waited for her time to dance.

V

Sylvester Stockton tossed restlessly upon his bed. The room, big as it was, smothered him, and a breeze drifting in and bearing with it a rift of moon seemed laden only with the cares of the world he would have to face next day.

"They don't understand," he thought. "They don't see, as I do, the underlying misery of the whole damn thing. They're hollow optimists. They smile because they think they're always going to be happy."

"Oh, well," he mused drowsily, "I'll run up to Rye tomorrow and endure more smiles and more heat. That's all life is—just smiles and heat, smiles and heat."

Notes:

"The Smilers' was written in St Paul in September 1919 as "A Smile for Sylvo". After failing at his attempt to make a fast success as an advertising writer in New York, Fitzgerald returned to St Paul to rewrite his first novel. This Side of Paradise was accepted by Scribners in September, and Fitzgerald devoted the rest of the year to writing short stories for ready money. He submitted "The Smilers" to Scribner's Magazine, which rejected it. After Harold Ober, his literary agent, was unable to place the story in one of the magazines that paid well, Fitzgerald sold it to the Smart Set for $35: "I want to keep in right with Menken+Nathan as they're the most powerful critics in the country." Although the Smart Set under editors H. L. Mencken and George Jean Nathan was an influential magazine among literary people, its limited circulation did not allow for generous payment. Fitzgerald sold stories to the Smart Set when they were unplaceable in the mass-circulation magazines—including two of his masterpieces, "The Diamond as Big as the Ritz" and "May Day".

Although "The Smilers" was written soon after acceptance of This Side of Paradise, it is still very much a college literary magazine piece—self-conscious and blatantly ironic. This story shows the didactic streak that marked several of Fitzgerald's early stories, such as "The Four Fists" and "The Cut-Glass Bowl". The moralizing quality in his work—especially the stories—has been obscured by Fitzgerald's image as the Boswell of the Jazz Age. Near the end of his life he noted that he sometimes wishes he had gone into musical comedy, "but I guess I am too much a moralist at heart and really want to preach at people in some acceptable form rather than to entertain them."

The Popular Girl

Along about half-past ten every Saturday night Yanci Bowman eluded her partner by some graceful subterfuge and from the dancing floor went to point of vantage overlooking the country-club bar. When she saw her father she would either beckon to him, if he chanced to be looking in her direction, or else she would dispatch a waiter to call attention to her impendent presence. If it were no later than half past ten—that is, if he had had no more than an hour of synthetic gin rickeys—he would get up from his chair and suffer himself to be persuaded into the ballroom.

"Ballroom," for want of a better word. It was that room, filled by day with wicker furniture, which was always connotated in the phrase "Let's go in and dance." It was referred to as "inside" or "downstairs." It was that nameless chamber wherein occur the principal transactions of all the country clubs in America.

Yanci knew that if she could keep her father there for an hour, talking, watching her dance, or even on rare occasions dancing himself, she could safely release him at the end of that time. In the period that would elapse before midnight ended the dance he could scarcely become sufficiently stimulated to annoy anyone.

All this entailed considerable exertion on Yanci's part, and it was less for her father's sake than for her own that she went through with it. Several rather unpleasant experiences were scattered through this past summer. One night when she had been detained by the impassioned and impossible-to-interrupt speech of a young man from Chicago her father had appeared swaying gently in the ballroom doorway; in his ruddy handsome face two faded blue eyes were squinted half shut as he tried to focus them on the dancers, and he was obviously preparing to offer himself to the first dowager who caught his eye. He was ludicrously injured when Yanci insisted upon an immediate withdrawal.

After that night Yanci went through her Fabian maneuver to the minute.

Yanci and her father were the handsomest two people in the Middle Western city where they lived. Tom Bowman's complexion was hearty from twenty years spent in the service of good whisky and bad golf. He kept an office downtown, where he was thought to transact some vague real-estate business; but in point of fact his chief concern in life was the exhibition of a handsome profile and an easy well-bred manner at the country club, where he had spent the greater part of the ten years that had elapsed since his wife's death.

Yanci was twenty, with a vague die-away manner which was partly the setting for her languid disposition and partly the effect of a visit she had paid to some Eastern relatives at an impressionable age. She was intelligent, in a flitting way, a romantic under the moon and unable to decide whether to marry for sentiment or for comfort, the latter of these two abstractions being well enough personified by one of the most ardent among her admirers. Meanwhile she kept house, not without efficiency, for her father, and tried in a placid unruffled tempo to regulate his constant tippling to the sober side of inebriety.

She admired her father. She admired him for his fine appearance and for his charming manner. He had never quite lost the air of having been a popular Bones man at Yale. This charm of his was a standard by which her susceptible temperament unconsciously judged the men she knew. Nevertheless, father and daughter were far from that sentimental family relationship which is a stock plant in fiction, but in life usually exists in the mind of only the older party to it. Yanci Bowman had decided to leave her home by marriage within the year. She was heartily bored.

Scott Kimblerly, who saw her for the first time this November evening at the country club, agreed with the lady whose house guest he was that Yanci was an exquisite little beauty. With a sort of conscious sensuality surprising in such a young man—Scott was only twenty-five—he avoided an introduction that he might watch her undisturbed for a fanciful hour, and sip the pleasure or the disillusion of her conversation at the drowsy end of the evening.

"She never got over the disappointment of not meeting the Prince of Wales when he was in this country," remarked Mrs. Orrin Rogers, following his gaze. "She said so, anyhow; whether she was serious or not, I don't know. I hear that she has her walls simply plastered with pictures of him."

"Who?" asked Scott suddenly.

"Why, the Prince of Wales."

"Who has plaster pictures of him?"

"Why, Yanci Bowman, the girl you said you thought was so pretty."

"After a certain degree of prettiness, one pretty girl is as pretty as another," said Scott argumentatively.

"Yes, I suppose so."

Mrs. Rogers' voice drifted off on an indefinite note. She had never in her life compassed a generality until it had fallen familiarly on her ear from constant repetition.

"Let's talk her over," Scott suggested.

With a mock reproachful smile Mrs. Rogers lent herself agreeably to slander. An encore was just beginning. The orchestra trickled a light overflow of music into the pleasant green-latticed room and the two score couples who for the evening comprised the local younger set moved placidly into time with its beat. Only a few apathetic stags gathered one by one in the doorways, and to a close observer it was apparent that the scene did not attain the gayety which was its aspiration. These girls and men had known each other from childhood; and though there were marriages incipient upon the floor tonight, they were marriages of environment, of resignation, or even of boredom.

Their trappings lacked the sparkle of the seventeen-year-old affairs that took place through the short and radiant holidays. On such occasions as this, thought Scott as his eyes still sought casually for Yanci, occurred the matings of the left-overs, the plainer, the duller, the poorer of the social world; matings actuated by the same urge toward perhaps a more glamorous destiny, yet, for all that, less beautiful and less young. Scott himself was feeling very old.

But there was one face in the crowd to which his generalization did not apply. When his eyes found Yanci Bowman among the dancers he felt much younger. She was the incarnation of all in which the dance failed—graceful youth, arrogant, languid freshness and beauty that was sad and perishable as a memory in a dream. Her partner, a young man with one of those fresh red complexions ribbed with white streaks, as though he had been slapped on a cold day, did not appear to be holding her interest, and her glance fell here and there upon a group, a face, a garment, with a far-away and oblivious melancholy.

"Dark-blue eyes," said Scott to Mrs. Rogers. "I don't know that they mean anything except that they're beautiful, but that nose and upper lip and chin are certainly aristocratic—if there is any such thing," he added apologetically.

"Oh, she's very aristocratic," agreed Mrs. Rogers. "Her grandfather was a senator or governor or something in one of the Southern states. Her father's very aristocratic looking too. Oh, yes, they're very aristocratic; they're aristocratic people."

"She looks lazy."

Scott was watching the yellow gown drift and submerge among the dancers.

"She doesn't like to move. It's a wonder she dances so well. Is she engaged? Who is the man who keeps cutting in on her, the one who tucks his tie under his collar so rakishly and affects the remarkable slanting pockets?"

He was annoyed at the young man's persistence, and his sarcasm lacked the ring of detachment.

"Oh, that's"—Mrs. Rogers bent forward, the tip of her tongue just visible between her lips—"that's the O'Rourke boy. He's quite devoted, I believe."

"I believe," Scott said suddenly, "that I'll get you to introduce me if she's near when the music stops."

They arose and stood looking for Yanci—Mrs. Rogers, small, stoutening, nervous, and Scott Kimberly, her husband's cousin, dark and just below medium height. Scott was an orphan with half a million of his own, and he was in this city for no more reason than that he had missed a train. They looked for several minutes, and in vain. Yanci, in her yellow dress, no longer moved with slow loveliness among the dancers.

The clock stood at half past ten.

II

"Good evening," her father was saying to her at that moment in syllables faintly slurred. "This seems to be getting to be a habit."

They were standing near a side stairs, and over his shoulder through a glass door Yanci could see a party of half a dozen men sitting in familiar joviality about a round table.

"Don't you want to come out and watch for a while?" she suggested, smiling and affecting a casualness she did not feel.

"Not tonight, thanks."

Her father's dignity was a bit too emphasized to be convincing.

"Just come out and take a look," she urged him. "Everybody's here, and I want to ask you what you think of somebody."

This was not so good, but it was the best that occurred to her.

"I doubt very strongly if I'd find anything to interest me out there," said Tom Bowman emphatically. "I observe that f'some insane reason I'm always taken out and aged on the wood for half an hour as though I was irresponsible."

"I only ask you to stay a little while."

"Very considerate, I'm sure. But tonight I happ'n to be interested in a discussion that's taking place in here."

"Come on, father."

Yanci put her arm through his ingratiatingly; but he released it by the simple expedient of raising his own arm and letting hers drop.

"I'm afraid not."

"I'll tell you," she suggested, concealing her annoyance at this unusually protracted argument, "you come in and look, just once, and then if it bores you you can go right back."

He shook his head.

"No, thanks."

Then without another word he turned suddenly and reentered the bar. Yanci went back to the ballroom. She glanced easily at the stag line as she passed, and making a quick selection murmured to a man near her, "Dance with me, will you, Carty? I've lost my partner."

"Glad to," answered Carty truthfully.

"Awfully sweet of you."

"Sweet of me? Of you, you mean."

She looked up at him absently. She was furiously annoyed at her father. Next morning at breakfast she would radiate a consuming chill, but for tonight she could only wait, hoping that if the worst happened he would at least remain in the bar until the dance was over.

Mrs. Rogers, who lived next door to the Bowmans, appeared suddenly at her elbow with a strange young man.

"Yanci," Mrs. Rogers was saying with a social smile, "I want to introduce Mr. Kimberly. Mr. Kimberly's spending the weekend with us, and I particularly wanted him to meet you."

"How perfectly slick!" drawled Yanci with lazy formality.

Mr. Kimberly suggested to Miss Bowman that they dance, to which proposal Miss Bowman dispassionately acquiesced. They mingled their arms in the gesture prevalent and stepped into time with the beat of the drum. Simultaneously it seemed to Scott that the room and the couples who danced up and down upon it converted themselves into a background behind her. The commonplace lamps, the rhythm of the music playing some paraphrase of a paraphrase, the faces of many girls, pretty, undistinguished or absurd, assumed a certain solidity as though they had grouped themselves in a retinue for Yanci's languid eyes and dancing feet.

"I've been watching you," said Scott simply. "You look rather bored this evening."

"Do I?" Her dark-blue eyes exposed a borderland of fragile iris as they opened in a delicate burlesque of interest. "How perfectly kill-ing!" she added.

Scott laughed. She had used the exaggerated phrase without smiling, indeed without any attempt to give it verisimilitude. He had heard the adjectives of the year—"hectic," "marvelous," and "slick"—delivered casually, but never before without the faintest meaning. In this lackadaisical young beauty it was inexpressibly charming.

The dance ended. Yanci and Scott strolled toward a lounge set against the wall, but before they could take possession there was a shriek of laughter and a brawny damsel dragging an embarrassed boy in her wake skidded by them and plumped down upon it.

"How rude!" observed Yanci.

"I suppose it's her privilege."

"A girl with ankles like that has no privileges."

They seated themselves uncomfortably on two stiff chairs.

"Where do you come from?" she asked of Scott with polite uninterest.

"New York."

This having transpired, Yanci deigned to fix her eyes on him for the best part of ten seconds.

"Who was the gentleman with the invisible tie," Scott asked rudely, in order to make her look at him, "who was giving you such a rush? I found it impossible to keep my eyes off him. Is his personality as diverting as his haberdashery?"

"I don't know," she drawled; "I've only been engaged to him for a week."

"My Lord!" exclaimed Scott, perspiring suddenly under his eyes.

"I beg your pardon. I didn't–"

"I was only joking," she interrupted with a sighing laugh. "I thought I'd see what you'd say to that."

Then they both laughed, and Yanci continued, "I'm not engaged to anyone. I'm too horribly unpopular." Still the same key, her languorous voice humorously contradicting the content of her remark. "No one'll ever marry me."

"How pathetic!"

"Really," she murmured; "because I have to have compliments all the time, in order to live, and no one thinks I'm attractive any more, so no one ever gives them to me."

Seldom had Scott been so amused.

"Why, you beautiful child," he cried, "I'll bet you never hear anything else from morning till night!"

"Oh yes I do," she responded, obviously pleased. "I never get compliments unless I fish for them."

"Everything's the same," she was thinking as she gazed around her in a peculiar mood of pessimism. Same boys sober and same boys tight; same old women sitting by the walls and one or two girls sitting with them who were dancing this time last year.

Yanci had reached the stage where these country-club dances seemed little more than a display of sheer idiocy. From being an enchanted carnival where jeweled and immaculate maidens rouged to the pinkest propriety displayed themselves to strange and fascinating men, the picture had faded to a medium-sized hall where was an almost indecent display of unclothed motives and obvious failures. So much for several years! And the dance had changed scarcely by a ruffle in the fashions or a new flip in a figure of speech.

Yanci was ready to be married.

Meanwhile the dozen remarks rushing to Scott Kimberly's lips were interrupted by the apologetic appearance of Mrs. Rogers.

"Yanci," the older woman was saying, "the chauffeur's just telephoned to say that the car's broken down. I wonder if you and your father have room for us going home. If it's the slightest inconvenience don't hesitate to tell—"

"I know he'll be terribly glad to. He's got loads of room, because I came out with someone else."

She was wondering if her father would be presentable at twelve.

He could always drive at any rate—and, besides, people who asked for a lift could take what they got.

"That'll be lovely. Thank you so much," said Mrs. Rogers.

Then, as she had just passed the kittenish late thirties when women still think they are persona grata with the young and entered upon the early forties when their children convey to them tactfully that they no longer are, Mrs. Rogers obliterated herself from the scene. At that moment the music started and the unfortunate young man with white streaks in his red complexion appeared in front of Yanci.

Just before the end of the end of the next dance Scott Kimberly cut in on her again.

"I've come back," he began, "to tell you how beautiful you are."

"I'm not, really," she answered. "And, besides, you tell everyone that."

The music gathered gusto for its finale, and they sat down upon the comfortable lounge.

"I've told no one that for three years," said Scott.

There was no reason why he should have made it three years, yet somehow it sounded convincing to both of them. Her curiosity was stirred. She began finding out about him. She put him to a lazy questionnaire which began with his relationship to the Rogerses and ended, he knew not by what steps, with a detailed description of his apartment in New York.

"I want to live in New York," she told him; "on Park Avenue, in one of those beautiful white buildings that have twelve big rooms in each apartment and cost a fortune to rent."

"That's what I'd want, too, if I were married. Park Avenue—it's one of the most beautiful streets in the world, I think, perhaps chiefly because it hasn't any leprous park trying to give it an artificial suburbanity."

"Whatever that is," agreed Yanci. "Anyway, Father and I go to New York about three times a year. We always go to the Ritz."

This was not precisely true. Once a year she generally pried her father from his placid and not unbeneficent existence that she might spend a week lolling by the Fifth Avenue shop windows, lunching or having tea with some former school friend from Farmover, and occasionally going to dinner and the theater with boys who came up from Yale or Princeton for the occasion. These had been pleasant adventures—not one but was filled to the brim with colorful hours—dancing at Montmartre, dining at the Ritz, with some movie star or supereminent society woman at the next table, or else dreaming of what she might buy at Hempel's or Waxe's or Thrumble's if her father's income had but one additional naught on the happy side of the decimal. She adored New York with a great impersonal affection—adored it as only a Middle Western or Southern girl can. In its gaudy bazaars she felt her soul transported with turbulent delight, for to her eyes it held nothing ugly, nothing sordid, nothing plain.

She had stayed once at the Ritz—once only. The Manhattan, where they usually registered, had been torn down. She knew that she could never induce her father to afford the Ritz again.

After a moment she borrowed a pencil and paper and scribbled a notification "To Mr. Bowman in the grill" that he was expected to drive Mrs. Rogers and her guest home, "by request"—this last underlined. She hoped that he would be able to do so with dignity. This note she sent by a waiter to her father. Before the next dance began it was returned to her with a scrawled O. K. and her father's initials.

The remainder of the evening passed quickly. Scott Kimberly cut in on her as often as time permitted, giving her those comforting assurances of her enduring beauty which not without a whimsical pathos she craved. He laughed at her also, and she was not so sure that she liked that. In common with all vague people, she was unaware that she was vague. She did not entirely comprehend when Scott Kimberly told her that her personality would endure long after she was too old to care whether it endured or not.

She liked best to talk about New York, and each of their interrupted conversations gave her a picture or a memory of the metropolis on which she speculated as she looked over the shoulder of Jerry O'Rourke or Carty Braden or some other beau, to whom, as to all of them, she was comfortably anesthetic. At midnight she sent another note to her father, saying that Mrs. Rogers and Mrs. Rogers' guest would meet him immediately on the porch by the main driveway. Then, hoping for the best, she walked out into the starry night and was assisted by Jerry O'Rourke into his roadster.

III

"Good night, Yanci." With her late escort she was standing on the curbstone in front of the rented stucco house where she lived. Mr. O'Rourke was attempting to put significance into his lingering rendition of her name. For weeks he had been straining to boost their relations almost forcibly onto a sentimental plane; but Yanci, with her vague impassivity, which was a defense against almost anything, had brought to naught his efforts. Jerry O'Rourke was an old story. His family had money; but he—he worked in a brokerage house along with most of the rest of his young generation. He sold bonds— bonds were now the thing; real estate was once the thing—in the days of the boom; then automobiles were the thing. Bonds were the thing now. Young men sold them who had nothing else to go into.

"Don't bother to come up, please." Then as he put his car into gear, "Call me up soon!"

A minute later he turned the corner of the moonlit street and disappeared, his cut-out resounding voluminously through the night as it declared that the rest of two dozen weary inhabitants was of no concern to his gay meanderings.

Yanci sat down thoughtfully upon the porch steps. She had no key and must wait for her father's arrival. Five minutes later a roadster turned into the street, and approaching with an exaggerated caution stopped in front of the Rogers' large house next door. Relieved, Yanci arose and strolled slowly down the walk. The door of the car had swung open and Mrs. Rogers, assisted by Scott Kimberly, had alighted safely upon the sidewalk; but to Yanci's surprise Scott Kimberly, after escorting Mrs. Rogers to her steps, returned to the car. Yanci was close enough to notice that he took the driver's seat. As he drew up at the Bowman's curbstone Yanci saw that her father was occupying the far corner, fighting with ludicrous dignity against a sleep that had come upon him. She groaned. The fatal last hour had done its work–Tom Bowman was once more hors de combat.

"Hello," cried Yanci as she reached the curb.

"Yanci," muttered her parent, simulating, unsuccessfully, a brisk welcome. His lips were curved in an ingratiating grin.

"Your father wasn't feeling quite fit, so he let me drive home," explained Scott cheerfully as he got himself out and came up to her.

"Nice little car. Had it long?"

Yanci laughed, but without humor.

"Is he paralyzed?"

"Is who paralyze'?" demanded the figure in the car with an offended sigh.

Scott was standing by the car.

"Can I help you out, sir?"

"I c'n get out. I c'n get out," insisted Mr. Bowman. "Just step a li'l' out my way. Someone must have given me some 'stremely bad whisk'."

"You mean a lot of people must have given you some," retorted Yanci in cold unsympathy.

Mr. Bowman reached the curb with astonishing ease; but this was a deceitful success, for almost immediately he clutched at a handle of air perceptible only to himself, and was saved by Scott's quickly proffered arm. Followed by the two men, Yanci walked toward the house in a furor of embarrassment. Would the young man think that such scenes went on every night? It was chiefly her own presence that made it humiliating for Yanci. Had her father been carried to bed by two butlers each evening she might even have been proud of the fact that he could afford such dissipation; but to have it thought that she assisted, that she was burdened with the worry and the care! And finally she was annoyed with Scott Kimberly for being there, and for his officiousness in helping to bring her father into the house.

Reaching the low porch of tapestry brick, Yanci searched in Tom Bowman's vest for the key and unlocked the front door. A minute later the master of the house was deposited in an easy-chair.

"Thanks very much," he said, recovering for a moment. "Sit down. Like a drink? Yanci, get some crackers and cheese, if there's any, won't you, dear?"

At the unconscious coolness of this Scott and Yanci laughed.

"It's your bedtime, Father," she said, her anger struggling with diplomacy.

"Give me my guitar," he suggested, "and I'll play you tune."

Except on such occasions as this, he had not touched his guitar for twenty years. Yanci turned to Scott.

"He'll be fine now. Thanks a lot. He'll fall asleep in a minute and when I wake him he'll go to bed like a lamb."

"Well–"

They strolled together out the door.

"Sleepy?" he asked.

"No, not a bit."

"Then perhaps you'd better let me stay here with you a few minutes until you see if he's all right. Mrs. Rogers gave me a key so I can get in without disturbing her."

"It's quite all right," protested Yanci. "I don't mind a bit, and he won't be any trouble. He must have taken a glass too much, and this whisky we have out here–you know! This has happened once before–last year," she added.

Her words satisfied her; as an explanation it seemed to have a convincing ring.

"Can I sit down for a moment, anyway?" They sat side by side upon a wicker porch setee.

"I'm thinking of staying over a few days," Scott said.

"How lovely!" Her voice had resumed its die-away note.

"Cousin Pete Rogers wasn't well to-day, but tomorrow he's going duck shooting, and he wants me to go with him."

"Oh, how thrilling! I've always been mad to go, and Father's always promised to take me, but he never has."

"We're going to be gone about three days, and then I thought I'd come back and stay over the next week-end–" He broke off suddenly and bent forward in a listening attitude.

"Now what on earth is that?"

The sounds of music were proceeding brokenly from the room they had lately left–a ragged chord on a guitar and half a dozen feeble starts.

"It's father!" cried Yanci.

And now a voice drifted out to them, drunken and murmurous, taking the long notes with attempted melancholy:

Sing a song of cities,

Ridin on a rail,
A niggah's ne'er so happy
As when he's out-a jail.

"How terrible!" exclaimed Yanci. "He'll wake up everybody in the block."

The chorus ended, the guitar jangled again, then gave out a last harsh sprang! and was still. A moment later these disturbances were followed by a low but quite definite snore. Mr. Bowman, having indulged his musical proclivity, had dropped off to sleep.

"Let's go to ride," suggested Yanci impatiently. "This is too hectic for me."

Scott arose with alacrity and they walked down to the car.

"Where'll we go?" she wondered.

"I don't care."

"We might go up half a block to Crest Avenue–that's our show street– and then ride out to the river boulevard."

IV

As they turned into Crest Avenue the new cathedral, immense and unfinished, in imitation of a cathedral left unfinished by accident in some little Flemish town, squatted just across the way like a plump white bulldog on its haunches. The ghosts of four moonlit apostles looked down at them wanly from wall niches still littered with the white, dusty trash of the builders. The cathedral inaugurated Crest Avenue. After it came the great brownstone mass built by R. R. Comerford, the flour king, followed by a half mile of pretentious stone houses put up in the gloomy 90's. These were adorned with monstrous driveways and porte-cocheres which had once echoed to the hoofs of good horses and with huge circular windows that corseted the second stories.

The continuity of these mausoleums was broken by a small park, a triangle of grass where Nathan Hale stood ten feet tall with his hands bound behind his back by stone cord and stared over a great bluff at the slow Mississippi. Crest Avenue ran along the bluff, but neither faced it nor seemed aware of it, for all the houses fronted inward toward the street. Beyond the first half mile it became newer, essayed ventures in terraced lawns, in concoctions of stucco or in granite mansions which imitated through a variety of gradual refinements the marble contours of the Petit Trianon. The houses of this phase rushed by the roadster for a succession of minutes; then the way turned and the car was headed directly into the moonlight which swept toward it like the lamp of some gigantic motorcycle far up the avenue.

Past the low Corinthian lines of the Christian Science Temple, past a block of dark frame horrors, a deserted row of grim red brick—an unfortunate experiment of the late 90's—then new houses again, bright-red brick now, with trimmings of white, black iron fences and hedges binding flowery lawns. These swept by, faded, passed, enjoying their moment of grandeur; then waiting there in the moonlight to be outmoded as had the frame, cupolaed mansions of lower town and the brownstone piles of older Crest Avenue in their turn.

The roofs lowered suddenly, the lots narrowed, the houses shrank up in size and shaded off into bungalows. These held the street for the last mile, to the bend in the river which terminated the prideful avenue at the statue of Chelsea Arbuthnot. Arbuthnot was the first governor—and almost the last of Anglo-Saxon blood.

All the way thus far Yanci had not spoken, absorbed still in the annoyance of the evening, yet soothed somehow by the fresh air of Northern November that rushed by them. She must take her fur coat out of storage next day, she thought.

"Where are we now?"

As they slowed down, Scott looked up curiously at the pompous stone figure, clear in the crisp moonlight, with one hand on a book and the forefinger of the other pointing, as though with reproachful symbolism, directly at some construction work going on in the street.

"This is the end of Crest Avenue," said Yanci, turning to him. "This is our show street."

"A museum of American architectural failures."

"What?"

"Nothing," he murmured.

"I should have explained it to you. I forgot. We can go along the river boulevard if you'd like—or are you tired?"

Scott assured her that he was not tired—not in the least.

Entering the boulevard, the cement road twisted under darkling trees.

"The Mississippi—how little it means to you now!" said Scott suddenly.

"What?" Yanci looked around. "Oh, the river."

"I guess it was once pretty important to your ancestors up here."

"My ancestors weren't up here then," said Yanci with some dignity. "My ancestors were from Maryland. My father came out here when he left Yale."

"Oh!" Scott was politely impressed.

"My mother was from here. My father came out here from Baltimore because of his health."

"Oh!"

"Of course we belong here now, I suppose"—this with faint condescension—"as much as anywhere else."

"Of course."

"Except that I want to live in the East and I can't persuade Father to," she finished.

It was after one o'clock and the boulevard was almost deserted. Occasionally two yellow disks would top a rise ahead of them and take shape as a late-returning automobile. Except for that, they were alone in a continual rushing dark. The moon had gone down.

"Next time the road goes near the river let's stop and watch it," he suggested.

Yanci smiled inwardly. This remark was obviously what one boy of her acquaintance had named an international petting cue, by which was meant a suggestion that aimed to create naturally a situation for a kiss. She considered the matter. As yet the man had made no particular impression on her. He was good-looking, apparently well-to-do and from New York. She had begun to like him during the dance, increasingly as the evening had drawn to a close; then the incident of her father's appalling arrival had thrown cold water upon this tentative warmth; and now—it was November, and the night was cold. Still—

"All right," she agreed suddenly.

The road divided; she swerved around and brought the car to a stop in an open place high above the river.

"Well?" she demanded in the deep quiet that followed the shutting off of the engine.

"Thanks."

"Are you satisfied here?"

"Almost. Not quite."

"Why not?"

"I'll tell you in a minute," he answered. "Why is your name Yanci?"

"It's a family name."

"It's very pretty." He repeated it several times caressingly. "Yanci—it has all the grace of Nancy, and yet it isn't prim."

"What's your name?" she inquired.

"Scott."

"Scott what?"

"Kimberly. Didn't you know?"

"I wasn't sure. Mrs. Rogers introduced you in such a mumble."

There was a slight pause.

"Yanci," he repeated; "beautiful Yanci, with her dark-blue eyes and her lazy soul. Do you know why I'm not quite satisfied, Yanci?"

"Why?"

Imperceptibly she had moved her face nearer until as she waited for an answer with her lips faintly apart he knew that in asking she had granted.

Without haste he bent his head forward and touched her lips.

He sighed, and both of them felt a sort of relief—relief from the embarrassment of playing up to what conventions of this sort of thing remained.

"Thanks," he said as he had when she first stopped the car.

"Now are you satisfied?"

Her blue eyes regarded him unsmilingly in the darkness.

"After a fashion; of course, you can never say—definitely."

Again he bent toward her, but she stooped and started the motor. It was late and Yanci was beginning to be tired. What purpose there was in the experiment was accomplished. He had had what he asked. If he liked it he would want more, and that put her one move ahead in the game which she felt she was beginning.

"I'm hungry," she complained. "Let's go down and eat."

"Very well," he acquiesced sadly. "Just when I was enjoying—the Mississippi."

"Do you think I'm beautiful?" she inquired almost plaintively as they backed out.

"What an absurd question!"

"But I like to hear people say so."

"I was just about to—when you started the engine."

Downtown in a deserted all-night lunch room they ate bacon and eggs. She was pale as ivory now. The night had drawn the lazy vitality and languid color out of her face. She encouraged him to talk to her of New York until he was beginning every sentence with, "Well now, let's see—"

The repast over, they drove home. Scott helped her put the car in the little garage, and just outside the front door she lent him her lips again for the faint brush of a kiss. Then she went in.

The long living room which ran the width of the small stucco house was reddened by a dying fire which had been high when Yanci left and now was faded to a steady undancing glow. She took a log from the fire box and threw it on the embers, then started as a voice came out of the half darkness at the other end of the room.

"Back so soon?"

It was her father's voice, not yet quite sober, but alert and intelligent.

"Yes. Went riding," she answered shortly, sitting down in a wicker chair before the fire. "Then went down and had something to eat."

"Oh!"

Her father left his place and moved to a chair nearer the fire, where he stretched himself out with a sigh. Glancing at him from the corner of her eye, for she was going to show an appropriate coldness, Yanci was fascinated by his complete recovery of dignity in the space of two hours. His graying hair was scarcely rumpled; his handsome face was ruddy as ever. Only his eyes, crisscrossed with tiny red lines, were evidence of his late dissipation.

"Have a good time?"

"Why should you care?" she answered rudely.

"Why shouldn't I?"

"You didn't seem to care earlier in the evening. I asked you to take two people home for me, and you weren't able to drive your own car."

"The deuce I wasn't!" he protested. "I could have driven in—in a race in an arana, areaena. That Mrs. Rogers insisted that her young admirer should drive, so what could I do?"

"That isn't her young admirer," retorted Yanci crisply. There was no drawl in her voice now. "She's as old as you are. That's her niece—I mean her nephew."

"Excuse me!"

"I think you owe me an apology." She found suddenly that she bore him no resentment. She was rather sorry for him, and it occurred to her that in asking him to take Mrs. Rogers home she had somehow imposed on his liberty. Nevertheless, discipline was necessary—there would be other Saturday nights. "Don't you?" she concluded.

"I apologize, Yanci."

"Very well, I accept your apology," she answered stiffly.

"What's more, I'll make it up to you."

Her blue eyes contracted. She hoped—she hardly dared to hope that he might take her to New York.

"Let's see," he said. "November, isn't it? What date?"

"The twenty-third."

"Well, I'll tell you what I'll do." He knocked the tips of his fingers together tentatively. "I'll give you a present. I've been meaning to let you have a trip all fall, but business has been bad." She almost smiled—as though business was of any consequence in his life. "But then you need a trip. I'll make you a present of it."

He rose again, and crossing over to his desk sat down.

"I've got a little money in a New York bank that's been lying there quite a while," he said as he fumbled in a drawer for a check book. "I've been intending to close out the account. Let—me—see. There's just—" His pen scratched. "Where the devil's the blotter? Uh!"

He came back to the fire and a pink oblong paper fluttered into her lap.

"Why, Father!"

It was a check for three hundred dollars.

"But can you afford this?" she demanded.

"It's all right," he reassured her, nodding. "That can be a Christmas present, too, and you'll probably need a dress or a hat or something before you go."

"Why," she began uncertainly, "I hardly know whether I ought to take this much or not! I've got two hundred of my own downtown, you know. Are you sure—"

"Oh, yes!" He waved his hand with magnificent carelessness. "You need a holiday. You've been talking about New York, and I want you to go down there. Tell some of your friends at Yale and the other colleges and they'll ask you to the prom or something. That'll be nice. You'll have a good time."

He sat down abruptly in his chair and gave vent to a long sigh. Yanci folded up the check and tucked it into the low bosom of her dress.

"Well," she drawled softly with a return to her usual manner, "you're a perfect lamb to be so sweet about it, but I don't want to be horribly extravagant."

Her father did not answer. He gave another little sigh and relaxed sleepily into his chair.

"Of course I do want to go," went on Yanci.

Still her father was silent. She wondered if he were asleep.

"Are you asleep?" she demanded, cheerfully now. She bent toward him; then she stood up and looked at him.

"Father," she said uncertainly.

Her father remained motionless; the ruddy color had melted suddenly out of his face.

"Father!"

It occurred to her—and at the thought she grew cold, and a brassiere of iron clutched at her breast—that she was alone in the room. After a frantic instant she said to herself that her father was dead.

V

Yanci judged herself with inevitable gentleness—judged herself very much as a mother might judge a wild, spoiled child. She was not hard-minded, nor did she live by any ordered and considered philosophy of her own. To such a catastrophe as the death of her father her immediate reaction was a hysterical self-pity. The first three days were something of a nightmare; but sentimental civilization, being as infallible as Nature in healing the wounds of its more fortunate children, had inspired a certain Mrs. Oral, whom Yanci had always loathed, with a passionate interest in all such crises. To all intents and purposes Mrs. Oral buried Tom Bowman. The morning after his death Yanci had wired her maternal aunt in Chicago, but as yet that undemonstrative and well-to-do lady had sent no answer.

All day long, for four days, Yanci sat in her room upstairs, hearing steps come and go on the porch, and it merely increased her nervousness that the doorbell had been disconnected. This by order of Mrs. Oral! Doorbells were always disconnected! After the burial of the dead the strain relaxed. Yanci, dressed in her new black, regarded herself in the pier glass, and then wept because she seemed to herself very sad and beautiful. She went downstairs and tried to read a moving-picture magazine, hoping that she would not be alone in the house when the winter dark came down just after four.

This afternoon Mrs. Oral had said carpe diem to the maid, and Yanci was just starting for the kitchen to see whether she had yet gone when the reconnected bell rang suddenly through the house. Yanci started. She waited a minute, then went to the door. It was Scott Kimberly.

"I was just going to inquire for you," he said.

"Oh! I'm much better, thank you," she responded with the quiet dignity that seemed suited to her role.

They stood there in the hall awkwardly, each reconstructing the half-facetious, half-sentimental occasion on which they had last met. It seemed such an irreverent prelude to such a somber disaster. There was no common ground for them now, no gap that could be bridged by a slight reference to their mutual past, and there was no foundation on which he could adequately pretend to share her sorrow.

"Won't you come in?" she said, biting her lip nervously. He followed her to the sitting room and sat beside her on the lounge. In another minute, simply because he was there and alive and friendly, she was crying on his shoulder.

"There, there!" he said, putting his arm behind her and patting her shoulder idiotically. "There, there, there!"

He was wise enough to attribute no ulterior significance to her action. She was overstrained with grief and loneliness and sentiment; almost any shoulder would have done as well. For all the biological thrill to either of them he might have been a hundred years old. In a minute she sat up.

"I beg your pardon," she murmured brokenly. "But it's—it's so dismal in this house today."

"I know just how you feel, Yanci."

"Did I—did I—get—tears on your coat?"

In tribute to the tenseness of the incident they both laughed hysterically, and with the laughter she momentarily recovered her propriety.

"I don't know why I should have chosen you to collapse on," she wailed. "I really don't just go 'round doing it in-indiscriminately on anyone who comes in."

"I consider it—a compliment," he responded soberly, "and I can understand the state you're in." Then, after a pause, "Have you any plans?"

She shook her head.

"Va-vague ones," she muttered between little gasps. "I tho-ought I'd go down and stay with my aunt in Chicago a while."

"I should think that'd be the best—much the best thing." Then, because he could think of nothing else to say, he added, "Yes, very much the best thing."

"What are you doing—here in town?" she inquired, taking in her breath in minute gasps and dabbing at her eyes with a handkerchief.

"Oh, I'm here with—with the Rogerses. I've been here."

"Hunting?"

"No, I've just been here."

He did not tell her that he had stayed over on her account. She might think it fresh.

"I see," she said. She didn't see.

"I want to know if there's any possible thing I can do for you, Yanci. Perhaps go downtown for you, or do some errands—anything. Maybe you'd like to bundle up and get a bit of air. I could take you out to drive in your car some night, and no one would see you."

He clipped his last word short as the inadvertency of this suggestion dawned on him. They stared at each other with horror in their eyes.

"Oh, no, thank you!" she cried. "I really don't want to drive."

To his relief the outer door opened and an elderly lady came in. It was Mrs. Oral. Scott rose immediately and moved backward toward the door.

"If you're sure there isn't anything I can do—"

Yanci introduced him to Mrs. Oral; then leaving the elder woman by the fire walked with him to the door. An idea had suddenly occurred to her.

"Wait a minute."

She ran up the front stairs and returned immediately with a slip of pink paper in her hand.

"Here's something I wish you'd do," she said. "Take this to the First National Bank and have it cashed for me. You can leave the money here for me any time."

Scott took out his wallet and opened it.

"Suppose I cash it for you now," he suggested.

"Oh, there's no hurry."

"But I may as well." He drew out three new one-hundred-dollar bills and gave them to her.

"That's awfully sweet of you," said Yanci.

"Not at all. May I come in and see you next time I come West?"

"I wish you would."

"Then I will. I'm going East tonight."

The door shut him out into the snowy dusk and Yanci returned to Mrs. Oral. Mrs. Oral had come to discuss plans.

"And now, my dear, just what do you plan to do? We ought to have some plan to go by, and I thought I'd find out if you had any definite plan in your mind."

Yanci tried to think. She seemed to herself to be horribly alone in the world.

"I haven't heard from my aunt. I wired her again this morning. She may be in Florida."

"In that case you'd go there?"

"I suppose so."

"Would you close this house?"

"I suppose so."

Mrs. Oral glanced around with placid practicality. It occurred to her that if Yanci gave the house up she might like it for herself.

"And now," she continued, "do you know where you stand financially?"

"All right, I guess," answered Yanci indifferently; and then with a rush of sentiment, "There was enough for t-two; there ought to be enough for o-one."

"I didn't mean that," said Mrs. Oral. "I mean, do you know the details?"

"No."

"Well, I thought you didn't know the details. And I thought you ought to know all the details—have a detailed account of what and where your money is. So I called up Mr. Haedge, who knew your father very well personally, to come up this afternoon and glance through his papers. He was going to stop in your father's bank, too, by the way, and get all the details there. I don't believe your father left any will."

Details! Details! Details!

"Thank you," said Yanci. "That'll be—nice."

Mrs. Oral gave three or four vigorous nods that were like heavy periods. Then she got up.

"And now if Hilma's gone out I'll make you some tea. Would you like some tea?"

"Sort of."

"All right, I'll make you some ni-nice tea."

Tea! Tea! Tea!

Mr. Haedge, who came from one of the best Swedish families in town, arrived to see Yanci at five o'clock. He greeted her funereally; said that he had been several times to inquire for her; had organized the pallbearers and would now find out how she stood in no time. Did she have any idea whether or not there was a will? No? Well, there probably wasn't one.

There was one. He found it almost at once in Mr. Bowman's desk—but he worked there until eleven o'clock that night before he found much else. Next morning he arrived at eight, went down to the bank at ten, then to a certain brokerage firm, and came back to Yanci's house at noon. He had known Tom Bowman for some years, but he was utterly astounded when he discovered the condition in which that handsome gallant had left his affairs.

He consulted Mrs. Oral, and that afternoon he informed a frightened Yanci in measured language that she was practically penniless. In the midst of the conversation a telegram from Chicago told her that her aunt had sailed the week previous for a trip through the Orient and was not expected back until late spring.

The beautiful Yanci, so profuse, so debonair, so careless with her gorgeous adjectives, had no adjectives for this calamity. She crept upstairs like a hurt child and sat before a mirror, brushing her luxurious hair to comfort herself. One hundred and fifty strokes she gave it, as it said in the treatment, and then a hundred and fifty more—she was too distraught to stop the nervous motion. She brushed it until her arm ached, then she changed arms and went on brushing.

The maid found her next morning, asleep, sprawled across the toilet things on the dresser in a room that was heavy and sweet with the scent of spilled perfume.

VI

To be precise, as Mr. Haedge was to a depressing degree, Tom Bowman left a bank balance that was more than ample—that is to say, more than ample to supply the post-mortem requirements of his own person. There was also twenty years' worth of furniture, a temperamental roadster with asthmatic cylinders and two one-thousand-dollar bonds of a chain of jewelry stores which yielded 7.5 per cent interest. Unfortunately these were not known in the bond market.

When the car and the furniture had been sold and the stucco bungalow sublet, Yanci contemplated her resources with dismay. She had a bank balance of almost a thousand dollars. If she invested this she would increase her total income to about fifteen dollars a month. This, as Mrs. Oral cheerfully observed, would pay for the boarding-house room she had taken for Yanci as long as Yanci lived. Yanci was so encouraged by this news that she burst into tears.

So she acted as any beautiful girl would have acted in this emergency. With rare decision she told Mr. Haedge that she would leave her thousand dollars in a checking account, and then she walked out of his office and across the street to a beauty parlor to have her hair waved. This raised her morale astonishingly.

Indeed, she moved that very day out of the boarding house and into a small room at the best hotel in town. If she must sink into poverty, she would at least do so in the grand manner.

Sewed into the lining of her best mourning hat were the three new one-hundred-dollar bills, her father's last present. What she expected of them, why she kept them in such a way, she did not know, unless perhaps because they had come to her under cheerful auspices and might through some gayety inherent in their crisp and virgin paper buy happier things than solitary meals and narrow hotel beds. They were hope and youth and luck and beauty; they began, somehow, to stand for all the things she had lost in that November night when Tom Bowman, having led her recklessly into space, had plunged off himself, leaving her to find the way back alone.

Yanci remained at the Hiawatha Hotel for three months, and she found that after the first visits of condolence her friends had happier things to do with their time than to spend it in her company. Jerry O'Rourke came to see her one day with a wild Celtic look in his eyes, and demanded that she marry him immediately. When she asked for time to consider he walked out in a rage. She heard later that he had been offered a position in Chicago and had left the same night.

She considered, frightened and uncertain. She had heard of people sinking out of place, out of life. Her father had once told her of a man in his class at college who had become a worker around saloons, polishing brass rails for the price of a can of beer; and she knew also that there were girls in this city with whose mothers her own mother had played as a little girl, but who were poor now and had grown common; who worked in stores and had married into the proletariat. But that such a fate should threaten her—how absurd! Why, she knew everyone! She had been invited everywhere; her great-grandfather had been governor of one of the Southern states!

She had written to her aunt in India and again in China, receiving no answer. She concluded that her aunt's itinerary had changed, and this was confirmed when a post card arrived from Honolulu which showed no knowledge of Tom Bowman's death, but announced that she was going with a party to the east coast of Africa. This was a last straw. The languorous and lackadaisical Yanci was on her own at last.

"Why not go to work for a while?" suggested Mr. Haedge with some irritation. "Lots of nice girls do nowadays, just for something to occupy themselves with. There's Elsie Prendergast, who does society news on the Bulletin, and that Semple girl—"

"I can't," said Yanci shortly with a glitter of tears in her eyes. "I'm going East in February."

"East? Oh, you're going to visit someone?"

She nodded.

"Yes, I'm going to visit," she lied, "so it'd hardly be worth while to go to work." She could have wept, but she managed a haughty look. "I'd like to try reporting sometime, though, just for the fun of it."

"Yes, it's quite a lot of fun," agreed Mr. Haedge with some irony. "Still, I suppose there's no hurry about it. You must have plenty of that thousand dollars left."

"Oh, plenty!"

There were a few hundred, she knew.

"Well, then I suppose a good rest, a change of scene would be the best thing for you."

"Yes," answered Yanci. Her lips were trembling and she rose, scarcely able to control herself. Mr. Haedge seemed so impersonally cold. "That's why I'm going. A good rest is what I need."

"I think you're wise."

What Mr. Haegde would have thought had he seen the dozen drafts she wrote that night of a certain letter is problematical. Here are two of the earlier ones. The bracketed words are proposed substitutions:

Dear Scott: Not having seen you since that day I was such a silly ass and wept on your coat, I thought I'd write and tell you that I'm coming East pretty soon and would like you to have lunch [dinner] with me or something. I have been living in a room [suite] at the Hiawatha Hotel, intending to meet my aunt, with whom I am going to live [stay], and who is coming back from China this month [spring]. Meanwhile I have a lot of invitations to visit, etc., in the East, and I thought I would do it now. So I'd like to see you—

This draft ended here and went into the wastebasket. After an hour's work she produced the following:

My dear Mr. Kimberly: I have often [sometimes] wondered how you've been since I saw you. I am coming East next month before going to visit my aunt in Chicago, and you must come and see me. I have been going out very little, but my physician advises me that I need change, so I expect to shock the proprieties by some very gay visits in the East—

Finally in despondent abandon she wrote a simple note without explanation or subterfuge, tore it up and went to bed. Next morning she identified it in the wastebasket and decided it was the best one after all and sent him a fair copy. It ran:

Scott: Just a line to tell you I will be at the Ritz-Carlton Hotel from February seventh, probably for ten days. If you phone me some rainy afternoon I'll invite you to tea.

Sincerely, Yanci Bowman.

VII

Yanci was going to the Ritz for no more reason than that she had once told Scott Kimberly that she always went there. When she reached New York—a cold New York, a strangely menacing New York, quite different from the gay city of theaters and hotel-corridor rendezvous that she had known—there was exactly two hundred dollars in her purse.

It had taken a large part of her bank account to live, and she had at last broken into her sacred three hundred dollars to substitute pretty and delicate quarter-mourning clothes for the heavy black she had laid away.

Walking into the hotel at the moment when its exquisitely dressed patrons were assembling for luncheon, it drained at her confidence to appear bored and at ease. Surely the clerks at the desk knew the contents of her pocketbook. She fancied even that the bell boys were snickering at the foreign labels she had steamed from an old trunk of her father's and pasted on her suitcase. This last thought horrified her. Perhaps the very hotels and steamers so grandly named had long since been out of commission!

As she stood drumming her fingers on the desk she was wondering whether if she were refused admittance she could muster a casual smile and stroll out coolly enough to deceive two richly dressed women standing near. It had not taken long for the confidence of twenty years to evaporate. Three months without security had made an ineffaceable mark on Yanci's soul.

"Twenty-four sixty-two," said the clerk callously.

Her heart settled back into place as she followed the bell boy to the elevator, meanwhile casting a nonchalant glance at the two fashionable women as she passed them. Were their skirts long or short?—longer, she noticed.

She wondered how much the skirt of her new walking suit could be let out.

At luncheon her spirits soared. The head waiter bowed to her. The light rattle of conversation, the subdued hum of the music soothed her. She ordered supreme of melon, eggs Susette and an artichoke, and signed her room number to the check with scarcely a glance at it as it lay beside her plate. Up in her room, with the telephone directory open on the bed before her, she tried to locate her scattered metropolitan acquaintances. Yet even as the phone numbers, with their supercilious tags, Plaza, Circle, and Rhinelander, stared out at her, she could feel a cold wind blow at her unstable confidence. These girls, acquaintances of school, of a summer, of a house party, even of a week-end at a college prom—what claim or attraction could she, poor and friendless, exercise over them? They had their loves, their dates, their week's gayety planned in advance. They would almost resent her inconvenient memory.

Nevertheless, she called four girls. One of them was out, one at Palm Beach, one in California. The only one to whom she talked said in a hearty voice that she was in bed with grippe, but would phone Yanci as soon as she felt well enough to go out. Then Yanci gave up the girls. She would have to create the illusion of a good time in some other manner. The illusion must be created—that was part of her plan.

She looked at her watch and found that it was three o'clock. Scott Kimberly should have phoned before this, or at least left some word. Still, he was probably busy—at a club, she thought vaguely, or else buying some neckties. He would probably call at four.

Yanci was well aware that she must work quickly. She had figured to a nicety that one hundred and fifty dollars carefully expended would carry her through two weeks, no more. The idea of failure, the fear that at the end of that time she would be friendless and penniless had not begun to bother her.

It was not the first time that for amusement, for a coveted invitation or for curiosity she had deliberately set out to capture a man; but it was the first time she had laid her plans with necessity and desperation pressing in on her.

One of her strongest cards had always been her background, the impression she gave that she was popular and desired and happy. This she must create now, and apparently out of nothing. Scott must somehow be brought to think that a fair portion of New York was at her feet.

At four she went over to Park Avenue, where the sun was out, walking and the February day was fresh and odorous of spring and the high apartments of her desire lined the street with radiant whiteness. Here she would live on a gay schedule of pleasure. In these smart not-to-be-entered-without-a-card women's shops she would spend the morning hours acquiring and acquiring, ceaselessly and without thought of expense; in these restaurants she would lunch at noon in company with other fashionable women, orchid-adorned always, and perhaps bearing an absurdly dwarfed Pomeranian in her sleek arms.

In the summer—well, she would go to Tuxedo, perhaps to an immaculate house perched high on a fashionable eminence, where she would emerge to visit a world of teas and balls, of horse shows and polo. Between the halves of the polo game the players would cluster around her in their white suits and helmets, admiringly, and when she swept away, bound for some new delight, she would be followed by the eyes of many envious but intimidated women.

Every other summer they would, of course, go abroad. She began to plan a typical year, distributing a few months here and a few months there until she—and Scott Kimberly, by implication—would become the very auguries of the season, shifting with the slightest stirring of the social barometer from rusticity to urbanity, from palm to pine.

She had two weeks, no more, in which to attain to this position. In an ecstasy of determined emotion she lifted up her head toward the tallest of the tall white apartments.

"It will be too marvelous!" she said to herself.

For almost the first time in her life her words were not too exaggerated to express the wonder shining in her eyes.

VIII

About five o'clock she hurried back to the hotel, demanding feverishly at the desk if there had been a telephone message for her. To her profound disappointment there was nothing. A minute after she had entered her room the phone rang.

"This is Scott Kimberly."

At the words a call to battle echoed in her heart.

"Oh, how do you do?"

Her tone implied that she had almost forgotten him. It was not frigid—it was merely casual.

As she answered the inevitable question as to the hour when she had arrived, a warm glow spread over her. Now that, from a personification of all the riches and pleasure she craved, he had materialized as merely a male voice over the telephone, her confidence became strengthened. Male voices were male voices. They could be managed; they could be made to intone syllables of which the minds behind them had no approval. Male voices could be made sad or tender or despairing at her will. She rejoiced. The soft clay was ready to her hand.

"Won't you take dinner with me tonight?" Scott was suggesting.

"Why"—perhaps not, she thought; let him think of her tonight—"I don't believe I'll be able to," she said. "I've got an engagement for dinner and the theater. I'm terribly sorry."

Her voice did not sound sorry—it sounded polite. Then as though a happy thought had occurred to her as to a time and place where she could work him into her list of dates, "I'll tell you: Why don't you come around here this afternoon and have tea with me?"

He would be there immediately. He had been playing squash and as soon as he took a plunge he would arrive. Yanci hung up the phone and turned with a quiet efficiency to the mirror, too tense to smile.

She regarded her lustrous eyes and dusky hair in critical approval. Then she took a lavender tea gown from her trunk and began to dress.

She let him wait seven minutes in the lobby before she appeared; then she approached him with a friendly, lazy smile.

"How do you do?" she murmured. "It's marvelous to see you again. How are you?" And, with a long sigh, "I'm frightfully tired. I've been on the go ever since I got here this morning; shopping and then tearing off to luncheon and a matinee. I've bought everything I saw. I don't know how I'm going to pay for it all."

She remembered vividly that when they had first met she had told him, without expecting to be believed, how unpopular she was. She could not risk such a remark now, even in jest. He must think that she had been on the go every minute of the day.

They took a table and were served with olive sandwiches and tea. He was so good-looking, she thought, and marvelously dressed. His gray eyes regarded her with interest from under immaculate ash-blond hair. She wondered how he passed his days, how he liked her costume, what he was thinking of at that moment.

"How long will you be here?" he asked.

"Well, two weeks, off and on. I'm going down to Princeton for the February prom and then up to a house party in Westchester County for a few days. Are you shocked at me for going out so soon? Father would have wanted me to, you know. He was very modern in all his ideas."

She had debated this remark on the train. She was not going to a house party. She was not invited to the Princeton prom. Such things, nevertheless, were necessary to create the illusion. That was everything—the illusion.

"And then," she continued, smiling, "two of my old beaus are in town, which makes it nice for me."

She saw Scott blink and she knew that he appreciated the significance of this.

"What are your plans for this winter?" he demanded. "Are you going back West?"

"No. You see, my aunt returns from India this week. She's going to open her

Florida house, and we'll stay there until the middle of March. Then we'll come up to Hot Springs and we may go to Europe for the summer."

This was all the sheerest fiction. Her first letter to her aunt, which had given the bare details of Tom Bowman's death, had at last reached its destination. Her aunt had replied with a note of conventional sympathy and the announcement that she would be back in America within two years if she didn't decide to live in Italy.

"But you'll let me see something of you while you're here," urged Scott, after attending to this impressive program. "If you can't take dinner with me tonight, how about Wednesday—that's the day after tomorrow?"

"Wednesday? Let's see." Yanci's brow was knit with imitation thought. "I think I have a date for Wednesday, but I don't know for certain. How about phoning me tomorrow, and I'll let you know? Because I want to go with you, only I think I've made an engagement."

"Very well, I'll phone you."

"Do—about ten."

"Try to be able to—then or any time."

"I'll tell you—if I can't go to dinner with you Wednesday I can go to lunch surely."

"All right," he agreed. "And we'll go to a matinee."

They danced several times. Never by word or sign did Yanci betray more than the most cursory interest in him until just at the end, when she offered her hand to say good-by.

"Good-by, Scott."

For just the fraction of a second—not long enough for him to be sure it had happened at all, but just enough so that he would be reminded, however faintly, of that night on the Mississippi boulevard—she looked into his eyes. Then she turned quickly and hurried away.

She took her dinner in a little tea room around the corner. It was an economical dinner which cost a dollar and a half. There was no date concerned in it at all, and no man—except an elderly person in spats who tried to speak to her as she came out the door.

IX

Sitting alone in one of the magnificent moving-picture theaters—a luxury which she thought she could afford—Yanci watched Mae Murray swirl through splendidly imagined vistas, and meanwhile considered the progress of the first day. In retrospect it was a distinct success. She had given the correct impression both as to her material prosperity and as to her attitude toward Scott himself. It seemed best to avoid evening dates. Let him have the evenings to himself, to think of her, to imagine her with other men, even to spend a few lonely hours in his apartment, considering how much more cheerful it might be if—Let time and absence work for her.

Engrossed for a while in the moving picture, she calculated the cost of the apartment in which its heroine endured her movie wrongs. She admired its slender Italian table, occupying only one side of the large dining room and flanked by a long bench which gave it an air of medieval luxury. She rejoiced in the beauty of Mae Murray's clothes and furs, her gorgeous hats, her short-seeming French shoes. Then after a moment her mind returned to her own drama; she wondered if Scott were already engaged, and her heart dipped at the thought. Yet it was unlikely. He had been too quick to phone her on her arrival, too lavish with his time, too responsive that afternoon.

After the picture she returned to the Ritz, where she slept deeply and happily for almost the first time in three months. The atmosphere around her no longer seemed cold. Even the floor clerk had smiled kindly and admiringly when Yanci asked for her key.

Next morning at ten Scott phoned. Yanci, who had been up for hours, pretended to be drowsy from her dissipation of the night before.

No, she could not take dinner with him on Wednesday. She was terribly sorry; she had an engagement, as she had feared. But she could have luncheon and go to a matinee if he would get her back in time for tea.

She spent the day roving the streets. On top of a bus, though not on the front seat, where Scott might possibly spy her, she sailed out Riverside Drive and back along Fifth Avenue just at the winter twilight, and her feeling for New York and its gorgeous splendors deepened and redoubled. Here she must live and be rich, be nodded to by the traffic policemen at the corners as she sat in her limousine—with a small dog—and here she must stroll on Sunday to and from a stylish church, with Scott, handsome in his cutaway and tall hat, walking devotedly at her side.

At luncheon on Wednesday she described for Scott's benefit a fanciful two days. She told of a motoring trip up the Hudson and gave him her opinion of two plays she had seen with—it was implied—adoring gentlemen beside her. She had read up very carefully on the plays in the morning paper and chosen two concerning which she could garner the most information.

"Oh," he said in dismay, "you've seen Dulcy? I have two seats for it—but you won't want to go again."

"Oh, no, I don't mind," she protested truthfully. "You see, we went late, and anyway I adored it."

But he wouldn't hear of her sitting through it again—besides he had seen it himself. It was a play Yanci was mad to see, but she was compelled to watch him while he exchanged the tickets for others, and for the poor seats available at the last moment. The game seemed difficult at times.

"By the way," he said afterwards as they drove back to the hotel in a taxi, "you'll be going down to the Princeton prom tomorrow, won't you?"

She started. She had not realized that it would be so soon or that he would know of it.

"Yes," she answered coolly. "I'm going down tomorrow afternoon."

"On the 2:20, I suppose," Scott commented; and then, "Are you going to meet the boy who's taking you down—at Princeton?"

For an instant she was off her guard.

"Yes, he'll meet the train."

"Then I'll take you to the station," proposed Scott. "There'll be a crowd and you may have trouble getting a porter."

She could think of nothing to say, no valid objection to make. She wished she had said that she was going by automobile, but she could conceive of no graceful and plausible way of amending her first admission.

"That's mighty sweet of you."

"You'll be at the Ritz when you come back?"

"Oh, yes," she answered. "I'm going to keep my rooms."

Her bedroom was the smallest and least expensive in the hotel.

She concluded to let him put her on the train for Princeton; in fact, she saw no alternative. Next day as she packed her suitcase after luncheon the situation had taken such hold of her imagination that she filled it with the very things she would have chosen had she really been going to the prom. Her intention was to get out at the first stop and take the train back to New York.

Scott called for her at half past one and they took a taxi to the Pennsylvania Station. The train was crowded as he had expected, but he found her a seat and stowed her grip in the rack overhead.

"I'll call you Friday to see how you've behaved," he said.

"All right. I'll be good."

Their eyes met and in an instant, with an inexplicable, only half-conscious rush of emotion, they were in perfect communion. When Yanci came back, the glance seemed to say, ah, then–

A voice startled her ear:

"Why, Yanci!"

Yanci looked around. To her horror she recognized a girl named Ellen Harley, one of those to whom she had phoned upon her arrival.

"Well, Yanci Bowman! You're the last person I ever expected to see. How are you?"

Yanci introduced Scott. Her heart was beating violently.

"Are you coming to the prom? How perfectly slick!" cried Ellen. "Can I sit here with you? I've been wanting to see you. Who are you going with?"

"No one you know."

"Maybe I do."

Her words, falling like sharp claws on Yanci's sensitive soul, were interrupted by an unintelligible outburst from the conductor. Scott bowed to Ellen, cast at Yanci one level glance and then hurried off.

The train started. As Ellen arranged her grip and threw off her fur coat Yanci looked around her. The car was gay with girls whose excited chatter filled the damp, rubbery air like smoke. Here and there sat a chaperon, a mass of decaying rock in a field of flowers, predicting with a mute and somber fatality the end of all gayety and all youth. How many times had Yanci herself been one of such a crowd, careless and happy, dreaming of the men she would meet, of the battered hacks waiting at the station, the snow-covered campus, the big open fires in the clubhouses, and the imported orchestra beating out defiant melody against the approach of morning.

And now–she was an intruder, uninvited, undesired. As at the Ritz on the day of her arrival, she felt that at any instant her mask would be torn from her and she would be exposed as a pretender to the gaze of all the car.

"Tell me everything!" Ellen was saying. "Tell me what you've been doing. I didn't see you at any of the football games last fall."

This was by way of letting Yanci know that she had attended them herself.

The conductor was bellowing from the rear of the car, "Manhattan Transfer next stop!"

Yanci's cheeks burned with shame. She wondered what she had best do—meditating a confession, deciding against it, answering Ellen's chatter in frightened monosyllables—then, as with an ominous thunder of brakes the speed of the train began to slacken, she sprang on a despairing impulse to her feet.

"My heavens!" she cried. "I've forgotten my shoes! I've got to go back and get them."

Ellen reacted to this with annoying efficiency.

"I'll take your suitcase," she said quickly, "and you can call for it. I'll be at the Charter Club."

"No!" Yanci almost shrieked. "It's got my dress in it!"

Ignoring the lack of logic in her own remark, she swung the suitcase off the rack with what seemed to her a super-human effort and went reeling down the aisle, stared at curiously by the arrogant eyes of many girls. When she reached the platform just as the train came to a stop she felt weak and shaken. She stood on the hard cement which marks the quaint old village of Manhattan Transfer and tears were streaming down her cheeks as she watched the unfeeling cars speed off to Princeton with their burden of happy youth.

After half an hour's wait Yanci got on a train and returned to New York. In thirty minutes she had lost the confidence that a week had gained for her. She came back to her little room and lay down quietly upon the bed.

X

By Friday Yanci's spirits had partly recovered from their chill depression. Scott's voice over the telephone in mid-morning was like a tonic, and she told him of the delights of Princeton with convincing enthusiasm, drawing vicariously upon a prom she had attended there two years before. He was anxious to see her, he said. Would she come to dinner and the theater that night? Yanci considered, greatly tempted. Dinner—she had been economizing on meals, and a gorgeous dinner in some extravagant show place followed by a musical comedy appealed to her starved fancy, indeed; but instinct told her that the time was not yet right. Let him wait. Let him dream a little more, a little longer.

"I'm too tired, Scott," she said with an air of extreme frankness; "that's the whole truth of the matter. I've been out every night since I've been here, and I'm really half dead. I'll rest up on this house party over the week-end and then I'll go to dinner with you any day you want me."

There was a minute's silence while she held the phone expectantly.

"Lot of resting up you'll do on a house party," he replied; "and, anyway, next week is so far off. I'm awfully anxious to see you, Yanci."

"So am I, Scott."

She allowed the faintest caress to linger on his name. When she had hung up she felt happy again. Despite her humiliation on the train her plan had been a success. The illusion was still intact; it was nearly complete. And in three meetings and half a dozen telephone calls she had managed to create a tenser atmosphere between them than if he had seen her constantly in the moods and avowals and beguilements of an out-and-out flirtation.

When Monday came she paid her first week's hotel bill. The size of it did not alarm her—she was prepared for that—but the shock of seeing so much money go, of realizing that there remained only one hundred and twenty dollars of her father's present, gave her a peculiar sinking sensation in the pit of her stomach. She decided to bring guile to bear immediately, to tantalize Scott by a carefully planned incident, and then at the end of the week to show him simply and definitely that she loved him.

As a decoy for Scott's tantalization she located by telephone a certain Jimmy Long, a handsome boy with whom she had played as a little girl and who had recently come to New York to work. Jimmy Long was deftly maneuvered into asking her to go to a matinee with him on Wednesday afternoon. He was to meet her in the lobby at two.

On Wednesday she lunched with Scott. His eyes followed her every motion, and knowing this she felt a great rush of tenderness toward him. Desiring at first only what he represented, she had begun half unconsciously to desire him also. Nevertheless, she did not permit herself the slightest relaxation on that account. The time was too short and the odds too great. That she was beginning to love him only fortified her resolve.

"Where are you going this afternoon?" he demanded.

"To a matinee—with an annoying man."

"Why is he annoying?"

"Because he wants me to marry him and I don't believe I want to."

There was just the faintest emphasis on the word "believe." The implication was that she was not sure—that is, not quite.

"Don't marry him."

"I won't—probably."

"Yanci," he said in a low voice, "do you remember a night on that boulevard—"

She changed the subject. It was noon and the room was full of sunlight. It was not quite the place, the time. When he spoke she must have every aspect of the situation in control. He must say only what she wanted said; nothing else would do.

"It's five minutes to two," she told him, looking at her wrist watch. "We'd better go. I've got to keep my date."

"Do you want to go?"

"No," she answered simply.

This seemed to satisfy him, and they walked out to the lobby. Then Yanci caught sight of a man waiting there, obviously ill at ease and dressed as no habitue of the Ritz ever was. The man was Jimmy Long, not long since a favored beau of his Western city. And now—his hat was green, actually! His coat, seasons old, was quite evidently the product of a well-known ready-made concern. His shoes, long and narrow, turned up at the toes. From head to foot everything that could possibly be wrong about him was wrong. He was embarrassed by instinct only, unconscious of his gaucherie, an obscene specter, a Nemesis, a horror.

"Hello, Yanci!" he cried, starting toward her with evident relief.

With a heroic effort Yanci turned to Scott, trying to hold his glance to herself. In the very act of turning she noticed the impeccability of Scott's coat, his tie.

"Thanks for luncheon," she said with a radiant smile. "See you tomorrow."

Then she dived rather than ran for Jimmy Long, disposed of his outstretched hand and bundled him bumping through the revolving door with only a quick, "Let's hurry!" to appease his somewhat sulky astonishment.

The incident worried her. She consoled herself by remembering that Scott had had only a momentary glance at the man, and that he had probably been looking at her anyhow. Nevertheless, she was horrified, and it is to be doubted whether Jimmy Long enjoyed her company enough to compensate for the cut-price, twentieth-row tickets he had obtained at Black's Drug Store.

But if Jimmy as a decoy had proved a lamentable failure, an occurrence of Thursday offered her considerable satisfaction and paid tribute to her quickness of mind. She had invented an engagement for luncheon, and Scott was going to meet her at two o'clock to take her to the Hippodrome. She lunched alone somewhat imprudently in the Ritz dining room and sauntered out almost side by side with a good-looking young man who had been at the table next to her. She expected to meet Scott in the outer lobby, but as she reached the entrance to the restaurant she saw him standing not far away.

On a lightning impulse she turned to the good-looking man abreast of her, bowed sweetly and said in an audible, friendly voice, "Well, I'll see you later."

Then before he could even register astonishment she faced about quickly and joined Scott.

"Who was that?" he asked, frowning.

"Isn't he darling-looking?"

"If you like that sort of looks."

Scott's tone implied that the gentleman referred to was effete and overdressed. Yanci laughed, impersonally admiring the skillfulness of her ruse.

It was in preparation for that all-important Saturday night that on Thursday she went into a shop on Forty-second Street to buy some long gloves. She made her purchase and handed the clerk a fifty-dollar bill so that her lightened pocketbook would feel heavier with the change she could put in. To her surprise the clerk tendered her the package and a twenty-five-cent piece.

"Is there anything else?"

"The rest of my change."

"You've got it. You gave me five dollars. Four-seventy-five for the gloves leaves twenty-five cents."

"I gave you fifty dollars."

"You must be mistaken."

Yanci searched her purse.

"I gave you fifty!" she repeated frantically.

"No, ma'am, I saw it myself."

They glared at each other in hot irritation. A cash girl was called to testify, then the floor manager; a small crowd gathered.

"Why, I'm perfectly sure!" cried Yanci, two angry tears trembling in her eyes. "I'm positive!"

The floor manager was sorry, but the lady really must have left it at home. There was no fifty-dollar bill in the cash drawer. The bottom was creaking out of Yanci's rickety world.

"If you'll leave your address," said the floor manager, "I'll let you know if anything turns up."

"Oh, you damn fools!" cried Yanci, losing control. "I'll get the police!"

And weeping like a child she left the shop. Outside, helplessness overpowered her. How could she prove anything? It was after six and the store was closing even as she left it. Whichever employee had the fifty-dollar bill would be on her way home now before the police could arrive, and why should the New York police believe her, or even give her fair play?

In despair she returned to the Ritz where she searched through her trunk for the bill with hopeless and mechanical gestures. It was not there. She had known it would not be there. She gathered every penny together and found that she had fifty-one dollars and thirty cents. Telephoning the office, she asked that her bill be made out up to the following noon—she was too dispirited to think of leaving before then.

She waited in her room, not daring even to send for ice water. Then the phone rang and she heard the room clerk's voice, cheerful and metallic.

"Miss Bowman?"

"Yes."

"Your bill, including tonight, is ex-act-ly fifty-one twenty."

"Fifty-one twenty?" Her voice was trembling.

"Yes, ma'am."

"Thank you very much."

Breathless, she sat there beside the telephone, too frightened now to cry. She had ten cents left in the world!

XI

Friday. She had scarcely slept. There were dark rings under her eyes, and even a hot bath followed by a cold one failed to arouse her from a despairing lethargy. She had never fully realized what it would mean to be without money in New York; her determination and vitality seemed to have vanished at last with her fifty-dollar bill. There was no help for it now—she must attain her desire today or never.

She was to meet Scott at the Plaza for tea. She wondered—was it her imagination, or had his manner been consciously cool the afternoon before? For the first time in several days she had needed to make no effort to keep the conversation from growing sentimental. Suppose he had decided that it must come to nothing—that she was too extravagant, too frivolous. A hundred eventualities presented themselves to her during the morning—a dreary morning, broken only by her purchase of a ten-cent bun at a grocery store.

It was her first food in twenty hours, but she self-consciously pretended to the grocer to be having an amusing and facetious time in buying one bun. She even asked to see his grapes, but told him, after looking at them appraisingly—and hungrily—that she didn't think she'd buy any. They didn't look ripe to her, she said. The store was full of prosperous women who, with thumb and first finger joined and held high in front of them, were inspecting food. Yanci would have liked to ask one of them for a bunch of grapes. Instead she went up to her room in the hotel and ate her bun.

When four o'clock came she found that she was thinking more about the sandwiches she would have for tea than of what must occur there, and as she walked slowly up Fifth Avenue toward the Plaza she felt a sudden faintness which she took several deep breaths of air to overcome. She wondered vaguely where the bread line was. That was where people in her condition should go—but where was it? How did one find out? She imagined fantastically that it was in the phone book under B, or perhaps under N, for New York Bread Line.

She reached the Plaza. Scott's figure, as he stood waiting for her in the crowded lobby, was a personification of solidity and hope.

"Let's hurry!" she cried with a tortured smile. "I feel rather punk and I want some tea."

She ate a club sandwich, some chocolate ice cream and six tea biscuits. She could have eaten much more, but she dared not. The eventuality of her hunger having been disposed of, she must turn at bay now and face this business of life, represented by the handsome young man who sat opposite watching her with some emotion whose import she could not determine just behind his level eyes.

But the words, the glance, subtle, pervasive and sweet, that she had planned, failed somehow to come.

"Oh, Scott," she said in a low voice, "I'm so tired."

"Tired of what?" he asked coolly.

"Of—everything."

There was a silence.

"I'm afraid," she said uncertainly—"I'm afraid I won't be able to keep that date with you tomorrow."

There was no pretense in her voice now. The emotion was apparent in the waver of each word, without intention or control.

"I'm going away."

"Are you? Where?"

His tone showed strong interest, but she winced as she saw that that was all.

"My aunt's come back. She wants me to join her in Florida right away."

"Isn't this rather unexpected?"

"Yes."

"You'll be coming back soon?" he said after a moment.

"I don't think so. I think we'll go to Europe from—from New Orleans."

"Oh!"

Again there was a pause. It lengthened. In the shadow of a moment it would become awkward, she knew. She had lost—well? Yet, she would go on to the end.

"Will you miss me?"

"Yes."

One word. She caught his eyes, wondered for a moment if she saw more there than that kindly interest; then she dropped her own again.

"I like it—here at the Plaza," she heard herself saying.

They spoke of things like that. Afterwards she could never remember what they said. They spoke—even of the tea, of the thaw that was ended and the cold coming down outside. She was sick at heart and she seemed to herself very old. She rose at last.

"I've got to tear," she said. "I'm going out to dinner."

To the last she would keep on—the illusion, that was the important thing. To hold her proud lies inviolate—there was only a moment now. They walked toward the door.

"Put me in a taxi," she said quietly. "I don't feel equal to walking."

He helped her in. They shook hands.

"Good-by, Scott," she said.

"Good-by, Yanci," he answered slowly.

"You've been awfully nice to me. I'll always remember what a good time you helped to give me this two weeks."

"The pleasure was mine. Shall I tell the driver the Ritz?"

"No. Just tell him to drive out Fifth. I'll tap on the glass when I want him to stop."

Out Fifth! He would think, perhaps, that she was dining on Fifth. What an appropriate finish that would be! She wondered if he were impressed. She could not see his face clearly, because the air was dark with the snow and her own eyes were blurred by tears.

"Good-by," he said simply.

He seemed to realize that any pretense of sorrow on his part would be transparent. She knew that he did not want her.

The door slammed, the car started, skidding in the snowy street.

Yanci leaned back dismally in the corner. Try as she might, she could not see where she had failed or what it was that had changed his attitude toward her. For the first time in her life she had ostensibly offered herself to a man—and he had not wanted her. The precariousness of her position paled beside the tragedy of her defeat.

She let the car go on—the cold air was what she needed, of course. Ten minutes had slipped away drearily before she realized that she had not a penny with which to pay the driver.

"It doesn't matter," she thought. "They'll just send me to jail, and that's a place to sleep."

She began thinking of the taxi driver.

"He'll be mad when he finds out, poor man. Maybe he's very poor, and he'll have to pay the fare himself." With a vague sentimentality, she began to cry.

"Poor taxi man," she was saying half aloud. "Oh, people have such a hard time—such a hard time!"

She rapped on the window and when the car drew up at a curb she got out. She was at the end of Fifth Avenue and it was dark and cold.

"Send for the police!" she cried in a quick low voice. "I haven't any money!"

The taxi man scowled down at her.

"Then what'd you get in for?"

She had not noticed that another car had stopped about twenty-five feet behind them. She heard running footsteps in the snow and then a voice at her elbow.

"It's all right," someone was saying to the taxi man. "I've got it right here."

A bill was passed up. Yanci slumped sideways against Scott's overcoat.

Scott knew—he knew because he had gone to Princeton to surprise her, because the stranger she had spoken to in the Ritz had been his best friend, because the check of her father's for three hundred dollars had been returned to him marked "No funds." Scott knew—he had known for days.

But he said nothing; only stood there holding her with one arm as her taxi driver drove away.

"Oh, it's you," said Yanci faintly. "Lucky you came along. I left my purse back at the Ritz, like an awful fool. I do such ridiculous things—"

Scott laughed with some enjoyment. There was a light snow falling, and lest she should slip in the damp he picked her up and carried her back toward his waiting taxi.

"Such ridiculous things," she repeated.

"Go to the Ritz first," he said to the driver. "I want to get a trunk."

The Staying Up All Night

The warm fire.
The comfortable chairs.
The merry companions.
The stroke of twelve.
The wild suggestion.
The good sports.
The man who hasn't slept for weeks.
The people who have done it before.
The long anecdotes.
The best looking girl yawns.
The forced raillery.
The stroke of one.
The best looking girl goes to bed.
The stroke of two.
The empty pantry.
The lack of firewood.
The second best looking girl goes to bed.
The weather-beaten ones who don't.
The stroke of four.
The dozing off.
The amateur "life of the party."
The burglar scare.
The scornful cat.
The trying to impress the milkman.
The scorn of the milkman.
The lunatic feeling.
The chilly sun.
The stroke of six.
The walk in the garden.
The sneezing.
The early risers.
The volley of wit at you.
The feeble come back.
The tasteless breakfast.

The miserable day.
8 P. M.—Between the sheets.

Princeton—The Last Day

The last light wanes and drifts across the land,
The low, long land, the sunny land of spires.
The ghosts of evening tune again their lyres
And wander singing, in a plaintive band
Down the long corridors of trees. Pale fires
Echo the night from tower top to tower.
Oh sleep that dreams and dream that never tires,
Press from the petals of the lotus-flower
Something of this to keep, the essence of an hour!
No more to wait the twilight of the moon
In this sequestrated vale of star and spire;
For one, eternal morning of desire
Passes to time and earthy afternoon.
Here, Heracletus, did you build of fire
And changing stuffs your prophecy far hurled
Down the dead years; this midnight I aspire
To see, mirrored among the embers, curled
In flame, the splendor and the sadness of the world.

Marching Streets

Death slays the moon and the long dark deepens,
Hastens to the city, to the drear stone-heaps,
Films all eyes and whispers on the corners,
Whispers to the corners that the last soul sleeps.
Gay grow the streets now torched by yellow lamplight,
March all directions with a long sure tread.
East, west they wander through the blinded city,
Rattle on the windows like the wan-faced dead.
Ears full of throbbing, a babe awakens startled,
Sends a tiny whimper to the still gaunt room.
Arms of the mother tighten round it gently,
Deaf to the patter in the far-flung gloom.
Old streets hoary with dear, dead foot-steps
Loud with the tumbrils of a gold old age
Young streets sand-white still unheeled and soulless,
Virgin with the pallor of the fresh-cut page.
Black streets and alleys, evil girl and tearless,
Creeping leaden footed each in thin, torn coat,
Wine-stained and miry, mire choked and winding,
Wind like choking fingers on a white, full throat.
White lanes and pink lanes, strung with purpled roses,
Dance along the distance weaving o'er the hills,
Beckoning the dull streets with stray smiles wanton,
Strung with purpled roses that the stray dawn chills.
Here now they meet tiptoe on the corner,
Kiss behind the silence of the curtained dark;
Then half unwilling run between the houses,
Tracing through the pattern that the dim lamps mark.
Steps break steps and murmur into running,
Death upon the corner spills the edge of dawn
Dull the torches waver and the streets stand breathless;
Silent fades the marching and the night-noon's gone.

www.ingramcontent.com/pod-product-compliance
Lightning Source LLC
Chambersburg PA
CBHW030413310726
48979CB00002B/395

* 9 7 9 8 8 8 0 9 0 4 0 9 9 *